DAVID G BAILEY was born in Lincolnshire a[...] Isle of Ely, also studying in the Fens and the Bl[...] the USA, Caribbean and South America as well a[...] in the Midlands, he travels to write reports on ins[...] markets around the world.

Researching and producing for publication reports the length of novels may have instilled more discipline in David's creative writing. In 2021 his first novel *Seventeen* came out, an adventure fantasy story aimed at and beyond young adults.

From *Seventeen*'s mainly masculine world of Pirates, Knights, Army and Westerners, *Them Roper Girls* returns to our own. With humour and compassion it traces in their own voices the lives of four sisters over more than sixty years from their 1950s childhood, as each tries to make her own way in the world against many challenges – as often from within the family as outside it!

To read more of and about David's work, including a quarterly newsletter and new content daily comprising extracts from diaries and other writing over more than fifty years, visit his website www.davidgbailey.com.

Them Roper Girls

David G Bailey

SilverWood

Published in 2022 by SilverWood Books

SilverWood Books Ltd
14 Small Street, Bristol, BS1 1DE, United Kingdom
www.silverwoodbooks.co.uk

ISBN 978-1-80042-226-1 (paperback)
ISBN 978-1-80042-227-8 (hardback)

British Library Cataloguing in Publication Data
A CIP catalogue record for this book is
available from the British Library

Page design and typesetting by SilverWood Books

'What you put into fiction isn't the things that happen to you, it's the things that happen to you make you think up.'

Kingsley Amis

To Wendy,

You never read me, and read me from the start; yet loved and feed me,
I hold you in my heart. With the best of my love, always.

Contents

Them Roper Girls' Family Pretty Tree

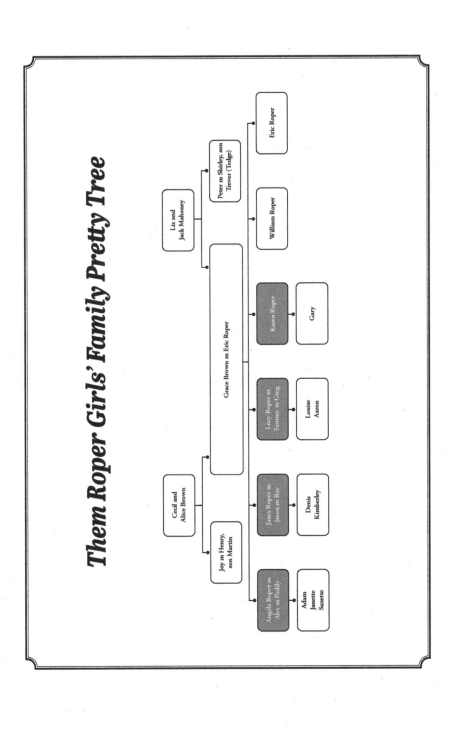

Part One:
The Fifties and Sixties

1

Angela

Me and Jan. My first memory, left on our own in the house, me and Jan. Aunt Molly from next door – not a real aunt, you know what I mean – is supposed to look after us. Mum had to be taken into hospital pretty sharpish for the birth – maybe she didn't have time to make plans, and Dad is away.

But Aunt Molly won't have us round her house to sleep. She's all right though, that's all right. She sees us up to bed with a broom in her hands and leans it against the wall. Says we can use it to bang on that same wall, it must go through to her house, if anything happens. Jan is still in nappies, but I swear I get up a hundred times in the night to make sure I don't pee the bed for Aunt Molly to find out in the morning. I do anyway though. I do still pee it.

I always tell my sisters they had it a lot easier. For one thing, I was the one who was always looking after them. They say I was a bit hard on them. They never seem to think it was a bit hard on me.

I haven't thought back to those years in the longest time, but lately Paddy has been stirring up memories, wanting to know about my childhood, drinking only tea between us. That makes me sound like a lonely old bat with her carer, and I'm not – not lonely I mean, and Paddy's not my carer neither if it comes to that. If I'd had a whole house to myself and just whoever else I want to invite in to share it when I was younger, what a luxury it would have been.

Dad was a soldier when our mum Grace met him. He'd tell us war stories which, if we'd realised, was as good a proof as any that he was never in the war. Perhaps he was doing national service – they had that in them days you know. They got married within six months of meeting, best man an army pal of his who Mum said she never met except on that day, and I got born within six months of that.

I suppose Private Eric Roper – in some of his stories he was a captain, but he would wink when he gave himself that rank – must have had to accept some kind of discipline in the forces. Maybe he used his whole stock up then. I would *never* use the word discipline to talk about Dad.

They may have been a bit previous about having me, and Janet was born within the next twelve months – did you know they call them Irish twins when there's that short a space between them? Longer than real twins, but Jan and I have always been close.

He didn't have an accent or anything but there was some talk of Dad being from Ireland. That's what I thought they meant when I first heard them talking about us as Irish twins. Not that they didn't call us worse things than that. I wouldn't have minded gypsy – has a kind of romantic ring to it, you know, the gypsy prince (not Gypsy King like that boxer, that is a bit much) – but they hardly used that word, nor travellers. Sometimes gyppos, more often vanners or diddicoys (I don't think pikies had been invented yet), all ugly words.

Lucy's arrival while I was left babysitting, I think we were living in a village somewhere near Thetford but can't be sure, was a year and something after Jan. I remember we would fight about whether she was mine or hers to play with. Mum was more than happy to let us look after her. Three kids was a lot to handle, I learned that early.

Whatever rumours you may have heard, all I can tell is I never knew Dad to say my third sister Karen, born another couple of years down the fifties, wasn't his. Mum had a wicked tongue, so if she did say that sometimes, that was her all over – probably just trying to get Dad to bite.

Others sometimes say they notice a difference in our looks, but I don't think kids care about that sort of thing, if they notice it at all. They might be cruel plenty of other ways, but not like that. Know what I think? It's cos they see so many supposed-to-be brothers and sisters on telly who look nothing like each other. In them days it would have been just *Crossroads* and *Corrie*, now there's *EastEnders* and *Emmerdale*, *Doctors* and all the rest – they just take it for granted. I've already said Dad was away sometimes. Maybe Mum got lonely. Who knows?

In any case we wouldn't all have to be the same, because while Dad was quite dark complexioned, black hair and sideboards when they came into fashion, Grace was more your classic blue-eyed blonde. That in itself didn't make her a beauty any more than it made her stupid, but I always thought it was a pretty good start. That she *was* a beauty her worst enemies never denied. She would complain about her nose being too small – Dad used to call her Pug sometimes, and I wondered why she didn't mind being compared to a dog as I thought he meant. She also made the best of her looks most of the time. It was a real shock to see her with straight hair later when she was suffering more than we knew.

I don't know about Jan with hers, but I would definitely have swapped my big hooter for Mum's little button. His first two girls had Dad's fleshy nose and his colouring, while you could have argued that Karen was similar to Mum except she had brown eyes, which stood out more against her fair skin. It was only Lucy among us girls who seemed to be a real joint project between our parents – his chunky build (I wasn't the first to call Luce thunder thighs) and her blue eyes, the hair a fudgy brown. Not that any of us ever got accused of falling out of the ugly tree and hitting every branch on the way down, like I heard Alex say about my best friend Sally Gregory. I know I shouldn't have laughed but I did.

Billy was definitely a Roper as they used to say – nobody would dream to deny he was Eric's son. Our parents were still together, or perhaps back together. I honestly can't say if Dad did time. I wouldn't say he favoured Billy – tell you the truth, he was less and less around by the time he was growing up – just for being a boy, named after Dad's dad, who we never knew. Probably some old Irish tinker, that's what I used to think when I was feeling mean about our dad. Billy was Mum's favourite from day one, then to be fair he come to dote on her as well. You've heard them talk about a man's man? I wouldn't say Billy ever got to be one, and if there even is such a thing I wouldn't call Mum a woman's woman. I'm not saying she was man-mad either though. Don't go thinking that.

Like I said they didn't call us travellers much, but Mum and Dad must have done quite a bit of moving around in their first married years, mainly East Anglia outside the big cities. What big cities, right? I suppose I mean Peterborough or Norwich although that, Norwich, was where Grace's family was from in the first place. Not so much villages either, they seemed to favour the little market towns. Just like I had no early memories of Swaffington where

I was born, Jan wouldn't of Washtown until we ended up back there.

I don't suppose Mum was in hospital long before she brought Lucy home. When she did, Dad's parents were there with us – Grandad and Nana. His stepfather really, but we always knew him as Grandad, not Grandad Jack any more than she was Nana Liz.

From Mum's side of the family, all we knew of was her sister, Aunt Joy. We'd all get birthday cards with a postal order from her. Mum would let us pick out a bar of chocolate or bag of sweets when she went to cash them in.

Mum was never what she used to call house-proud. I remember Nan, when Karen was born or some other time, cleaning ours 'from top to bottom' she told Mum, who thanked her, saying lucky it was only a bungalow then. 'I was going to do it before you came, but I knew you'd still go over it again, so I just put my feet up and had a fag instead.'

Grandad wouldn't dream of doing anything like housework, any more than Dad would. He stood outside our place near Thetford, smoking a Woodbine and looking sort of miserable that there wasn't more garden for him to get stuck into. Only a little bit of lawn by the garden path we shared with Aunt Molly, and various bits of that bald from where toys or house rubbish had been left on it too long.

Her husband Fred – we never called him 'uncle' for some reason – kept their garden very smart, separated from the path by a fence so little it wouldn't have been any obstacle to kids only a bit older than us. He had mowed our lawn once or twice with Aunt Molly standing guard, hanging out clothes or something, making sure he wouldn't be lured into a cup of coffee by Mum, though he was a lot older than her. Or *because* he was a lot older, know what I mean?

We kind of assumed Mum had fallen out with her family, because she never said much about them. Perhaps Aunt Joy years later would have told us a bit of their story if I'd have thought to talk to her about it. Lucy was the one for that, the family historian, at one time she was into doing one of them online research things, family trees and stuff. She got a bit mardy cos I laughed when she told us she was going to do that. Good luck to her – I didn't mean to be taking the mickey or anything. I just somehow had a picture in my head of a pretty tree, us all falling off it and landing on our feet, all the better for kissing a few leaves on the way down.

We hadn't seen much of Dad's folks either, for whatever reason. East Anglia is big but not so big that we'd ever been that far from Washtown, close enough for Jan to be born there during our travels though we only moved into the town itself later. All of us came to think of it as home, I suppose because it was the first place we'd ever been really settled. We started off living with Nan and Grandad, but that wasn't going to work for long, especially as our family continued to grow.

We were always in council houses or flats of one kind or another, like everyone was back then. I think Mum got pretty expert working the system so we were never without a place. She had good cards to play, a nap hand of children. It would have looked ugly if the council put us out on the street, grizzling and making a nuisance of ourselves.

I suppose they had family allowance at the least and perhaps some other kind of benefits. All us kids knew about money was that there wasn't much of it about and we had to be careful with what we got. We never had pocket money. Try telling that to today's lot and they look at you gone out, but we didn't notice. I know I'm starting to sound like Nan myself – nothing wrong with that being as I am one – but I don't mean to moan. I'm happy enough, really I am.

Grandad was a lorry driver, and Dad did some of that too. He was great with cars – always had one outside wherever we were living, never new, never ours. He didn't work from a garage, except he would go to one sometimes, to help out a mate he'd say. It was as if he never wanted to be tied down to a steady routine. Sometimes he did have plenty of money in his pocket, the best times. Even when we were real young he was never ashamed to take us all out to the club with him. It was Mum who preferred to make us stay at home while she went out with him, which I can understand better now.

He was a right one for clubs was Dad, more than pubs. He always said the beer was cheaper, the company better and the fruit machines paid out more. They were generally more welcome to children than proper pubs as well. There was a British Legion wherever we went – I suppose he got free membership there having been a captain an' all, ha ha. In Washtown our favourite place was the ex-servicemen's club, the Service, down near the library. Our uncle Pete kept it, a proper uncle. We knew we had to be quiet whenever there was anyone playing on one of the half a dozen snooker tables, unless it was only Dad against his brother when business was slack.

When we weren't bickering with each other, which was a lot of the time, Jan and me was very close. We never thought life might not be all that easy for Mum. She didn't go out to work regular after all like some of our friends' mums. I say friends, but we didn't have many, we always had each other's back in the outside world. At school we were the bookends, that's what Mrs Lawrence called us when we first joined her class at Rambert Road Primary – the oldest and the youngest in our same year. Irish twins, remember.

Mum and Dad maybe had mixed feelings about moving back to Washtown. If he'd made a bid for freedom from his parents it had obviously failed, and she wasn't one to stop needling him at any sign of affection he got from them. Not that she had to worry about that with Grandad, but when Nan would talk about what a good footballer he'd been as a boy, always reminding us that he 'had trials for the Town', my mum knew he would end up looking at her and that's exactly when she would mouth 'mummy's boy' at him, out of Nan's eyeline. He wouldn't say anything straight away but it would most likely spoil the day later.

It wasn't as if Grace didn't get on with Nan, not really. They had that solidarity women always manage to find when lined up against men, cos let's face it, they're all a pain. I don't know how many years it took me to realise that – maybe not till these last few when Paddy helped set me straight, ha ha. I'll be fair to Nan because I did love her, she never said anything *outright* bad about Mum, but there was always that little niggle. However young we were, girls are good at picking up on that sort of thing, like men never do.

We must have enjoyed being at Nan's because we would always stop on our way home from Rambert Road, trailing the younger kids with us as they gradually joined us at school. She was always at her kitchen sink looking out onto the road the time we came by, perhaps she saved her washing-up till then. We knew we had to be a bit quieter if Grandad was upstairs 'catching some kip'. She would sometimes be getting his tea ready, we hardly ever stayed to eat a meal but she was usually good for a jam sandwich. Strawberry was my favourite. We didn't have to fight over it because Jan preferred marmalade, and Nan always had both.

At least I didn't have to look after Billy so much as I did the younger girls. Mum kept him closer to her than she did any of us, then there was Karen – sometimes we thought Billy was the only one in the whole family she could stand – and Luce liked to mother him a bit too. Anyway, he hadn't hardly started primary school when I was getting near leaving.

I was all right at Rambert Road – I'm not a complete thicko just because I haven't got any qualifications. I was in the group that took the eleven-plus our year, like not everyone was, they knew it would be a total waste of time for some. I thought they did away with the whole thing for comprehensives, but now I heard some kids are taking it again.

I didn't do very well myself. I get tense when I have to sit quietly and do something on my own. With homework, we always used to go through it together, Jan and me. I was double upset because Jan wasn't in the gym where they set up the chairs for the exam – not that we would have tried to cheat or anything – and we would be separated whether I passed or not. I think she would have sailed through it, even as youngest in our class, but someone had decided she would be better with another year at little school before moving to one of the big ones.

In the summer holidays we all did our bit to earn some extra money, or help Mum to by going out to one of the villages around Washtown with her. Dad had a lorry-driving mate whose family owned plenty of land. Enough to keep us going right through till school again between picking strawberries, redcurrants, raspberries, blackberries, no problem getting our five a day but to be honest you soon got fed up with the very sight of them. Us kids weren't allowed to join in on apples, because of climbing the trees. When he wasn't away, Dad would take us down there in the morning, all five of us plus Mum, except sometimes Luce would cry off and manage to stay at Uncle Pete's. Otherwise it was the bus.

Dad would sometimes fetch us late afternoon as well. He had a go at picking strawberries when he arrived early one day, full of (I heard Mr Sealey say this, he probably didn't mean me to) 'piss and vinegar'. He lasted half an hour tops before going to sleep in the back of the van until we were finished, telling Mum he didn't know how she did it, his back was aching already. I don't know about the vinegar but I reckon he had definitely been on the piss that day.

Not too many summers were like that. We wouldn't always have been within reach of Mr Sealey's land, Dad wouldn't have known his son Bob, Mum would have been too pregnant to go fruiting some years. It's probably the one when I'd just left Rambert Road that sticks in my mind because it was nearabouts the last we would be properly together as a family. As a more or less happy family, anyway.

They say if you can remember the sixties you weren't there. The druggies and pop stars say that. I was there and I remember them too well sometimes: my first baby, first marriage, first suicide attempt (not necessarily in that order).

All of a sudden we not only had a second set of grandparents, it seemed we were going to live with them. Cecil and Alice were proper old people's names I thought at the time (Alice has made a bit of a comeback, I know). They pulled up in a little black Morris Minor was it – they used to be everywhere – when Mum had been nagging us all morning to get washed and dressed and help her tidy up, like she never usually bothered on Sundays. Dad would normally lay in if he was at home, so she must have pestered him as well, up earlier than usual at the kitchen table with a fag and a cuppa reading the *News of the World*. He flat out refused to put a necktie on.

Mum always said it was a shame we didn't get much height from our dad's side of the family, to make up for her own lack of it. She wasn't totally tiny – none of us are – and with her heels on she was more or less level with him. Grandad Cecil was no bigger than Mum, coming up our shared garden path wearing a blue V-necked pullover over a buttoned shirt and tie. Grandma Alice was clinging to him like she was sheltering from a strong wind, face against his upper arm, shorter again (without the benefit of heels I may be guessing now, it's hard to remember her in anything but bedroom slippers) and wearing an overcoat despite the hot day. It was already gone twelve, because Dad had been grumbling. He liked to be up the Service for Uncle Pete to serve his first pint on the stroke of opening time.

Karen had asked Mum if she wanted us all to line up like the Von Trapp children, except she said Von Craps, to do a little song and dance. Mum must have been a bit stressed because she didn't laugh like she normally might of. They didn't make any fuss of us – we weren't expecting presents, but they could have brought us a bag of sweets or something. Our new grandmother did pull a bottle of sherry out of her overcoat pocket, which her and Mum kept strictly between themselves. She had greeted us timidly, not with hugs but little finger handshakes, almost like she expected us to kiss the ring on her hand instead.

Sess, as Dad called him, was ushered back up the garden path before he had set foot indoors. I don't know how well they knew each other before that day, but they were close enough when they came back for their Sunday dinner past two. The women had made a fair dent in the sherry bottle while they were out, Mum giggling and hiding it in a cupboard when she heard them coming. She hadn't been in her usual hurry to send me out to fetch Dad home from the one session of the week when neither wife nor kids were ever allowed to join him for a drink. He had his arm round Grandad's shoulder – the poor man was short enough for that and didn't look any more comfortable than he had with his own wife hanging off his arm earlier.

After our roast, the men sat in front of the telly while the women watched Karen and me do the washing-up – for some reason Jan had been sent with Luce and Billy round to what I would always think of somehow as our proper nan's.

'Your father got a tidy little pay-off from the bank and he's already got a job lined up with a friend at the dairy, so it makes sense to invest a bit in a bigger place where there'll be room for us all. He says property prices are going up like billy-o. We're letting Joy and Henry keep our old house, and I told him I wanted to do something for you as well if we could before…you know, before it's too late.'

'Don't get morbid, Mum. You've got years left yet.'

'Are we going to move then?' Karen was never shy about butting in on adults' conversations. I was more of a listener and a worrier.

'We're thinking about it, love. You can pretend we really are in *The Sound of Music*, got to run away from the Nazis. That's what the bloody council are like,' Grace continued to her mum, 'always after you once you get a bit behind with the rent.'

Nothing more was said for a week or two after the visit, which to be honest didn't made that much impression on us girls despite Mum's admission to Karen they were thinking of moving. I was the only other one who heard her say it, and maybe I just shut it out of my mind. Our grandparents themselves, well we'd hardly seen Cecil between being rushed off to the pub then allowed to sleep through the football or whatever they were watching till his wife pronounced him fit to drive them home again. She was far more involved in talking to Mum than to any of us, only taking her coat off when dinner was about to be served and not asking how we were getting on at school like any normal adult would.

It was a Friday night we all got the big announcement – must have been, cos we had fish and chips still in the paper on our kitchen table, a special treat always on that night of the week if Dad happened to be flush. He and Mum had the fish, while we got a sausage with our chips, battered or saveloy whichever we liked. Other times we might get chips with just a fried egg to go with them, sometimes when Dad was away, and that was a treat too.

'Tell them then, Eric. The little gannets will have the grub down them and be away in five minutes if you don't.'

'You tell 'em. It's your folks.' They made us eat with a knife and fork, but Dad always just used his hands, one of them never far from the Sarson's bottle.

'Always me. Karen, stop stealing Billy's chips – you've got plenty of your own. Wasn't it good to meet your nana and grandad?' Lucy probably agreed with her. I kept my head down. I like to think I already guessed something bad was coming.

'Anyway, we'll soon be going to visit them back. They're in a place called Northampton, and we're all going to live in a bigger house than this. Well, Jan will stay here with your other nan and grandad because of her eleven-plus coming up, and we don't want to spoil her chances in that.'

'So you're basically abandoning me then?' Jan could be just as sharp as Karen at times, no pushover for anyone.

'I won't move. I'm not going anywhere. If she don't, I don't have to because I'm the oldest.' I couldn't keep quiet any longer.

'If she can stay with them, I can stay here with Uncle Pete and Aunt Shirley.' Lucy wasn't quite so keen to agree now.

'Is Northampton bigger than Washtown? Is it nearer to London?'

I don't know how or why, but as far back as that Karen had a thing about London, or at least about being anywhere else except where she was.

Billy just tucked into his chips while his sister was distracted from pinching more off him.

Dad ended up disappearing off to the club earlier than usual while we were still wrangling, clever enough to hold out the bait of Vimto and crisps for us all once we'd accepted things enough for Mum to agree to bring us along to him. We all ended up there of course, and before too long. I was probably the most upset and said the least. Mum had to explain that despite its name Northampton wasn't right up north near Scotland. She said it was somewhere in the Midlands, which meant Dad might be home a bit more as it was central for practically anywhere in the country and closer to the motorway network. Honestly, that didn't cut much ice with me, and nor did the talk of us perhaps getting separate bedrooms in a bigger house. I would rather keep sharing with Jan any day.

In July the new school year still seemed a long way away. I hadn't been pleased to leave Rambert Road, as I said, mainly because Jan wouldn't be coming with me. I argued that she should come to the new place with us, could just as easy take the eleven-plus there. Mum was firm for once – said Jan had a good chance of passing it and they wouldn't risk her future. That was something they'd never said about me when I was coming up to take it, about passing I mean.

We all knew Lucy was really Uncle Pete's pet, but maybe she thought

24

our aunt Shirley would have more influence talking to Mum. Anyway, it was her she got to come round and say they wouldn't mind having Lucy live with them and our cousin Tedge (everyone called him that, Trevor his real name was, about my age, but unlike us he would always be a child). I think the adults pretended to consider something they had no intention of carrying through on, a trick I learned soon enough myself as a parent.

I didn't know the phrase 'moonlight flit' until later, when Sally Gregory – she could be a right bitch – said that's what everyone was saying we'd done. To me it was only another of many moves in our early years, except I was expected to help Mum even more, and we'd accumulated enough furniture for Dad to load it up with Grandad and Pete onto one of his lorries. Billy wanted to ride sitting on the settee and watching telly until they explained to him you couldn't switch it on, plus it would be kind of dark under the tarpaulin. It wasn't moonlight either – you know it's daylight till 10 o'clock or whatever in summer.

'Go and have a last look round then, kids. First one back gets to post the keys through the front door – let the council come fetch if they want 'em that bad,' Dad said.

I'm glad I did go in. I wanted to cry, but I didn't. It surprised me to see how big the rooms looked bare, including the one that had been cramped with just me and Jan in it. Big and already in their emptiness somehow as if they'd turned their back on us.

I try not to look back on that time in Northampton more than I can help, except perhaps for the very first part before we had to start our new schools and were getting to know our new house – not right in the town but the outskirts, Duston. They were right, it was bigger than we had been used to with four bedrooms, one of them reserved for our new grandma (as we soon learned to call Alice – Nana didn't seem right somehow) and grandad.

I don't think Mum and Dad were being deliberately cruel in leaving Jan behind to do her last year at Rambert Road. She came with us until school started, us sharing a room just like forever, with the other three in the smallest bedroom for the time being.

Our grandparents had the second big bedroom, even though there was a grannie flat attached to the house by a conservatory from the kitchen. The flat wasn't ready to live in like the house was. Grandad Sess and Dad would work together to do it up properly then rent it out, helping with the family finances till they were in a better state, and perhaps Grandma and Grandad would move in there when they got really old.

25

Maybe it wasn't a bad plan, but like so many of Mum and Dad's big ideas in life it never quite worked out. If Grandad ever spent a night in the main house, it was only the first one or two. The job from his friend at the dairy didn't turn out to be quite what I'd imagined. He was a milkman, away in the morning before any of us were up, and when he got home mainly alone in his flat, sometimes knocking and banging about.

I suppose everyone was trying extra hard to make things work in them first days. Mum was never that strict with us anyway. Dad either hadn't got himself into the full swing of the local clubs or was slack on work – around enough anyway to put up a swing for us in the orchard at the bottom of the garden. I know, an orchard! All right no more than half a dozen trees, but they had fruit on them and everything. Apples were just coming into season, and was there a pear tree too? I never much liked pears so I may be wrong on that.

Grandad didn't wear a tie when he did his round, and Dad ribbed him when he put one on to go to the big park up the road for our one and only picnic. 'Bloody hell, Sess, we're going to have egg sandwiches on the grass, not to a garden party at Buckingham Palace.'

Grandma seemed uncomfortable in a different way. My first sight of her clinging to Cecil as they came up our path in Washtown was not right anymore – she seemed to have transferred to Mum, linking arms as we walked along the pavement and generally doing all her human business with her.

Jan and I went to the park on our own a few times after that, or sometimes having to drag Billy along. I mean he was a drag on us – he loved it. We never got on the tennis courts they had there but could still enjoy ourselves messing around on the swings. His presence gave us an excuse to do that, I suppose. We did get talking to some of the local girls, Jan more so than me. I remember one Jane Something was quite nice, there with a little sister. Later when I met her at school and tried to say hello, she just blanked me. She was in the year above I think.

A lot less often than when she'd first started pestering him for it, at least once during our last few days together Jan went out on the lorry with Dad. No doubt it was a special treat for her with our separation coming up. It wasn't that Dad never showed us affection, so it may have been his idea rather than Mum's. I didn't envy Jan the trip – I never fancied getting up in the early hours to go and sit in a dirty old lorry driving up to Scotland or wherever – but I did mind that she preferred it to spending time with me. It might have been different if it was Paris, but although he would be gone overnight sometimes, as far as I know he was strictly UK.

We were all surprised when Jan came into the kitchen bursting with excitement, we thought at first from her ride. Mum and Grandma were sitting there at the table, as they did an awful lot in them days before Alice took to her bed. 'Did you have a good time, love? Where's your Dad?'

'He told me to tell you he's gone to see a man about a dog.' For a reason we soon found out, Jan couldn't stop giggling when she said it.

'Not over the doorstep before he's off out boozing now,' Grandma remarked. If he heard that he didn't comment, appearing a moment later with a squirming puppy in his arms.

The little Alsatian was a favourite with everyone at first. Dad tried to tell us it was a good business deal, saying we could breed from him, take the pick of the litter every time and sell it on. Grandad was not impressed, reckoning it wasn't a true-bred. He was an expert in a lot of unexpected areas, or fancied he was, which soon started to rile Dad. Jan didn't remember any money changing hands when he'd got Fang in the first place, and he wasn't quick to produce the pedigree documents for inspection by Grandad. Whatever, it never got to the stage of breeding.

Dad didn't put his foot down when Jan wanted to take Fang to live with her back in Washtown. He got Nan and Grandad to do the dirty work when they came to pick her up and have our new house shown off to them. Looking back, I can see he was pretty good at that sort of thing – we all had a tendency to blame Mum for a lot that was perhaps more his fault.

What I still thought of as our real grandparents must have arrived before the Duston Legion opened, or else Dad would never have wasted his time drinking home brew before he took his own dad out, leaving Grandad Sess at home. His trip to the boozer in Washtown turned out to have been a forced march, totally out of character. In Northampton he would drink only at home, making his own beer from kits. He tried producing apple cider from the windfalls in our orchard – it still gives me a little kick to call it that, silly I know. It was just a few trees, and we didn't have it long. He said the cider was weak enough for us to taste, but taste rather than strength was its real problem – horrible (then again, the first time I tried proper cider a couple of years later I thought that was horrible too). Dad never had a good word to say about his efforts but would try every new batch as if hoping eventually Cecil would crack it. Our other grandad was no more impressed with it than he was interested in seeing the house, though he trailed along behind the women through all the rooms.

I don't know how old Dad was when Grandad came into the picture or if he ever formally adopted him and the younger Pete, who called him Dad. Eric never did – it was always Jack – but I think he still looked up to him a bit, which you couldn't say about Dad with many men. He had to look up to him physically cos as I said he wasn't tall, while Grandad was, and probably looked taller because he was wiry too, not run to fat like some of Dad's muscle had.

Jan had been straight at Grandad when they arrived, trying to make him love the much-mauled Fang – he spent more time in people's arms than on the floor, until he got too heavy to lift and developed a mind of his own.

'We don't need a guard dog, gal. I've got my gun under the bed,' was all he said. Nan had to tell her, whether it was true or not, that pets weren't allowed in their bungalows and that was the end of the matter.

'You'll still have him to come back to here in the school holidays, love,' Mum tried to console her. 'The others will look after him for you.'

'He's not theirs to look after – he's mine,' Jan sulked. She didn't cry until they left, and then more for that blessed dog than for us. My tears were proper people ones, at separation from my sister.

Things might not have been so hard if we were all going to the same school in Northampton. While Lucy, Karen and Billy could walk to the primary in the village, I had to get on a bus into town. I started to feel worse and worse as the days of our summer holidays disappeared. When we bought my school uniform – boring old navy-blue pullover and black skirt – I would not be persuaded how smart it looked. I have to admit I was pretty nasty to the other kids and would sometimes give Fang a pinch too. That's perhaps why he didn't like me very much.

Grandma's solution was to give me tablets, like she took herself to 'stop things getting too much'. If Mum was prepared to accept that advice for herself, she took a tougher line with me. 'She can't give in to it – we can't let her, Mum, or else she'll never do anything. She'll be all right once she gets there, make new friends and everything.'

Deep down, I knew I would have to do it. I couldn't skip school for the next five years or whatever it was. I tried to build myself up by saying that Jan didn't care about me anyway, that she cared more for Fang so I should find myself a new best friend. Still I couldn't stop feeling terrible whenever I thought about that first day, like I was going to be sick. I wasn't sleeping well, and I was getting headaches.

It turned out there was some physical reason too, or the mental stuff brought on the physical, because on the very day I was due to start at Northampton school – a Tuesday it was – I got my first period. Mum hadn't talked to us about them or anything, but we weren't totally naïve – I didn't think I was dying or anything like you hear some stupid girls do. I was frightened when I saw the blood in the toilet bowl until she reassured me and showed me how to use the towels. I was amazed when she then expected me to go to school as if nothing had happened. I threw a real fit. She would have had to drag me out of the house and she wasn't up for that fight, so I got to stay home. Dad didn't want to know about 'women's problems' when he got in, so I was allowed to sit it out on the promise that I would start school without fail the next Monday.

Although I had got my way, I didn't feel any the better for it – worse if anything. It wasn't much fun at home alone with Mum and Grandma, wrapped up in their own conversations all day long. They weren't always friends, don't get me wrong. Sometimes they would go at it hammer and tongs. My sympathies were always with Mum. Alice did nothing to get any of us on her side. All she said about my first period was 'She's starting young just like you did – get ready for trouble.'

I mean I didn't expect a soppy speech about becoming a woman or anything like that, but a *little* sympathy would have been nice. She was probably jealous of me taking Mum's time away from her while otherwise they would have been alone. At least I was someone to walk Fang, except they wouldn't have done it themselves anyway, just let him out into the garden to do his business where soon there were a lot more than windfalls in the grass under the apple trees.

It did me more harm than good to miss those first few days. I was thinking it would be like when the odd single new kid joined us at Rambert Road and we weren't all that nice to them. I hadn't realised it would be different primary schools coming together at the big one, other kids with similar fears to me, more opportunity to hide. Everyone else got a few days' head start on me, so it was like I *was* the only new kid, just what I'd dreaded.

The school was all girls, which didn't bother me in itself. I wasn't interested in boys, it was just one more change from Rambert Road. So was the fact we all now had single desks instead of sharing with another pupil. It wouldn't have been Jan, but it might have given me more chance to develop a close friendship with someone.

I couldn't believe how our younger kids seemed to have settled into their new school without any bother at all. Billy was too small to think about others' problems. Lucy always seemed to sail smoothly along in her own little world. Karen was the one that surprised me by being sympathetic when they got back from school to find me mooching about the house. She would never have admitted to fear of anything – from the earliest age she was always ready to take on Jan or me.

Karen being tough like that made me think of something Dad tried to teach us, when the police come round to talk to him after a fight in the street where the other fellow ended up in hospital. That makes it sound worse than it was, sorry. He knew the policeman – this was back in Washtown – and they sat at our kitchen table over a cuppa. The other man was never going to press charges anyway. We got shooed out, but afterwards Mum was nagging him, saying why did he have to keep getting in trouble, she wouldn't be left alone again to bring us all up for him. As he went out to the Service (to buy the copper a pint, he said), he saw us goggling – so this was before we learned our presence wouldn't stop their rows escalating – and said, 'You lot can all take this in as well. A Roper never backs down.'

No fear of that. I am quiet, but I'm not the oldest in our family for nothing. Feisty, that's what they call the gobby little tarts on Celebrity this and that nowadays. Nobody ever says that about me – disturbed is more like it. I only have to fight once in the playground, and even if I don't put the other girl in hospital they all know better than to tease me too far after that. So I fulfil that old bag Alice's promise of trouble within a couple of weeks, only not in the way she might have meant.

I survived. While I don't like to remember those times at Northampton, like I said right at the start, it's not so much for the school, more what happened the next summer. Already I couldn't wait to leave, but it's just one day after another once you've got that first one under your belt. You can find a way to keep going with or without friends. And I must be fair, it wasn't all bad. It did get better. I turned out to be good at netball and got a bit pally with one or two of the other girls in the school team, sorry their names have long gone.

Jan came to what we now called home for Christmas, naturally, Nan and Grandad bringing her up with their presents for us a day or two before. I think we were all disappointed they didn't stay on for Christmas – I was anyway. I don't know if they had finished the flat to their satisfaction, Grandad Cecil and Dad – as far as I could tell, there was never much cooperation between them even before the banging and hammering stopped. We saw very little of our live-in grandad and not much more of Dad, despite Mum's brave talk before we moved about Northampton being nearer to motorways and all that. I think his trips still sometimes took him back through Washtown, and he would pick up Jan for a ride if it didn't clash with her school.

There would have been room to put up Nan and Grandad somehow, just like between them and Uncle Pete they managed to house us all that very New Year's Eve back in Washtown when Mum and Dad went out to the Rugby Club dance and came home at three in the morning – Grandad made a point of mentioning the exact time on New Year's Day. Maybe they were invited and turned it down. Anyway, they weren't there that one Christmas dinner we all sat down together in Northampton: Dad carving the turkey at the head of the table, Mum to his right, Grandma beside her, Billy at Dad's other hand then Karen, Jan and me with Lucy between our grandparents. Cecil was at the end nearest to his bolthole, the conservatory being the only space we had big enough to seat us all, with a card table added to the kitchen one. We don't have a photo or anything of the day, but that's the picture in my mind, clear as anything.

Me and Jan still stuck together except it wasn't the same anymore. Maybe we had both changed. I wouldn't say I felt more mature because I had my periods and was going to wear a bra to school after Christmas – I was annoyed that was one of my presents, just boring old underwear. There was no question then of thinking what sort might look nice, far less attract boys. We were still taught to be mortified if any of them ever got a glimpse of your knickers, not flashing them at every opportunity or going without them. Nobody would have dreamed of that unless they were a bit funny in the head. Jan seemed somehow quieter. Before, I would have sworn I knew every little thing about her. Now I wasn't anything like as sure.

It was really Christmas for Fang, who'd never had so much exercise and fuss. Jan swore he remembered her straight away. I don't know about that, but obviously he soon did since she monopolised him while she was with us. Wherever Jan had found his name, his teeth definitely grew to meet it. I didn't dare pinch him anymore. He never got as big as some Alsatians, and was pretty much all black, none of the brown trimmings – things Grandad Cecil had stopped pointing out proved he wasn't a true-bred.

Aunt Joy and Uncle Henry came round for Christmas night tea, the postal-order gifts replaced by book tokens for us girls and a toy drum for

Billy that got vanished pretty much by Boxing Day. I overheard Grandma say to Mum that her sister had bought it purpose to irritate them, knowing she wouldn't have to put up with the din herself.

Mum and Joy were friendly enough together, at the same sort of distance I was already feeling between me and Jan. Alice was more clingy to Mum when Joy was around, practically ignoring her. I heard Mum try to apologise, saying she had told her not to be so rude.

'Don't worry, Grace – water off a duck's back. Believe me, I've got the better of the deal, you'll find out soon enough. It would have broken up me and Henry if she'd still had her hooks in us. Don't let her take over your life is all I'll say.'

'Now you tell me – bit late with us under the same roof!' Mum tried to laugh it off – it was Christmas after all – a sort of nervous laugh though.

On Boxing Day it was our turn to go to Aunt Joy's for tea after bubble and squeak in the morning, made by Dad with loads of smoke in the kitchen before he disappeared to meet Uncle Henry at the pub. I think Henry was originally Polish or something. He never said very much – no harm in him, Dad always used to say, for all his size and serious look.

Me and Jan and Karen joined them and Henry's son in knockout whist for a penny a game. I say Henry's son not because Martin wasn't Aunt Joy's as well – he was, but the spit of his dad from the start, same crewcut as we used to call it then and a big, fair face, a year or two older than me. Dad insisted the money was for real, out of our own pockets, and warned us in advance he wouldn't let us off anything – we'd have to pay another penny if we wanted to take up our dog's lives on seven and six. Uncle Henry staked us girls sixpence each. Martin already had a pile of coppers ready to play with. When our money was gone, the two men sat on switching to brag or crib, which none of us could understand. Martin sat and watched them so he probably soon would.

Henry may already have told Dad over their lunchtime pints of bitter. Aunt Joy waited until her husband was slicing the big ham joint for tea to announce that they would be moving to London in the New Year. Grandma pursed her lips, as if pinching in any comment. Mum hugged her sister and Karen asked if she could go to live with them there. The big property wheeler-dealer Cecil asked what about their house, which to be fair had until recently been his. Henry and Joy were going to let it out and rent something small for themselves in London until they were sure Henry could make a go of it down there as an electrician, about to become his own boss for the first time.

Grandma did open her mouth for the sparkling wine Aunt Joy had ready to drink with our tea – more than one bottle of it as well. Apart from Grandad's foul cider, that Boxing Day may have been the first time I tasted alcohol, with lemonade in it admittedly, but then years later that's how I would drink it too. The difference was I didn't know as a kid to call it a spritzer. Mum had her share, grew a bit tearful when she said she would be left to look after the old folks all on her own now. Not that Grandad took much looking after. I suppose she meant Grandma Alice, and I could see what she meant.

If I could do the arithmetic, Mum might have been able to give us her own news that day. I don't know whether it was hers alone to tell – at that point perhaps she was keeping her options open. In my childhood memories she is pregnant as often as not, and we wouldn't have connected it with sex in those days. By now I knew where babies came from. It just didn't occur to me that our mum and dad would still be up to that sort of thing. I probably bought into the half-understood family jokes that Eric had kept twisting till he got a boy then stuck.

More recently our Christmas breakfast Buck's Fizzes – as you get older you want to start drinking earlier in the day, don't you? (although I have been doing my best to wind the clock back lately) – worked as a kind of pregnancy test. That was how our Adam guessed and I learned when I was first going to be a nana. There would have been no clue at the time I'm talking about, no accepted reason for Mum to avoid Aunt Joy's wine (she would never have touched Grandad's stuff, out of concern for her own well-being). Is it true what they used to say that pregnant women would get a medical prescription for a pint of Guinness a day? I don't know, I never liked that stuff so didn't bother to ask the doctor when my time came.

I can't remember if there was a sit-down revelation that we would soon be having another little brother or sister, or what reaction Dad might have had to the news. Don't ask me to think about why there had been such a gap between Billy, who'd already started school at least, and the newcomer. Mum and Dad were both supposed to be Catholics, but they weren't practising ones so why would they have worried about contraception? I mean worried about using some – it was obviously never a consideration in their earlier years together when we were all coming along like clockwork.

The other thing is there might have been a freeze in their relations. If what was said about Karen was true there must have been, surely, for some time, but nobody was saying Lucy and Billy weren't his. With Billy, you could be sure of it just from looking at him. Perhaps the fresh start in moving to Northampton had made them daft as newly-weds again, if so like any honeymoon that didn't last long. Perhaps it was just an accident. I say I don't really want to think about it, but somehow after all these years it still turns over in my mind sometimes.

I can't say if I was the first person to tell Jan. I would have bet on it before Christmas when we used to send each other letters, but somehow that all tailed off in the New Year. We did have a phone fitted up in the conservatory, which Grandad took precautions against us using. Apparently he was doing it in advance of renting out the little flat, or that was the excuse he gave for getting it to be coin-operated. Dad refused to touch it, saying it was a matter of principle – if he had to pay for it, he'd rather go down to the red booth on the corner, where he could get a bit of privacy.

So through that spring and early summer, as my periods continued Mum's had stopped. I didn't see her boobs getting bigger, but couldn't help noticing my own were. After the shock of that first time, I didn't suffer much with periods, apart from the inconvenience and faff (less so when we moved on from the bulky old towels to tampons). Mum did suffer a lot with her pregnancy. It may have been her extreme sickness in the mornings, hard to hide with four kids getting ready for school and one bathroom in the main house, that made her give us the news in the first place. Alice rarely left the house at all nowadays, but I know she took Mum to get some medication for it.

Grandma was the expert on pills and potions. 'It's like bloody Boots in here,' Dad hollered once when struggling to park his Brylcreem in the little cabinet above the sink in our toilet, without counting all the stuff she had stashed in her bedside table.

As the baby grew in Mum's belly, so did her own mum's clinginess. She was never out of bed when we left for school nowadays, and if we caught her at the kitchen table on our return it wasn't long before she would be scurrying back upstairs. Karen asked Mum right out if Grandma was ill, and if so what was the matter with her? Mum gave some vague reply about suffering with her nerves. That's good enough to cover most of the different things people are diagnosed with today, never mind the fancy names and their middle-page spreads in *The Mirror*. I know what I'm talking about. Nerves, anxiety, better to put it that way even if terror is more what it feels like to me.

I had no more sympathy for her then than the other kids did, except Lucy might sometimes linger through *Crossroads* when it was her turn to take Alice's tea up – whatever was the matter, it didn't affect her appetite.

Grandad seemed to have no contact with his wife beyond adding a small television – our main one was black and white then, the kids can't imagine it when I tell them that – to the radio in their upstairs bedroom, solely occupied by her (though no doubt she would have been overjoyed for Mum to move in with her). There was a constant murmur from the telly or wireless behind her closed door however late we went to bed ourselves. Grandad was mainly invisible to us between his milk round and home brewery. There was no more talk of renting out the flat, so he had it pretty much to himself.

Jan passed her eleven-plus, so perhaps our move to Northampton did someone some good. No, I shouldn't be catty – it wasn't her choice and perhaps she suffered more from the separation than she ever let on. Whatever faults your parents have, they're still your mum and dad, as I only realised when we were all scattered. Although Jan must have been the first one in our family ever to get to grammar or high school, she never made a big deal of it and nor did anyone else. It could even have worked against her. Later people would sometimes say she didn't make the most of the opportunity, as if it had cost them a lot to give it to her and wasn't something she'd worked to earn herself.

We didn't go on many holidays when we were children, so we were all excited by the prospect of a week at the Clacton Butlin's that summer. Apart from his lorry-driving, Dad had more mysterious sources of income, not reliable but sometimes spectacular, often – we would later realise – involving things that fell off the back of lorries. He could be generous and thoughtful, but I wouldn't be surprised either if the holiday was payment in kind or taking up some friend's late forced cancellation.

Aunt Joy, Uncle Henry and Martin joined us on the coast. Mum said her sister was worried that Henry would collapse from working so hard if he didn't take a break, and Dad was pleased to have a drinking partner along. Joy was one of the few people who called on our payphone, and Mum would sometimes ring out to her when she got a handful of coins together.

Mum had been fretful when Dad first broke what he must have thought would be a lovely surprise on us. 'I don't know if Mum will want to go that far, Eric.' (We didn't yet understand the dependency between them was growing in two directions.)

'Good cos she's not invited, not unless Sess wants to stump up for their own chalet. You need a break from her. Grace, for Christ's sake, haven't we got enough kids of our own without making Alice another one in her own little Wonderland. You might not feel up to a holiday for a while after you pop out

35

Eric or Erica' – he had decided that the latest addition would have his name one way or another – 'so let's take the chance while we can.'

'And what about if I pop the bab out there as you put it? It's not as easy as shelling peas. I'll be close to full term, you know.'

'All right. Take to your bed already then. Get in with your ma, why don't you? I'm going to Butlin's. I'll see if I can't get some pretty little redcoat to help me look after the kids, unless you want to keep them cooped up here as well.'

So we went on what would be the best and worst holiday of my life. Have you ever been to a Butlin's? I think there's still some left – not in Clacton though, because we checked one year. When we went as kids, they were still super-popular, and for us it was fabulous. The pools alone were enough to keep us occupied for lots of the day, and the beach right there on the site, not to mention all the other activities. Here we did at last play tennis. Not for long mind. We soon found none of us could hit the ball over the net.

There were enough boozers on site, plus a big snooker hall, to satisfy Dad and Uncle Henry, so we hardly left it all week except for the first day. We'd set off at sparrow fart as Dad called it and were there before they would let us into the chalets. We dumped Billy on Mum and Joy, catching up in one of the cafes, while the rest of us piled into Dad's borrowed van.

They managed to find a club in one of the back streets away from the prom. The bloke smoking behind the bar wasn't overenthusiastic about having a bunch of kids come in but made an exception for Martin, who looked almost big enough to drink and I know for a fact did do sometimes. He was like his dad's shadow so had no interest in coming with when Dad allowed us to head off to the proper seaside. He said we'd meet at three by a big tower with a clock on it we'd passed on a green overlooking the beach, which we did, except we had to send Karen to fetch them out of the club.

Dad had a huge wad in his pocket – I'd never seen so much money. He gave us each a note, a quid or ten bob I can't remember which. You'd laugh at that now, but believe me it was really generous then. He didn't say he wanted change either, so we spent it all or pretended we had. I made out I was annoyed because Dad hadn't given it all to me to take care of as the oldest, but secretly I was glad not to have it to risk losing or having to dole it out to them – that would have been sure to lead to fights.

We walked up and down that prom a dozen times, sometimes on the beach below (the tide was way out so we didn't go as far as the sea), sometimes just looking at all the shops selling souvenirs and tat. We'd have a giggle at the dirty postcards – big fat wives and henpecked husbands wearing hats, busty women wearing stockings and bending over. There was a little boating lake, a skating rink no use since none of us could skate, amusement arcades every so often before there was a whole bundle of them in the main funfair right at the end of the prom. It wasn't like now where you get a day ticket for everything – every ride you had to pay for individually. Me and Lucy were the most careful at hanging on to our money. Karen was the least, first off buying a kiss me quick plastic bowler hat for some reason and then going on the waltzers and down the big tower slide. To be fair, she treated us all to 99s as well.

We went on the slot machines and games in the arcades, always checking the trays at the bottom in case someone had been careless enough to leave a payout behind. Can you believe that game where you feed in pennies and hope they'll push others three trays lower down off the edge is on telly nowadays? Fun enough but my Lord, on telly, no matter if the stakes are a bit bigger than ours back then.

Maybe I remember so clearly the carefree feeling of those few hours with my sisters because it was such a rarity, and not just because Jan wasn't living at home anymore. Looking back, I can see the pattern of adult life already there, the men and women separated when out together. Us at tables for weddings, christenings, funerals, while they hung about at the bar, sometimes bringing our drinks over but otherwise keeping an eye on us only to make sure no other men were getting near. When we *could* just sit that is. If there wasn't food to serve or organise, there would be kids demanding our attention, pushed onto us by the men. I'm not saying we wanted it any other way – they would have been miseries sitting with us while their mates were at the bar. Anyway, it was a great feeling that day, money in our pockets (given us by a man, so what?) and no responsibilities, nothing to do except enjoy ourselves.

Sorry if I'm harping on about that fun time too much. I don't want to start thinking about what happened after. We had a few days of great weather, no need to be indoors at all – just as well because the chalets weren't exactly roomy – falling dead asleep whenever we did get to bed, which was at no fixed time, no school the next day. Practically at the end of our week Mum at last gave in to our constant pleading to dip her toes in the water.

Her belly was really big – like she had a football up her jumper, as Billy said. She had some light floaty dresses she would put on over her swimwear, but she wasn't going to wear a bikini. One-pieces were still common enough then anyway. That's what Aunt Joy wore. She would just lay in the sun all day long if you let her, which gave us someone to look after the towels and all that other stuff you were so happy to take to the beach in the morning but was such a drag to take home at night.

Lucy had hold of Mum's other hand. None of us could swim, but we would splash about in the shallows for hours, even after we lost our beach ball, letting it float a bit too far out for any of us to get it back. Dad would come down with us in the morning once he got back with his paper. If he had any trunks, we never saw them, but he would sometimes turn up his trouser legs – his shirt sleeves were always rolled up tight against his muscles, right to the lorry-driver's tan line on one arm – to walk along the shore. He would carefully dry his feet and put his socks and shoes back on when it was pub time, meeting Henry and Martin there. Martin always had some sporting or other activity organised for him and his dad in the mornings – there were plenty of different things, ones you'd never think of, like archery or fencing. Dad joined them once for a football tournament, where he nearly got into a fight. He had a drink with the other bloke in the Pig and Whistle on site later, so it couldn't have been anything too serious.

Mum suddenly paused. We thought she was just messing around, pretending not to want to go on. Then she turned to me and whispered, 'Ange, run and tell your dad and Auntie Joy my waters have broke. They'll know what you mean. Run – it's important.'

Without understanding what she meant, I passed on the message. Aunt Joy instantly set about gathering up her things while Dad ran towards Mum, now walking further into the sea with Lucy still holding her hand, until it got a bit deep for her. He didn't care about his creased trousers when he ran in after them, me keeping up as best I could.

'What you doing, you daft mare? We need to get you to hospital. No time for a bloody dip!'

'I'm not walking over that beach as if I've just wet myself, Eric. Let me get some water over my whole body so people will think I've been swimming.'

'Swimming? You can't swim. People can see you're preggers fit to bust, for Christ's sake – what does it matter?'

She would not be diverted until she had splashed her face, leaving only her hair still dry.

Aunt Joy helped Mum to the front seat of the van. They hadn't told me to look out for the other kids but Jan could do that. I don't know why I jumped in the back, wish I hadn't, but they weren't going to waste time dragging me out.

When they took her into the ward we thought everything would be all right, seeing the white and blue coats fuss about her, asking calm questions. Dad didn't panic until they asked if he would be attending the birth. 'You go, Joy, if anybody has to. She managed the others on her own. I don't want to faint or nothing.'

She shook her head at him. 'Take care of Ange then if that's not too much trouble. Don't worry, honeybunch, everything will be all right now – won't be long at all.'

Too long for Dad to sit still though. I refused to be left in the waiting room, which was not limited to expectant fathers. In fact, I don't think there were any others there. He reluctantly let me go with him for 'a bit of fresh air'. He'd been smoking like he was in a pub, and in honour of the occasion bought himself the biggest cigar the nearest grocery had – not all that big – along with a fresh packet of Park Drive. The woman behind the counter (English she was in them days) said she couldn't sell him alcohol from the off-licence section because we weren't in pub opening hours. She agreed it was a stupid rule – why would you need to buy it if the pubs *were* open? – and she understood the birth of a new baby was worth celebrating, but she wasn't budging. He bought me a tin of pop and a Bounty, counting out the change rather than producing a single note.

We're just back to our places in the waiting room when Aunt Joy comes rushing in with a white-coated young man holding the door for her. 'Eric, I can't do that on my own – you have to decide. Grace is out of it. Come and see – it's awful.'

For a minute it's like we're playing ring-a-ring-a-roses, her grabbing his sleeve and pulling him to the door and me hanging on to his other arm. 'What's happened, mate?' he asks the kid in the white coat, who mutters something about 'severe complications' but won't meet his eye.

Dad still thinks everything will be all right. He wants me to go in to meet the baby – they won't tell him boy or girl – which makes Aunt Joy shriek. 'God no, please not, Eric. You go, it's your place but not her.'

She keeps me outside in the corridor, no seats there, I'm crying and begging to be told what's going on. She's crying just as hard, however much she tries to control herself. No taller than me, she doesn't have to stoop to give me a tight hug, letting me go only to put her hands on my shoulders with my back to the wall.

'Angela, I'm going to tell you because you're the oldest. You'll need to help your sisters and little Billy but above all help your mum. Your little brother, he's been born...*deformed*.'

'What. Like Johnny Woods at school?' She doesn't know who Johnny is, he just come into my mind, a boy with a withered arm. 'But he'll be all right, won't he?'

'I don't know, honeybunch – that's what they have to decide.'

I take Aunt Joy by surprise and she's too slow to stop me bursting past her into the delivery room. I see Dad standing at the bed, holding Mum's hand, her face all screwed up, I can't see his with his back to me. I scare a nurse bending over a sink with a bin beside it – clinical waste it says – a baby in her arms on a dark red towel. My brother Eric's face is all screwed up too, he's not making a sound, and he doesn't have any arms or legs.

2

Karen

I let my sister – my oldest sister, as she never fails to let you know – have a good run to avoid giving you the immediate impression this is going to be one of those books where you hear a cacophony of female voices, like that group biography of the Nolan Sisters I read one time. It must have been in one of my own sisters' houses I found it lying about, a tatty paperback (I won't say tacky – the girls had to make a living): it's true what they would always say about me, that I'd read anything. There they are, Coleen and Bernie and Linda and whoever all trilling away turn and turn about, until one or the other drops off the perch, and without contributions from one or two more who fell out over top billing at Blackpool or whatever it was.

Don't think I'll be rambling on like Ange either – I just want to have a quick word about our childhood. I wouldn't want to leave you only her version – talk about unreliable memoirs. She never stopped moaning from then to now about how she had to be a mother to all of us, never had a proper childhood of her own. If you hear any of that kind of whingeing from me, please shoot me. I'm surprised she didn't use that as another excuse for not passing the eleven-plus. Let's face it, that wasn't like other exams where you have to revise for them and absorb knowledge, but an intelligence test, pure and simple. Maybe she just wasn't that bright. I wouldn't be surprised if Paddy or someone had to write her story up for her. Don't expect anyone to be ghosting for me. What you hear is my own voice *in propria persona*.

You will have noticed the snidey way Ange got in the bit about Dad not really being my dad, as if it was an amusing anecdote and nobody got hurt. She's right that I didn't suffer from it *consciously* as a child, because she's wrong in that I didn't find out about it till much later. Even so, I think it was somehow always there, helped make me whatever I became. It was just that one time Mum said it to him in my presence (perhaps not deliberately so, but she didn't take it back when she saw me there). I never considered him as anything but Dad – it wasn't as if another candidate was suddenly sprung on me, and I wouldn't ever give Mum the satisfaction of asking. Equally, I didn't think of the others as half-sisters, we were all in it together and they never made me feel any different.

I can't speak for the earliest years of Ange's childhood, naturally. I wouldn't trust her on that either is all I'll say. I mean she peed herself the night Lucy was born – no big deal surely; she would have been what, two or three at most? Never mind bravely looking after her Irish-twin sister, at that age was she really up to assessing the sexual dynamic between Grace, the old witch Molly with the broomstick next door and her hapless husband? As to looking out for the rest of us, well I suppose she *was* like Mum in the sense that she was there from my earliest consciousness. And to be fair, she did stay around longer than Mum if you look at it in one way, before she started playing her own loony tunes.

There's a lot I could take exception to in Ange's account, tell you a different tale of, but what's the point? It would be like painting the Golden Gate Bridge, except there was little gold in our childhood – I think we're all agreed on that if nothing else. More like polishing a turd it might be, as a Sisyphean task.

The temptation is there of getting as gabby as my oldest sister – how can I not concede her the title, hers by birth, ha ha as she might say? – because I can touch-type. The thoughts and words come flooding out instead of being more measured if you're writing by hand – not that Ange ever did any of that either except maybe shopping lists. So calm down, Karen, calm down. That's something people have told me a lot over the years, from before it became compulsory to say it in that stupid Scouse accent.

You know what, I'm not going there. Who cares about the squabbles of a lot of snot-nosed kids? I don't have to justify myself either to older or younger siblings. Billy could never say I didn't keep an eye out for him – someone had to at Colditz – but if he'd ever tried to call me Mum he wouldn't have survived for long.

Chip on the shoulder, *moi*? That was something people used to say about me. It only half made me laugh when someone varied it by saying I was well balanced really, a chip on *both* shoulders. I should look up where that phrase comes from. I always think of it as like a fish-shop chip, but is that right? Does it make you chippy just because you like fighting? Ask Ange – maybe I learned how to fight the first time she started dragging me about the house by the hair, nearly having a fit because I wouldn't do what she told me when she was playing Mummy. More like *Mommie Dearest*.

I dare say I'll have more to write about Grace, our real mummy, in due course. We all came out of her barrel even if it wasn't always Dad that loaded the bullets. And I see Ange didn't mention the other kids he did have, did admit to.

All in good time.

3

Lucy

That was a bad time. I didn't know anything could go wrong with babies. I hardly knew what happened when they came. I wasn't in the hospital to see it, thanks God I say, especially after hearing Ange's descriptions of it. Well, not so much that to tell you the truth. It was hearing her wake up night after night screaming. I never asked, but I think she was wetting the bed again.

At first Mum tried to put a brave face on it. She had to stay in the hospital at Clacton to make sure she was all right. If they checked her up mentally as well as physically it would have been good. I had no idea whether she was hurt or not. It was already our last day at Butlin's so we had to go home. Dad seemed happy to have the chance of driving. He always liked driving.

Uncle Henry took Martin back to their home, while Aunt Joy stayed with Mum. Dad tried to give her money for a B & B, but she wouldn't take it. 'She's my sister, Eric,' she said, almost as if she was blaming him already. Maybe she could sleep at the hospital. I suppose they would have taken Mum off the maternity ward, if she even made it there in the first place.

None of us said much in the van on the way home, which was normal only for Billy. At the time we all thought it kind of passed over his head, that he didn't register he was going to be an older brother, before he wasn't again. Now, I think he took in a lot more than we realised.

I'm sure Dad wouldn't have rung our payphone to tell Grandad Cecil and

Grandma Alice what had happened. They would have expected to see us all coming home, Mum still fat.

Grandma was up in her bedroom when we arrived. No surprise there. Dad didn't go to her. He struggled to speak. 'She lost the baby, Sess. It was shit-awful bad. Get your missus up to see to her grandkids or do it yourself. I'm choking. I've got to go out for a bit. Heading back to Clacton first thing. Yeah, we think Grace will be OK, except for the shock. It weren't as if we hardly had the bab to lose.'

Grandad seemed at a bit of a loss, Grandma already shouting from upstairs for her Grace. 'Come with me, Lucy, help me break it to her.' He took me by the hand. That was a first.

I tried to help by going up with him. I thought Ange had somehow done her bit at the hospital, even if nobody could have helped there.

He was as tongue-tied as Dad had been. 'Ally, I'm sorry...prepare yourself... Do you want to get back in bed?'

'Tell me what's going on, you daft bugger. I'm ready. I know it's bad just from the look on your fizz. Does Lucy have to tell me? What's happened to my girl?' She was practically shouting at poor Grandad.

'She lost the baby, that's what Eric said. I don't know any more.'

'Lost it? She was full term near as dammit. He caused it, bouncing her all over the country so he could have his precious holiday. No wonder he's ashamed to face me. I'm sorry, Lucy, I know he's your dad. No need to cry. You've been a big help to Grandad – he's hopeless, isn't he?

'Will you go to the shop with him and get some ham in? Nice stuff, Wiltshire,' she turned back to order him. 'Make sure there's some eggs. I know there's oven chips being as you've been feeding me on them all week.'

Her tone softened as she spoke to me again. 'You all like ham egg and chips, don't you, precious?'

Another first, her calling me precious. I nearly said we liked them best with fish-shop chips but somehow it didn't seem...What's the word I'm looking for? Karen would know, for sure. It was too *solemn* for fish-shop chips, that's perhaps it. It didn't feel like we deserved any sort of a treat. I knew Dad wasn't treating himself at the pub, whatever others might think. I could see he was really upset.

I wasn't sorry that Ange would be sharing with Jan rather than me while we were still on school holidays. Karen had been getting in with Billy in the other room for us three, but the night we came home she asked if I wanted to.

45

'Why?'

'Dunno. Thought you might be scared. Or upset.'

'No, you can have him.'

'And what about if our new little brother comes looking for one of his sisters to slip into bed for a cuddle with?'

'That's sick, Karen. Don't you dare say anything like that to Ange.'

'Why not? She's the oldest – she should be the bravest. And she's the one he might recognise, isn't she? She'd be the favourite.'

I was annoyed with myself for feeling a little bit of comfort at that thought, however stupid it was. 'I don't care what you say, Kar. I would have liked to see him as well.'

'Whatever for? Did you want another little nit like this one, always under your feet?' The way she stroked already sleeping Billy's hair made me know she didn't mean it. So I turned my back on her and faced the wall. Me and Ange would always say goodnight to each other, but I hadn't got into that habit with Karen.

She wasn't quite ready to let me sleep, despite me letting her have the last word.

'It's all for the best, you know.'

'What is?' I didn't give her the satisfaction of turning round.

'That he died. I wonder if he had a name. We'll have to call him something other than dead bab, won't we?'

'Why are you trying to be so horrible? If you don't care about him, think about Mum in hospital.'

'Grandma said it, said they couldn't look after the kids they'd got already, why did they want more? I expect she was worried he might take some of Mum's attention off her – she's a big baby herself.'

'She called me "precious" tonight.'

'You're everyone's precious, aren't you? I can't stand her, but I think she was right about that. We're more than enough.'

I didn't have time to get into any bad dreams before Dad was in the bedroom holding Karen round the waist off the floor in front of him, her feet kicking out furiously. 'Hush baby, you'll wake the others.'

'Like you wouldn't have woke them as well, killing Grandma.'

'She took me by surprise. Christ, she's normally like Dracula, never seen after nightfall – how was I to know she'd be sitting up waiting to give me a hard time?'

'Dracula's *always* seen after nightfall.' Karen could never resist correcting someone. 'He only appears at night.'

'All right, clever clogs. I meant to say Alissula, his ugly sister. You can't see her in a mirror either, cos she cracks 'em all. I wasn't going to hit her, let alone kill her. I left my gun with the silver bullets in Washtown for one thing. Honest. Go to sleep now. You too Lucy Lastic – I know you're listening to everything, even if you didn't sneak out onto the stairs like your naughty sister.'

He was gone in the morning. Unless he had buried as well as killed Grandma during the rest of the night, she went with him. I couldn't remember the last time she'd left the house.

They decided it was best to give Mum a bit more space when she came home. I thought when I first saw her, or hoped for a second I suppose, that it had all been some sick joke, the sort Karen might play. She still had what women in the street used to call her baby bump, so I thought maybe she hadn't had our brother after all. He was still waiting to come out, his whole life ahead of him. But the rest of her body told the true story. Her face had taken a little tan from the Clacton sun and the look of someone who's had a proper physical and emotional tanning. Her hair hung shockingly straight, all the curly bounce hosed out of it. Her nose was red as a child's playbox button, hand clutching hankie never more than a few moments from dabbing at it or her matching eyes. The baby had come, he'd had his time, as I'd heard Grandma say with what sounded like satisfaction about the death of some old comedian she used to like on telly.

So we went back to Washtown, me and Ange and Jan. Mum wouldn't be separated from Billy – perhaps that was when she started getting more kind of possessive with him. I hadn't thought of that before. That wouldn't do him, or probably her, any favours. It certainly put Karen's nose out of joint. She refused to move to Washtown, so we left her to have a tug-of-war with Mum over our little brother – the living one.

What did we know? It was the way, back then. There was no question of having a funeral with a tiny little coffin like they do nowadays. From what you hear, our baby Eric went straight into the hospital furnace, if not out with its rubbish. We came to know his name. It was more and more the only time Mum said 'Eric' with affection, when she mentioned him.

Not that she did mention him much. I expect you're thinking, hearing about a baby born like that in the sixties, that it was thalidomide. Our brother was a child of thalidomide. I'm not saying that for sure – how can we check now? I wouldn't want to look up if the dates were right – or wrong I suppose. In a way, it would have been good. Not like Karen said about him dying, in a nasty way. It might have taken away some of the fear all Grace's daughters – and I mean all of us, whatever Kar might say – had when it came to our time. Better some criminal medication than a fault in Mum's genes we could have inherited. We might have remembered the five of us had been all right, but it wasn't a topic any of us could think clearly about. Maybe Mum was just too old by then to have another healthy child, but wouldn't there have been some signs of that? Surely they had ultrasound?

There was definitely no compensation. I mean money to put it crudely – what else compensation could there be? It wasn't like Mum to miss out on any state benefits available. That shows how deranged she was. Or perhaps it wasn't until later all that came along. When people who felt entitled for everything to be perfect in their lives started having to bring up those poor little babies with their horrible, obvious imperfections. By then all the evidence would have disappeared. Mum and Dad could hardly investigate for themselves.

I'm going to be honest about our return to Washtown. I was glad. I liked it better living with Uncle Pete and Aunt Shirley than I did with Mum and Dad. It was so much quieter, for one thing. Tedge could be boisterous but he was a sweet kid, and he idolised me. None of us were embarrassed by him anymore. Kids who didn't know him would sometimes call him names like mong or spazmo, but it took a lot to rile him (then you wouldn't want to do it again, mind). Everybody would get called spaz or spastic back then but I never liked it, perhaps because of him. Uncle Pete would go mad if he heard it, from adult or child. He and Aunt Shirley must have had Tedge when they were super-young, because he was well older than me (even though I never felt like he was), and Uncle Pete was younger than Dad.

They may have been scared to have another child, but they were always a great aunt and uncle. Karen always tries to put herself as the outcast in the family, the loner, but she had Billy at her beck and call. Ange and Jan had each other, and for all we'd shared a room best part of a year, Ange didn't think twice about wanting Jan not me when she came back in the holidays. So who did that leave me? Grandma and Grandad? Well, I can honestly say I made some effort with them, young though I was. An effort like none of the others ever did. If they always said I was the favourite with Pete and Shirley, perhaps I'd spent a bit more time with Tedge than any of them ever would.

Ange and Jan were still together back in Washtown, staying at Nana and

Grandad's. Jan had the usual major paddy on being separated again from Fang, begging Grandad to take him back to live with them.

'It's him or your sister,' he tried to joke, but it nearly backfired when she rattled right back that sure Ange could stay in Northampton with the others, she'd look after her dog so well they wouldn't know he was there.

'No lass, it was a mistake ever to have him. Maybe that can't be changed, but we can't have him with us. The council will already be wondering about another kid in an old folks' bungalow.'

At least that sounded a better excuse than Aunt Shirley's – that Fang's hairs would be bad for Tedge's asthma, for all my cousin was often said to be chesty. I felt a bit sorry for Jan, but I was never a dog person. Anyway, she had always made it very clear whose dog he was, nothing to do with us.

You might have thought a year apart would have let my two older sisters find some new friends. I hadn't seen much sign of that for Ange up in Northampton. Back in Washtown, I would never see her out except with Jan, who did have other options. She and I had gone to Brownies together, and during our separation she had graduated to the Guides. She tried to get Ange interested, with no luck.

I think Jan was away at a Guides' camp when I got run over. That would account for me being out in the street with Ange. We were messing about as we walked along, not fighting exactly – she was that much older and could still be scary – but maybe play-fighting you could call it. I ended up actually in the street, not on the pavement, and got hit by a motorbike. That's what I was told, I should say. I don't have any proper memory of that bit.

It was from the Service we would speak to Mum and Dad once a week, since neither Washtown house had a phone. Uncle Pete would normally call us to the club one to speak to our parents in turn, but that night he brought Nan and put her on first.

'Grace, how are you? No, he's here and the kids as well – not Jan, you remember she's away for the week. I know, we should speak more often. We'd come up and see you, but it's such a long way to bring them all. Why not get Eric to fetch you down here? We'll find a way between us to put everyone up. No, don't get nervous, love. Yes, there is something I have to tell you. Don't get worked up – Jack said I shouldn't, but I had to. No, it was Lucy. Grace?'

'Kids, get out from under people's feet. Go put the ashtrays out on the tables please. What's up, Mum? Has she hung up? I said you should have asked to speak to Eric first.'

'Shut up, Pete. Yes, Eric, Eric, can you try to quieten her down – everyone's fine. I know – she didn't give me a chance to tell her.'

Dad was apparently more prepared to listen. We had been almost outside Nan and Grandad's bungalow, to which Ange – open-mouthed as usual – pointed the bloke who picked me up and carried me in, leaving his bike slewed across the road.

'Cuts and bruises is all, son, a bump on the head, she's fine now – you can speak to her in a minute. I don't know what sort of bike. He was a nice young lad, almost crying himself. Hush up, your brother was just the same. It was an accident – not everything's somebody's fault. If you don't like the way we're looking after your kids, come and do a better job yourself, that's all I'll say. She's fine. Come and see for yourself sometime, you can't be working seven days a week. I'll put you on to Pete now – he can tell you whether it was a "proper" bike or a bloody moped. I thought you might be more interested in how your daughter is than bashing some kid's face in.'

I got on eventually and played the brave little soldier Dad called me. I could hardly make out what Mum was saying when she came on – 'couldn't stand to lose another one' through her horrible hiccupping sobs.

Ange told them of course she had been watching me but I just stepped right out into the street. As years passed, the story got to be more and more about her, another shock to her system, not to my bones. And secretly I would wonder if she had pushed me into the traffic. I was lucky in any case, hadn't seen a doctor, just got patched up from the cupboard above Nan's kitchen sink. As I always say, things were different then.

Believe it or not, that was probably one of our better calls. Karen found the long word for what they were normally like, relays of people at either end of the line – 'excruciating', it was.

'Hello, Lucy Lastic. How's my littlest little girl in Washtown?'

'Fine, Dad. How are you?'

'Not too bad. Do you want to speak to your sister here?'

'Does Karen want to speak to me?'

'Karen. Karen, you will if I say so.' He didn't even know to put his hand over the receiver.

Mum was worse than that. She would either be talking a mile a minute about how much she was missing us all and she'd soon be well enough for us to come back home, or it was as if she had to winch every word up separately from a deep well. We had all seen Dad drunk many times, but I think we all heard Mum that way before we saw her for ourselves.

If I'm totally honest, I suppose I can see why the other girls might have resented me a little bit. The trouble was they resented me an awful lot, especially Karen. They might have been jealous at my holiday in a little touring caravan going around the Norfolk coast with Uncle Pete, Aunt Shirley and Tedge. I heard Pete ask Dad's permission on one of those phone calls, explaining he wished he could take the others as well but it was only a four-berth. They always preferred the quieter places, self-catering. Uncle Pete didn't have the money to flash around like Dad in the early part of our week at Butlin's, which didn't stop us having a good time. The sea was still warm enough to go in, and Tedge loved it. He was getting a bit easier for people outside the family to understand. He wasn't stupid, just a little, 'backward' was the word most people used then, without meaning any harm by it – better than saying 'retarded' anyway, I always thought. The best way of describing him was the way Uncle Pete always did. Tedge marched to a different drum. That was it.

I wonder if they still make kids write compositions about what they did in their school holidays. I would love to see whatever I wrote that year, back at Rambert Road, now the only Roper apart from Tedge. Mum obviously wasn't well enough to have us back with her by the time the school year started, despite all her promises and I-swear-its.

I hadn't minded our school in Northampton. If I had, I hope I wouldn't have made the fuss Ange did. Uncle Pete tipped me off – you should cry up for yourself sometimes, gal. When I asked what, he said it was like speaking up, except it worked better. It was a girl thing. 'Turn on them waterworks and you'll get your own way from a man more often than not.'

I would have done it if needed to stay in Washtown, suppose Mum had wanted us back with her. Using Jan, I could say that I was now coming up to the eleven-plus so they mustn't risk me failing it. Karen always thinks she's the smartest one because she went to university. I could ask what good it did her in the end, but all I'll say is that we weren't stupid, any of us. I reckoned I had a good chance of passing without being much fussed either way. I wasn't dreaming about going to London or having a big career. The others used to kid me for playing with dolls, but I don't see anything wrong in wanting to have a family. My Sindy was always part of a happy family too – I could make sure of that.

I was tempted to squeeze a few crocodile tears out when Aunt Shirley said I would have to stay with them if I didn't mind, cos Mum was still a bit poorly and couldn't cope with us all yet. Poor Mum, but curiosity got the better of the tears.

'What's the matter with her?'

Aunt Shirley was good at sighs. 'I don't honestly know, Lucy. I mean we all know she lost the baby. That must have been terrible, enough to floor anyone.'

'Could she have kept him, little Eric?'

'How do you mean, kept him?'

'Well, I heard Grandma Alice say that whatever he looked like, we would have found a way to love him.'

'Who did she say that to?'

'I'm not sure, but I remember it was Dad who answered her.'

'What did he say?'

'He said "Don't be so bloody stupid. You didn't see him. It wasn't like a" – and then he said the F-word – "birthmark." Then he stormed out.'

'One day you might be able to talk to your mum about it, Luce, but not yet please. Maybe your Aunt Joy next time you see her – she was at the hospital too, wasn't she?'

'Yes she was. I mean I thought he just died, not like they had a choice.'

'That's what I thought as well. I'm not trying to duck the question. I hope you know I'll always try to give you a straight answer. Sometimes you do have to make hard choices in life, and you don't ever know if you've made the right one.'

'Like Tedge's school?' I had heard raised voices between her and Uncle Pete – a rare thing – about whether they should send my cousin to a different school when he had to leave Rambert Road. I mean not the Grammar obviously – are you joking me? – but not the Clarkson either, a different one.

'Yeah, a bit like Tedge's school, but that's one of the easier ones to tell you the truth. I've made that choice. Uncle Pete just has to make it as well now.'

'Maybe you can cry up if you need to.'

'Oh, I can do that all right.' I liked to see her smile.

None of us understood then the effort Aunt Joy must have made trekking from London to East Anglia and back by public transport on a Sunday. She took us to the Wimpy on the marketplace for burgers and chips before she had to catch her train back. It must have been just before half-term because I remember her warning us to expect Mum to be 'not herself. You know she's not well, don't you?'

'That's what we hear.' Maybe Aunt Joy didn't know the signs like Jan and me. We could already tell Ange was working up to go off on one. 'That's *all* we hear, but nobody ever tells us what's the matter with her. *Why* can't we be there with them? What difference does it make to her? She only ever sits gassing with her own mum anyway. It's not as if she really ever looked after us – I had to do most of it.'

'It's all right, love.' Aunt Joy reached across the table to put a hand on Ange's, which was clenched into a fist with the edge jittering up and down on the red-and-white tablecloth. 'I know it's hard to understand. The truth is our mum – Grandma Alice – isn't very well herself. You may not see it, but the amount of time your mum spends with her is kind of like looking after her.'

'They kind of like drinking sherry.' I always tried to lighten the mood when I could. Pathetic really – I almost agree with Karen sometimes.

'And vodka,' Aunt Joy said, more to herself than us. It seemed from her frown I had only succeeded in making her more miserable. 'I just wanted to say, before I go, that she's a lot thinner than she was, your mum. Your gran's gone the other way, so don't be surprised at that, or if what she says doesn't always seem to make sense. The doctors are trying to get her the right tablets to sort things out, so hopefully it will all be a lot better when we get together for Christmas.'

Hopefully. It wouldn't have a lot of competition to beat that half-term when Dad came down to fetch us, and Nan did one of her special Sunday roasts for us all. It felt strange to be sitting at a dinner table again with Karen and Billy, who was no more talkative than ever. Dad always said what could you expect, he could hardly get a word in himself with all the women in the family. He'd been saying that since Billy was late as a toddler with his first words. I don't know what Dad's excuse was for him being slow at reading.

Mum hadn't come. Dad made some lame excuse about not enough room in the van when Nan asked where she was, but surely Billy could have sat on her lap. Nan said what a shame, she would have liked to see Grace, and how was she doing, but continued fussing around her vegetables without listening much to Dad's answer. I think he realised, because after he'd started to say she wasn't doing too bad, he kind of tailed off and then muttered 'She's a fucking nightmare.' He'd turned away from Nan and saw me looking straight at him. He put a finger to his lips as if to say our secret. I didn't need to keep it long, because during the next week everyone could see he wasn't far off in describing life in Northampton.

Grandad Sess was still like a ghost, occasionally heard before we fully woke up in the morning getting ready for his round, or rustling about in his den in the evenings. Not Casper the Friendly Ghost, but he was harmless. Risking being called a lick-arse by the others, I went to see him one night. It felt strange knocking on a door in our own house, but not wrong.

He got my name right, so that was a good start.

'Hello, Grandad. I just wondered if you wanted some company.'

'Er...yes, come on in if you like.'

I'd meant did he want to come and join us in the living room to watch telly together. I didn't quite know how to say that without seeming rude, so I went in and sat through *Coronation Street* with him. Everything was spick and span, a lot tidier than the main house.

'We're all watching *Corrie* as well, you know.'

'I bet, but can you hear it?'

He had a point. There would be Billy having what we called his crazy half hour before bed, running round like a whirling dervish Mum would always say, whatever that was. Ange and Jan would be bickering or gossiping on the settee together, legs comfortably entwined or wrestling with each other. Then Karen would be doing a running commentary, supposed to be funny, making out it was a rubbish programme though she would never miss it. So no, it wasn't always easy to hear the latest goings-on at the Rovers when we were all together. Still, I watched it with the family on the Wednesday again and never returned to his room.

He had at least turned out to say hello when we arrived, behind only Fang. If you ask me, he didn't seem any more pleased to see Jan than the rest of us. The dog I mean. We all had to troop up to Grandma Alice's room to say hello, one by one. Ange and Jan said they just got a quick ask about how they were doing at school. I said it had gone the same with me, no point in mentioning what she did say. 'And how's my dearest Lucy, the only one who really cares for her old gran?'

It was a shock to see her, despite Aunt Joy's warning. You would have thought she had a switched-off Baby Glow in there with her under the covers if not for the evidence of fatness in the slack folds of many chins. Her eyes looked smaller than ever – she wasn't wearing her glasses – in that bloated face.

Karen had told us she was a vampire, sucking all the life out of Mum. Although I've never seen a fat vampire, I understood what she meant in a way, because as much as she had bulked up, Mum seemed to have – I was going to say slimmed down but you might think that meant she was more attractive than before. No, she was all skin and bone. Nobody had anorexia back then so it wasn't that, but she did look haggard like some of its sufferers do when you see them on telly.

I said we went to see Grandma Alice on our own, but Mum was lurking behind us all, as if she was afraid Grandma might grass her up for something if she wasn't in sight. If Mum looked weak, she showed no lack of energy or animation in the first hour or so after our arrival. Dad had more or less dumped us all on the house, saying he was going out but would be home with chips later. He said that to us – I was watching and there was not so much as a hello between him and Mum.

'Oh my babies, how you've all grown.' She was lying or frantic – it hadn't been *that* long. 'Me and Grandma are so looking forward to having you back with us. It's for a week, isn't it? When are you going back?'

That was typical of her conversation then. A burst of enthusiasm followed by self-doubt, an almost pleading question about something that might or might not be related to what had gone before. 'And you'll be passing that eleven-plus just like your clever sister Janet did – I know from Aunt Shirley what a good girl you are. Or is it Karen who's the clever one?'

Then there was 'Little Eric – I mean Billy' – she stuck a hand over her mouth, with eyes begging you to allow her the lapse – 'he's loving his football at school, little though he is. Don't think your dad will be coming home tonight. You'll have to whistle for your chips.'

We all noticed Mum was babying Grandma Alice more than before we'd been sent back to Washtown. She might as well have been in nappies. I know for a fact she didn't use the toilet properly cos I caught Mum trying to smuggle a smelly potty out of her room one day when I ran in from outside and up the stairs, busting for a pee myself.

I must confess over the years we've all been a bit guilty of putting Dad on a pedestal he didn't deserve. Never asked for either, to be fair to him. He had always spent odd nights away from home on his lorry. During the week of our half-term it didn't seem like he spent one at home. The worst wasn't when he went out for work but got dressed up in his blazer one night.

'Where are you going?'

'Out.'

'I can see that. Out with your fancy woman, no doubt.'

Dad didn't answer.

'Don't think I don't know. I'd say you were running away from your kids except I hear that bitch has got near as many as we have. Still, who else would have you? Not a great catch, are you?'

'Nope, so you've got nothing to worry about, have you?'

'Where are you going, Eric? Don't think I'll be leaving the door open for you to come in at any hour you like. I'll put the bolt on it.'

'Feel free. I can sleep in the wagon out in the street. Won't be the first time.'

'You'll be sleeping down Grosvenor Road, that's where you'll be sleeping, don't think I don't know. I might pay her a visit, see if she wants to take on our kids.'

'Might do a better job than you and that beached whale upstairs, popping pills and getting pissed together all day every day. Don't push me, Grace – think about them if not me.'

We would all be sitting in the living room as he adjusted his tie at the hall mirror, hoping and praying that he would get out without violence. They were both capable of starting, but he was always better at it. He never ended up crying.

Try as we would to sympathise with him – 'Can't blame him for wanting to get away from their nagging,' Karen would say, acting hard-nosed as ever – it was hard to hear Mum sobbing if he did come in late at night and she wasn't already out for the count. Hard to see her eyes dark with fatigue or…let's not beat about the bush, a proper shiner she had one morning during that half-term. Some holiday.

But don't hopes always rise for Christmas? Isn't there something in the build-up to it that makes you think it's going to be a great time. Whatever the evidence telling you it won't. As it happened, Mum and Dad were close during it. We weren't to know it was like that Christmas Day game of football in the First World War, a short break from the horrors before the horrors kept right on coming.

4

Grace

Worst thing I ever did meeting Eric Roper, let alone taking his name. Grace Roper. Give me enough rope to hang myself, he did that, but I wouldn't give him the satisfaction, not I. Five kids, I mean it's too much before I was twenty-five. I won't say I hadn't known other men before him – take that as biblical or not as you like. I'm free as a bird. What do I care what you say about me, what anyone says? I tried to be a mother, I was a mother, am a mother, just as good as many I could mention. Oh yes Mum, I'm thinking of you. I won't keep mum, BE LIKE DAD, KEEP MUM, but I can't keep mum any longer, not so dumb I'm not. Give me as much paper as you like, I'll fill it all – yes I know it may do me good, better than looking at your smug fucking face anyway.

He was handsome, course he was my Eric, and he'll be my Eric again one day, don't you worry you bitch. See how he sticks with you when he's got a kid by you, up the stick already that's what I heard. And don't you go accusing me about Karen. I'm saying nothing about that, some things are between a man and a wife. Eric my first and only lifetime husband, how many you on now Lil? Tell me that Lily Sheridan, don't keep shtum, Lily the colour of death, is that black lilies? Or white? White is something to do with death, isn't it? Or bad luck? Is it just bad luck? You were bad luck for me right enough Lily Sheridan and you'll be bad luck for him. Don't you worry – he knows to leave the table when his luck turns. He'll turn the tables on you then all right. He'll be your bad luck, mark my word. You're not prettier than me, nor younger, no better, no better than you should be. How could he? How could he start it with you?

Eric, Eric, you always used to look after me so much. I know Mum said it was a danger sign, the way you saw off my boyfriend when we first met. She never knew Harry was a big bully anyway but you did, spotted it straight away you did and rescued me. Didn't have to fight him that big lump you just looked at him, was it true you boxed for the Royal Hussars? Who knew when you were telling the truth or not? I didn't care, THAT WAS THE TRUTH, all I cared about was having you I wanted to have you and I was going to have you whatever the cost.

And what a cost. Five lovely kids you've got that's true enough, but don't be soft Mum – that's not like you and it's not true. Didn't Joy and me always used to hear about our own poor little lost brother, came before us and that was the only time Dad could give you a boy. How you made him know it. Never mind about your two lovely kids, your girls. What about them, Mum? What about us? Didn't we count? I won't have it from you no more, that's a fact, except there's no leaving you is there, whether you leave me or not? That's right Eric, don't think you'll get away, EVER, whether you leave or I leave or you try to make me leave.

And what, you want to have your say now Dad, bit late or what? I never wanted to know what the finances were about the house, as I recall you and Eric did all the signing between you, I wouldn't take sides. No, that's a lie – you may be my dad, but he's my husband. MY HUSBAND. It's still true. I stick to him and I stand by him. If he was too smart or too strong for you, then maybe it's your punishment for saying what you said only that one time but I'll take it with me to the grave. *He's probably like all pikies, thick as pigshit and twice as smelly.* Well what did you think of him when he come calling for me with his Brylcreem and aftershave? Like you could have stopped him anyway. Nobody could have stopped him – nobody could have stopped us. And he told me once he'd been looking for a dad all his life, once when I'd been slagging you off, but he had Jack I don't know what was wrong with Jack, always all right to me – maybe it's not the same if it's not your own blood. That was my flesh and blood there in the ward, more blood than flesh, just the opposite of Mum, that was all flesh it's a wonder we didn't have to winch her out of the fucking house. You can't stop me swearing FUCK FUCK FUCK – Doctor Shithead says I can write whatever I like in here so

I hope he was telling me the truth, but then what can he do? Can he punish me any worse?

I want my Billy here, maybe he could make it better, and I only want Billy so much because I can't have Eric, and I don't even know which Eric it is I want. Be good if somebody would help sort me out on that one – writing don't help there. And in case they ever read it, let me say I do love my girls as well, them poor Roper girls. Yes Karen, you too – you're a Roper just like the rest.

5

Karen

Was that last sentence the giveaway? Perhaps a little bit of wish fulfilment creeping in at the end of my bravura impersonation of Mum's voice? Her interior voice I never really heard of course. Only the fairies she was away with heard that. I'm sorry to hijack the story, I just got fed up with Lucy's so-precise sentences, and so boring, reaching for the right word and coming up every time with yet another thumping cliché.

I assume you got all the digs at me in her little tale in which she, of course, was the heroine? Didn't it strike you that she was very mature for a nine-year-old or whatever she would have been then?

The truth is we're all unreliable – you should take us all with a pinch of salt (I'll have that one off you, Luce). I mean none of us has a dispassionate record, for all the files in the various social services on the Ropers must have been thick enough; none of us was keeping diaries or any of that shit, and if we had been, I bet none of the big stuff would have been in there.

If I'm stealing the climax of your story off you, Luce, it's because I don't trust you to tell it straight. Remember you were away in Washtown, sitting down every night to a proper tea with Peter and Shirley and Tedge, starting to tag along to the Oliver Street youth club with Ange and Jan if they'd let you. Was there ever so much fuss made about such a crappy place?

Things got worse in Northampton between Bonfire Night and Christmas.

Dad did take us all out – Mum, Billy and me at any rate. Grandma and Grandad were locked in the house like little people in a clock, never seen together and her not even coming out when she was supposed to – the witching hour. So we did see the fireworks. We didn't have any of our own, I must ask the others if I'm dreaming one fantastic year when we did, Dad and Uncle Pete setting them off with their cigarette lighters. Maybe they were just burning all the rubbish we couldn't carry before making one of our many moonlight flits, but the memory of fireworks is strong.

If our grandparents were living separate lives, so were Mum and Dad. We never heard them laugh together anymore, much less play music downstairs like they used to; that was always a sign for Billy and me. We never let on to each other, but we knew it was safe to go to sleep on those nights. I don't remember seeing Dad and Grandad together in those months or much before, whether as friends or enemies. It was like we were all different spokes on a wheel, at the centre of which were Mum and Grandma Alice together. I tried to reach a hand across to Billy whenever he needed it as we went whirling round.

Why would she have killed herself? Could things really have been that bad? I may be making an assumption – the S-word is a little bit of a taboo in our family but it will keep popping up through the generations. I'm pretty sure I asked the question at the time, and if I didn't get a straight answer, what I did get made me think that way. On the other hand, she was buried in hallowed ground, not stuck outside the churchyard fence. I know that doesn't happen nowadays, but I've got a feeling it just might have still when I was a bairn.

The timing was either spiteful or tragic, again a matter of opinion. I tend to the former; more indulgent siblings might go the latter. Christmas Eve morning, Lucy had arrived with Ange and Jan the day before, courtesy Uncle Pete, who had to get back for his busy time at the Service. She would have gone all around the house like a dog in a new place if you let it, sniffing out our buried grandparents – him in his freezing little kennel where he might allow himself one bar of electric fire once or twice a year, she sweating in multiple layers of blubber, nightclothes and bedcovers in a radiator-superheated bedroom.

I don't know if she was already cold that morning. She must have been when I was the only one to go see her at the chapel of rest. We're a Catholic family, nominally at any rate, and the old black vulture with the white ruff did come circling. Maybe his motives were pure; after all, at that time of year he could probably have had a tot or two at most other houses without the grief.

'Aren't you coming in, Dad?' I had somehow assumed he would.

'No baby, I'll take the quacks' word for it that she's gone for good. You don't have to, you know.'

Once in there, the funeral assistant, undertaker or whatever hovering behind me in a grey pullover and necktie, I didn't know what to do. I didn't feel like crying; more like laughing if truth be told, perhaps a nervous reaction. I thought of sketching a cross on the dead forehead, but we weren't *that* Catholic. A kiss was out of the question. In the end, I just bowed my head, closed my eyes like hers were and turned to leave after I had counted slowly – in French, which we were learning at school – to a hundred.

'She was a right trouper,' the old pullie said to Dad.

'She's got more balls than all of us, mate,' he answered. That and his arm lightly over my shoulders for a moment were enough to justify my visit to the chapel.

I won't have Lucy claiming she was the one to discover the body. Ange is another one who likes to put herself centre stage at such moments – Gumpers both of them. Not that I want the credit myself. It was Mum, lurching that year like a drunk actress from one dreadful scene to another. 'I couldn't wake her' was the formula she used, over and over again: now I can never hear that phrase without fearing the worst, having to go and check on the sleeper, especially where – a not unfamiliar scenario – drugs and drink have been taken.

Dad appeared to have slept downstairs that night, still trying to turn his back to the world and face to the settee like a capless Andy Capp. He thumbed his braces over his shoulders when Mum stirred him, her voice gradually rising until 'I can't wake her' was a shriek. He went up the stairs in his vest and bare feet, but of course he couldn't wake her either.

It wasn't that bad a Christmas, all things considered. Dad rose to the occasion if you like, calling in the medical professionals – if ever a time justified sacrifice of his principles to use the hall payphone, this was surely it – and waiting to break the news to Grandad when he came in from his round. He had two bottles of beer for them, and not Grandad's home-brew stuff either. Aunt Joy also helped when she arrived that afternoon, as already scheduled. Cousin Martin didn't feel obliged to show any sort of grief, but we all kind of did, mainly for Mum's benefit.

Dad must have summoned Nan and Grandad from Washtown. She was all hugs for us kids, then down to the practicalities of getting a Christmas dinner done. Her sole reference to Grandma Alice was a robust 'That woman can't hurt anyone now', when Aunt Joy was tiptoeing around offering them her mother's bedroom. Mum and Dad shared their own bedroom over those few days for the first time in a long while, though I wonder if Mum knew it. He was doing his best to keep her calm in the way he knew best, by plying her with drink. The doctors made their contribution with sedatives. Perhaps they were emergency doctors; the ones the two women knew so well would surely have been aware there were cupboardfuls of prescription drugs in the house already, enough to put the lights out on the whole of Northampton.

So we had the presents – a bit odd opening the ones from Grandma Alice, boring stuff like clothes so to thank her would have felt like a lie except we didn't have to now. We had the turkey. We were introduced to eggnog, down to little Billy, mixed with lemonade. It was really good until it made me sick. I have a bottle every Christmas now – can drink it all by myself if I want.

Despite all that, it still wasn't right, and I don't mean just the empty seat at the dinner table. Perhaps she wouldn't have hauled herself downstairs anyway, even for a Christmas feast – would have had Lucy or Mum fetching and carrying it to her bed. That the atmosphere was not festive was no surprise. It was hectic I'd say, everyone on the point of hysteria. I didn't know then the saying that there's no problem alcohol doesn't make worse, but in this case any attempt at sobriety between death and funeral, over Christmas, might have been more disastrous yet.

Aunt Joy played her part in keeping things on the rails, along with Nan, allies then if not always. Trying to talk to us all individually, which was never Nana's way, Aunt Joy sounded like she was trying to convince herself of something, saying we shouldn't feel guilty or that the death was in any way our faults. Why would we? I didn't ever hear Mum rant against her sister for escaping their mother's clutches, as she perhaps thought she had herself at one point, and I doubt it would have occurred to me to think in that way unless Aunt Joy herself somehow put the idea in our heads.

Mum seemed to be struggling again to escape Grandma Alice after Christmas, in the endless walks she would take with Fang – that dog had never been so exercised. You didn't have to pick up their shit after them in those days, which Mum probably never would have had her own shit together enough to do. That was one side of the coin; the other was the days when she would be as if crawling back to her, spending all day in bed and then sometimes the next one too. I suppose both extremes were a sign of her grief; what united them was that she didn't give much of a toss for us whichever way the coin landed.

I doubt Dad was grief-stricken at the death of his mother-in-law, but I think he did try to show Mum some sympathy. He would do us a meal at times; we had no qualms about calling a fry-up a meal – still don't – but he didn't expect to have to do that every night. Grandad survived as before on his own, Mum manic or depressed never seemed to eat, so it was only Billy and me to cook for, our sisters already back in Washtown. Dad was just not up to, or perhaps up for is nearer the mark, looking after his kids full-time.

It was about then he introduced us to Lil. Although he tried to have us use the honorific 'Aunt', I drilled Billy hard that he must never do that. If he hadn't picked up on it I certainly had: this was the 'floozie', the 'scrubber', the 'slag', most often the 'bitch' and occasionally the 'whore' who occupied so much of Mum's ravaged mind. If I knew enough to associate those terms with sex, meeting Lil was something of an anti-climax. I never saw any sign of sexual attraction, let alone activity, between her and Dad, though later he would never deny he was little Eamon's father. While he never denied he was my father either, I think in the other case it wasn't just from gallantry. Lil was Irish, with a strong accent, and three kids at that time, all roughly of an age with us: Brenda was the oldest, Eddie, then Michael, who set off trying to lord it over our Billy until I set him right. They became best mates after that, and not just in childhood.

If she wasn't pretty, she did have big boobs, Lil. Maybe that was the lure (Mum was petite but perfectly proportioned), though I never saw them uncovered or in any way immodestly displayed. It was the middle of winter, a good time for the stews she seemed to cook every night, always enough for us to have a steaming bowlful each when Dad fetched us round to hers. To be honest, I preferred his fry-ups, except for the dumplings, which were great. I won't stoop to making the obvious pun on Dad also going mad for her dumplings.

I think Billy may have mentioned her name at some point in our home; I have a dim memory of him asking me if that was what had made Mum ill. I reassured him it couldn't be, though it might have led to one of the almighty rows which were one pole of her interactions with Dad that winter, the other being a chill apathy. I won't prolong the agony – not to drag the story out like my sisters tend to – so I'll guess it was February, still winter for sure, when they had her committed, or she looked for help herself. I've heard both versions. Our sisters stayed in Washtown. Billy and I were taken into care, as they used to say. And I won't be telling you anything about that particular episode, as old Forrest used to say.

Part Two:
Sixties and Seventies

6

The Twins

'I told you it wasn't much cop unless you like table tennis,' Janet said to her sister as they walked the twenty minutes from the Olly to their grandparents' bungalow off the Norwich Road.

'It was all right.'

'You should play yourself – you used to be able to beat me.'

'That was when I was just a kid, Jan. One of us had to grow up.'

'Don't start all that again. I know it must have been terrible what you saw at the hospital, then all the rest of it. God, I've heard it enough times to feel like I was there myself. But it's not our fault. We've just got to get on with it.'

'That's easy for you, with all the friends you've got there at the club. I see you were right busy while we were all away, making yourself a life outside the family.'

'Don't be such a drama queen, out of the family...'

'Who's the kid with the blonde hair, the one that looked about five years older than the others? Alex did they call him?'

'God's gift – that's what he thinks he is anyway. I don't think he's that much older. I see his little brother tonight giving you the once-over, but I doubt if Alex noticed you. They say all he thinks about is football and fighting.'

'Not fucking then?'

'Ange! Where'd you get that from? Don't tell me you've…?'

'Don't be daft, no, but I'd like to see Mum or Dad getting onto me about language. I don't remember them swearing about the house so much when we were little, do you?'

'No. I was so shocked when I first heard Dad use the F–word. Not even swearing like he was angry, he didn't know I was coming into the club behind him – must have used it about six times in the same sentence.'

'Mum's not so bad but he's got worse – he doesn't care who's around now. I might have been joking about fucking – you know I was – but sometimes I want to scream the words we're not supposed to say. I bet the boys don't put on that face like you just did when one of them says the word.'

'If you like him, why don't you try it? Give him another interest in life.'

'I never said I liked him. Did Grandad give you money for fish and chips to take back?'

Jan was the first Roper girl to start at the Oliver Street Youth Club in Washtown, up the road from the Hippodrome where they'd gone to watch Saturday morning films in their early childhood before it became a bingo hall. In her final year at Rambert Road and first at the Grammar she had a passion for table tennis, begun at the Brownies and continued into the Guides, both troops of which met at the Olly premises on Tuesdays. The youth club was on Fridays, and they also got the table out.

More than a few weddings could no doubt trace their origins to the Olly over the years. Only Lucy found it curious enough to mention that three of them involved the Roper family, once the girls finished their blasted childhood. For all its target age group corresponded more or less with secondary school – say eleven to eighteen – it was a sad sack indeed still going to it religiously once they could be served in a variety of pubs all around town – from fifteen at the latest, twelve in the case of girls if they had a dab of lipstick on. The lower limit was not strictly enforced at the Olly. There was usually a gaggle of primary-school kids, whether brought by older siblings on childcare duty or pitching up in little gangs of their own. The club drew the line at babies in prams, though more than one alumna, still age-eligible, must have pushed hers wistfully past it.

It was later, the times when Lucy and Karen would complete the four aces them Roper girls were in their youth, that one wag tried to rechristen the Friday-night Olly the Groparoper (the poor Draper girls fared even worse). Brian Jacobs didn't know that Alex was already with Ange by then. Instead of laughing, he cuffed Brian, who got off lightly at that.

Dark hair, dark eyes, full lips, Ange and Jan both had them, their faces alike enough to tell you they were sisters without ever believing them to be twins as Ange liked to claim. You would have thought Jan the older when she took her along for the first time, confidently through the door as usual while Angela behind her was like someone trying to sneak in at the flicks without paying. In another way, it was the opposite. They were both girls of course, still girls, but one was dolled up like a young woman while the other dressed more like a boy. Although they would each play different roles over the years, at that point Jan was Sporty and Ange was Sexy.

Discos, with an extension sometimes till ten, would soon come to replace the music initially limited to what the old gaffer on the door – his wife served the crisps and pop – deemed worthy of going on his record player. He subjected the kids to his Sinatra LPs until he let himself be persuaded to switch the needle to forty-five and play selected singles for those who had brought in their own. Selected by him from the ones they put forward, with criteria including his liking not only for the artist but the kid with the record. Elvis was the only banker. Girls had more luck getting plays than boys, which soon led to the situation where only they submitted them, on the lads' behalf as well as their own.

While you might see some of the girls bopping to their own numbers, the emphasis of the club remained on sports. A couple of ping-pong tables the boys tolerated, used themselves, for the first hour or two as long as the floor could be cleared for their football sharp at eight. They liked the girls to stand or sit in the recessed area where the snack counter was to watch them. Some (Ange) did, some (Jan) didn't. She wore shorts to play, not to show off her legs as Ange would in her defiantly non-sporting gear. In winter, Jan's tracksuit bottoms would go straight on the minute she got off the table, which might be after quite a while since none of the other girls were a match for her.

The same could be said of Alex at football. He was captain of the under-twelves through fourteens at the Grammar, which everyone expected to continue until he left. He might not get to sixth form if a proper team signed him up, as some people were already talking about – not just the Town, as Washtown FC was universally known within its limited catchment area, but maybe the Posh or even the Canaries.

'It was the tits, mate,' Brian Jacobs would say, keeping an eye open for Alex. Maybe it *was* her still developing curves that drew Alex to Ange in the first place. He would be glad enough himself to joke about that later. It was something a bit more romantic though, without wanting to get too soppy. Maybe it's coming it a bit strong to compare them to a prince and princess, a middle-class boy and council-house girl – no reverse snobbiness about that by the way, it's just the truth and better than a caravan any day – but for a brief spell, at the Olly, that's what they became.

Perhaps the girls were all looking for a safe landing, each in her own way and each with her own idea of what that meant, when their parents split and cut them adrift. Although she always denied it to her older sister, Jan had already felt a bit disconnected from the rest of them. The thing she hated their father for most was not what had made Grace support her staying in Washtown when they moved to Northampton. Grace wouldn't acknowledge it, wouldn't acknowledge anything other than normal paternal affection, for her sanity she said, which was ironic now she seemed to have mislaid that. She wasn't in the lorry as his eager daughter was. He would sometimes pull over in the middle of the night to 'catch forty winks' he would say, winking at her. She was often struggling to keep her own eyes open. The first time he allowed her to lay her head on his lap to sleep more comfortably it felt good. He stroked her hair until she dropped off. That's all he did. The first time, that's all he did.

That wasn't the *conscious* reason she hated him. That she had buried, trying her hardest to believe her mum and parroting the same mantra, for the sake of her own sanity. Luckily, she never had to discourage any of her sisters from riding with him. That had been her enthusiasm, and it had almost broken her.

Fang was perhaps her first love affair. He represented the innocent part of her lorry-driving days, the best part. If only he could have been with her on all the trips. He was a special gift from her dad, and she convinced herself he had a special, uncomplicated love for her. She hated it when he let the others fuss him, always finding an excuse to call him to her.

When Grace went to the psychiatric hospital in Braunton, Eric did not hang about. He sold up the house with the children's orchard, turfing his father-in-law onto the mercy of his other daughter, and by all accounts swindling him out of his share of the proceeds from the property. All accounts except his own. Eric never gave accounts.

'I would have taken Karen and Billy in, I told him that, cramped as we were,' Lil said when Jan asked if she could go and see Fang. 'But I couldn't have coped with a dog, especially a big one like that. I'm sorry it had to end that way, but I don't know that they marked the spot in the woods for you to visit

– probably thought it would upset you too much.'

Jan was able already to play the long game. 'No, it wouldn't. It would be a comfort to know just where it was, that's all. In the woods?'

'I really don't know, love.' Lil had gratefully accepted the girl's offer to help with the washing-up, unaware she was being rinsed for information. 'We couldn't have him here. I said I wouldn't have a gun in my house either. I made sure I saw your grandad load it right back in the boot. Oops, butterfingers – never mind, it's not my best china, no need to cry about dropping a stupid plate. It's all right, my love.'

The next day Grandad was loading up the boot again, taking her and Ange back to Washtown. This was when there was still some pretence that the family would keep in touch by alternate visits between there and Northampton. Lucy had already tired of it, and it would be the last time Jan set foot in Lil's house. She had to leave in Grandad's car. She didn't forgive him, but she still needed him.

She did not need Eric anymore. Instead of letting him hug her goodbye, she stood him off. 'You shot Fang. You murdered him. You didn't find him a good home at all. Did you even try?'

'I did try. He wasn't an easy dog to take on.'

'So you shot him.'

'We gave him a soldier's death.'

'We? We? Who pulled the trigger? Did you make Grandad do that as well? Didn't have the guts yourself?'

'Mind who you're talking to, girl.'

'A soldier's death? He was a dog. You shot my bloody dog, you bloody bastard.' And she attacked him with fists and feet, until Grandad came to pull her away, not having heard the build-up to the explosion, not asking his stepson or Jan for any explanation.

Maybe it would have been better that way, if there had been such an explosion. Jan would keep a lot to herself; as often as she might have lived out the scene in her mind, she did not confront her father. She took on the burden of guilt that he might have killed Fang as another way of punishing her.

If her sisters had any curiosity about the dog's fate, they never showed it. Years later, she was watching an *All Creatures Great and Small* repeat, where a squire has to have his favourite hunter put down. Declining the vets' offer to do the job, he has a bugler sound the tally-ho or whatever to make the animal prick up its ears before he puts a bullet behind one of them. 'You and your

71

horses,' Ray failed to josh her out of it. When she'd cried herself quiet, she decided they were going to have a dog. Her husband never knew to connect the two things.

She abandoned table tennis from one week to the next, without a word of explanation or anyone to ask her for one. She became a hippie. Her sports gear gave way to ankle-length skirts and cheese-cloth shirts, she let her hair grow long without putting flowers in it – she did after all still have to live in Washtown. The other bit she wasn't quite ready to buy into yet, despite the encouragement (determinedly unaggressive) of her new hippie boyfriend, was the free love. Like the sex – which she would discover was mostly what the free love was about – the drugs were still in the future for both of them.

Alex did not talk to Ange about free love. She was already living in his house, theoretically in separate bedrooms – the house was big enough to allow that comfortably, as well as rooms for his younger brother James and sister Helen. It was a case of observing the law as well as the proprieties, which Alex's solicitor father Simon surely knew. While he and his wife Gwen, with their en suite, did not police the landing, could they really have been unaware of the path trodden by Alex to her room? The nap was worn in only one direction – she never went to him, not because she was unwilling but as she always put it 'from respect to your parents'. She still addressed them, on the rare occasions she had to, as Mr and Mrs Reed.

It was mainly Mrs Reed who persuaded the Town Romeo and Juliet to have an abortion. To be fair to her, the possibility of criminal proceedings against her son was not the only motivation, and in justice to Alex, the fear of them was not a factor in his reluctant acquiescence. Both went with her to the clinic – privately, thank you Mr Reed – but it was Angela Roper, fourteen, who had to give a kind of birth and a kind of death.

Jan's hippie came from an even bigger house than Alex, of whom he was a classmate but not an intimate. She spoke to Jason Tyler first at the Olly, though he was no regular there. Not into either sports or fighting, he had his own little cool as one of the earliest smokers in school, and a sharp enough tongue to defend himself against jibes of effeminacy or gayness when it was still called worse things. Stevie Plater was rebuked by Monkie as form master for shouting at the teacher's enquiry as to why Jason couldn't do gym one day, 'Because he's having his period, sir.' He was more stung by Jason's comment as they left the classroom, detaining Plater by the arm in the doorway so a crowd had to hear him.

'Just for your info, matey, I'm not a girl. If I were, you wouldn't hardly be so interested in me.'

Alex did not have to consort with Ange at school, since she was at the Clarkson rather than the Grammar. He played football at every break and in the dinner hour, with a number of female admirers including overspill from the Olly among those in tight little gaggles watching the boys.

Jan made it clear to her elder sister that she would not be keeping an eye on him at school for her; that if she wanted a spy, she would have to look elsewhere. Other siblings were not available, with Karen in a grammar school at Northampton – academically fully entitled yet already with some 'behavioural issues' threatening her tenure – and Lucy after her eleven-plus fetching up also at the Clarkson. She wanted Uncle Pete to ask for a review of her result, but such an encounter with the authorities was too daunting for him. Aunt Shirley was more robust in declining to intervene. 'Love, you may just not have it in you – not everyone's bright, and the ones who are, it doesn't necessarily make them any more happier.' Children's educational attainments were something of a delicate issue with Tedge the way he was, so Lucy left it there.

Aside from a genuine distaste for following Alex around the schoolyard and telling tales on him to her sister, Jan would never have been seen amongst the girls watching the footballers and sometimes selected by them for further favour. With too few friends to form a successful lobby to get the gym opened for table tennis in the dinner break, once she lost interest in the sport she had fewer still.

She did have Jason though. While the teachers kept a watchful eye on intense mixed-sex relationships (intense same-sex ones were not on their radar), they could not entirely discourage friendships between boys and girls. Groups of boys still tended to hang around together, as did groups of girls, without much intermingling. If it was rare for couples to seek each other out exclusively between classes, it was not unknown. Rarer yet were acknowledged relationships where the girl – it was always the girl – was two years the junior, as was the case between Janet and Jason.

She liked the fact that Jason was different, that he was not ashamed to be seen with her, did not put up a strict barrier between chatting up and chatting. If he was prepared to hang out with her at breaks, she could put up with the sneers of other girls, the suggestions that she was giving him a lot more than kisses, the main currency of first and second-year relationships.

Although they did kiss, she also liked it that he did not force the pace, sexually or in other ways. He put her under no pressure to smoke when they moved to the lower surveillance areas of the school grounds, beyond sight of the main buildings, so he could do so. While he preferred Dylan or The Byrds, he had no objection to soul or pop music. She was touched when he bought her a Motown Chartbusters album the first year they were acknowledged boyfriend and girlfriend, without realising she had nothing to play it on.

She kept the LP at his house, where the two of them would have been free to get up to all that Alex and Ange were doing and more under the benevolent non-supervision of Jason's mother Jessica. Neither he nor Jan ever spoke of their respective fathers. It seemed from the size of the house, the cleaning woman sometimes in evidence and Jessica's general air of lounging or lying rather than doing anything more strenuous, that she had no need to work. She was active in the local Angles theatre; sometimes there would be groups of people in her living room, declaiming from scripts. Enlisted at times to help her learn a part, her son had so far resisted any attempts to get him on stage.

Jason had significant barriers to overcome with Jan, which again left him unfazed. He agreed at once when she said she would not have sex till she was sixteen, then inch by inch persuaded her to a much tighter definition of sex, like some stage or screen director ensuring he gets the shots he wants of his starlet, however many nudity-only-when-artistically-justified clauses she may have to cover her ass. Jan enjoyed the debate, came to enjoy granting the concessions he negotiated so earnestly, as long as he never forgot that she was the one in control, or made her feel it might be otherwise.

Jason's mother was naturally not involved in the minutiae of these quasi-contractual discussions carried out on her premises, as time went by with increasingly liberal use of her drink and dope supplies as well as free borrowing of her records. Meanwhile, Mrs Reed was falling down on the job. Active enough in terminating Ange's first pregnancy (unwanted by everyone except conceivably Ange herself), she must have neglected the lecture on preventive measures, since that girl was pregnant again when *she* turned sixteen.

'Are you mad, Ange? Jeez Louise, can't you see he's just taking advantage of you. I mean once might be an accident, but twice? Why don't you come back and live at Nan's if you can't keep him off you?'

'It's what adults do, Janet. Anyway, that's a good one, come back – don't you mean go back? I know you spend more time round that poof Jason's than you do at Nan and Grandad's. Don't blame me if he's not man enough to give you what you want.'

'Can you hear yourself? Better someone with a bit of restraint than someone who's not too fussy who he goes with. If you have a kid just be ready for it to have plenty of half-sisters and brothers as well. Anybody would think you're looking for somebody just like Dad.'

'That would be you, Jan – you were always his favourite. At least he's a proper man.'

Jan turned away. White-knuckled and with nails digging into the palms of her hands, but she turned away. She was unconcerned by the aspersions on her boyfriend. She thought it was just a laugh that time when Jason had encouraged her to do some undressing by coming back into the bedroom himself dressed up in items of his mum's clothing, under and outer. It was harder not to think of the times when she was Dad's 'favourite'. 'OK, I'll say no more. It's your funeral.'

'I'm sorry, Jan. Have your Jason if you want to keep playing at little kiddies' love stories. Maybe he'll grow up or out of it, whatever's the matter with him, but I'm a woman already – had to be since I was bringing all you lot up. And it might not be a funeral this time. It might be a wedding if you really want to know.'

7

Angela

I told Alex I would kill myself before I let them kill another baby of mine – of ours, I said, but he didn't seem to have any sense of that. He knew any baby of mine was his, which didn't stop him being mad jealous of me always. Perhaps he just didn't see himself as a father, while I'd always been worked like a mother so it came natural to me. I'd lost one, just like Mum – lost was the word I would use rather than look for a nastier one which others were quick enough to find.

He knew I meant it too. He'd seen me cut myself. He wasn't the only one who was jealous. In them days I still was. Remember I'd never had another boyfriend. More than that, I'd never had anything to call my own, always had to share with my sisters sooner or later. They weren't getting Alex – you could bet your britches on that, as Nan used to say.

Looking back, I can see I was still immature. Of course I was, for the love of Jesus look at my age! I don't like to say what it was. I had to be a lot stronger than the first time I fell, that I did know. I was fitter to stand up to Mr and Mrs Reed too. It's hard to be terrified of any man when you've seen him scared to fart out loud in his own house.

'And where will the newly-weds live then?' he asked, sarcastically I thought when I twigged he was talking about us. 'Have you turned your mind to that, Alexander?'

'Up to you, Dad. Ange says we can go round her Nan's, or round the council if we have to. They won't see a baby on the streets. I don't mind leaving school and getting a job either.'

'Getting a job with three O levels? And one of them in PE? Do you have any idea what you risk throwing away?'

'I'm not throwing away our baby.'

I was so proud of Alex at that moment.

Mr and Mrs Reed never sat together on the settee as we were now – they had their own armchair each. Gwen raised a hand, as if to wave to us, showing the back of it to her husband so maybe she was also suggesting he shut his yap. 'It's high time, Simon. Let's give the baby the chance of being born in wedlock.'

I know, she really did say that, 'born in wedlock'. Try to persuade kids to get hitched by using them words now, they'd look at you gone out.

'They are of an age to marry legally now,' Simon muttered.

Perhaps it was from being a lawyer that he always liked to have the last word. Actually, he wasn't as bad as I'm making him sound. I suppose he had a right to want the best for his children – don't we all? – and being honest, I'd have to say that none of us Roper girls might have been considered the best in many ways. He must have known his son fancied me something rotten – the evidence of that was in front of him. And I would sometimes catch him looking at me, usually when I wasn't right dressed, early morning or late evening, so the old man knew I did have something about me, some power.

Our Adam *was* born safely within wedlock, by about a fortnight. You can see him clear enough in all the wedding photos, a big bulge under my lacy pure-white wedding gown.

That's a joke, the dress and the photos. I did get a new top out of Mrs Reed, and she didn't go cheap on me either. No point in spending money on anything tight at the waist, but sometimes a wedding should be about spending money without any point to it. That's what I think. I'm not saying a professional photographer or anything fancy like that either, but somebody in that lawyer's family must have had a camera. Surely? Even a couple of Polaroids would be something. All I have is the pictures in my mind.

It was registry office, and not just because we were supposed to be Catholics and they were C of E. Alex and me didn't care a bit about that and I doubt they did either, though the Reeds might have pretended. My parents only bothered to pretend to be together, coming down from Northampton special. I don't know if Mum had to get time off for good behaviour from the loony bin, or if she was already out by then. It might sound cold to you, I still loved her and all that, I just couldn't be doing with looking after her at that point in my life. I often wonder, if she'd been around, whether we might between us have saved my first boy. Neither Alex nor me had the heart to use the name we'd chosen for him. I waited till this one was safely born – we did know in advance it was a boy – before saying his brand new name out loud. We'd chose it together, but I must admit it was Alex mainly.

'Adam was the first man, right? Let's call him that cos he'll be the first man in the next generation of our families, the leader of the pack.' (Do you remember that song? Didn't think so.)

Dad refused flat out to come round the Reeds' for 'supper' when he understood they didn't mean bringing chips back after the pub. For them it was somehow important to meet my parents. In the end, Simon had to introduce Gwen to Dad – 'All right, love?' He shook her hand real casual like – outside the registry.

Mum was kind of hiding behind him, reminding me of an earlier mind picture – Grandma Alice walking up our garden path for the first time. Simon stuck his hand out to her eventually when he realised Dad wasn't going to say anything else. 'It's a pleasure to meet you, Mrs Roper.' If he had added 'I've heard so much about you', it would have scared her shitless. She really thought nobody knew she'd been put away. Unlike Dad, locked up for different reasons, she was ashamed of it.

The women had met each other separate from the men the night before, when Gwen brought her youngest round Aunt Shirley's. I heard on Jeremy Vine the other day some young girl talking about how she got totally blotto on her hen night, and there was me wondering why she would want to risk spoiling the big day, then she said there were still another *five weeks* till her wedding. Talk about super-cautious. I can't remember where she said she'd been but I know it wasn't an old folks' bungalow in Washtown.

I'm being a bit unfair really. I did sleep at Nan and Grandad's the night before the wedding, but Aunt Shirley had us all round hers for a few drinks first. I wouldn't call it a hen night at all, even if it was just the women and girls of the family there – Tedge too, but he didn't count either way. Uncle Pete was having the stag party start off at the Service only on condition they mustn't take the piss – they would have to move on after one or two pints at most, when his regulars started coming in.

I suppose Helen was brought along to give Gwen Reed an excuse to leave early. She probably had no idea what to expect, though I think this was before the days when you might have a muscle-bound chap in budgie-smugglers under his fireman's uniform turn up. We wouldn't have known what to do! I was glad Aunt Joy came, more in support of Mum than to see me down the aisle. She couldn't have done that anyway – there was no aisle and no big reception, just a meal at Mr Reed's invitation. ('Very hoity-toity, a luncheon…at the Royal Northamptonshire Golf Club,' I heard Uncle Pete teasing Dad.)

The whole idea of having to spend the night before the wedding apart was news to me, tell you the truth. I did know something about bad luck for the groom to see the bride's dress in advance, but his mum hadn't bothered to make a big secret of the top I was going to wear, inviting a clearly uninterested husband to admire it while her equally unfussed son was also in the room. For Helen it was probably not Disney enough. She was a sweet kid. I got on all right with her – she didn't need looking after like my own sisters.

There you go, anyway. Gwen seemed to have her heart set on that little bit of tradition, etiquette or whatever they call it, me sleeping at Nan's that night. When I had first been in her house, her darling Alex couldn't hardly wait to get into my bed before we could really expect everyone else to be asleep, and I had to struggle to get him out of it in the morning. Now some nights he didn't appear. I knew I'd got fat, but it was a good fat surely, carrying his baby. I was torn, not wanting to think he didn't want me anymore yet not doing anything that might put Adam at risk.

Of course I got no advice from anyone who might have known something useful about sex during pregnancy. Sally Gregory said if I wanted the baby born a certain day, I only had to have sex from behind and that would bring it on. I thought that sounded disgusting and still do if it means up the bum. I assumed she meant that at the time, but she might have been talking doggy. When I asked Alex, joking like, if he fancied her, he said he would only give her one from behind so he didn't have to look at her ugly mug. Said he might wear a paper bag himself in case she turned round and hers had come off.

Sally wasn't there the night before my wedding – too tame for her (whatever Alex said, I kept a special eye on him when she was around). It was all family. I would have liked Jan and Lucy to be bridesmaids, along with Karen if she could have been arsed to come down from Northampton, and Billy as a page boy. When Mrs Reed said bridesmaids weren't 'appropriate' for a registry-office do, I wasn't going to kick up a fuss though (and probably saved myself a lot of hassle trying to herd them all together). I still had a tiny niggle that if we didn't play by their rules, the wedding might not happen. One of the rules was apparently that Mum and Dad had to sign some kind of permission because of my age. Dad would be leery of signing anything, but Mr Reed must have managed it. Once I got the ring on my finger, I told myself I would stick up for myself more.

Nana popped round and never got beyond the kitchen, sticking to a cup of tea while our two aunts and Mum started on a bottle of wine. I was caught between feeling I should be in with them and wanting to be with my sisters in the living room. Lucy wasn't old enough to be getting up to serious mischief I hoped, but then neither had I been. She was very knowing, had her life all mapped out. She'd organised us all into a game of rummy, a bit of a stretch for Tedge, but not as much as trumps would be. He generally puzzled his hand along until one of us was out, but if he said he'd won and could back it up with something like a run and a set, we would let him get away with it.

'Why aren't you getting married in church, Ange? I definitely want to,' Lucy started in while she was dealing out the cards.

'You'd better stay a virgin then,' Jan butted in. 'Only virgins can get married in church.'

'That's not true. They can't tell.'

'Bit nervous already, Lucy? Don't you know priests only have to put their hand on a girl's head to know if she's had sex or not?'

'That's a lie. That's an old wives' tale, isn't it, Ange? Even you could get married in church if you wanted, couldn't you?'

'Even me? Ta very much. The priests would put their hands on something else if they could, not your head, dirty old sods not allowed women of their own. You better ask your sister, the Holy Janet Maria, about anything to do with virginity. She's holding on to hers for grim death or till she gets wed, whichever comes first. Either that or Jason's waiting for someone to take his first.'

'I never said I'd wait till I'm married – just till I get to a respectable age.'

'You'll be as respectable as Nan if you wait for Jason.'

'I think I will wait till my wedding night.' Lucy wasn't interested in us – it was all about her. 'I've told Tommy and he's fine with that.'

'Is he really? And who might he be? Tedge, is Tommy a friend of yours?'

Tedge clapped his hands in apparent delight, which could have been a yes or no. To be perfectly honest, I didn't care about Lucy and her little boyfriends. This was the night before my wedding, *my* wedding.

8

Janet

'You look like shit on toast. How was the stag night, as if I need to ask?'

'It got kind of ugly.' Jason had answered the door in his underpants. 'Are you going to the wedding like that?'

'What do you mean?'

'Your dress. Is it one of Lucy's you put on by mistake?'

'Leave off, Grandad. You above all should be pleased to see me in a mini. Aren't you?' She made a grab at his crotch, startling him enough to jump back, before trying to recover the moment.

'Course I am, but only for me, I mean if you're really feeling that frisky today...'

'Too late, you missed your chance. Most men would be glad to have me sexually assault them, not scared. Tell me about it getting ugly.'

'Men against boys it was really, and before you say it, yes I was one of the boys. Lucky I spewed in the toilets at the Griffin or I wouldn't have made it round the marketplace on the streak.'

'On the what? You didn't?'

''Fraid so, babe. The rest of them started egging Alex on – he wasn't shy. They were saying he should give it a last airing around town before it got locked away forever.'

'And you had to join in?'

'He kind of dared me. I know I'm not best man or anything, but when you think of it I am the only one of his mates who'll be there today.'

'You're my plus one – don't kid yourself the golden boy thinks you're one of his best mates. Oh my God, don't tell me my father got involved in the streaking. I assume he was still with you?'

'Glad he was. He said he didn't have a stopwatch to time us like that *Chariots of Fire* shit but he'd watch over our clothes – they sometimes get nicked to leave the runners balls to the wind.'

'Let me get this right. You and Alex – just the two of you – ran round the market totally naked. Yeah, that would be ugly.'

'Fair enough, but that wasn't what I meant. It was a bit later in the Standard. Some of the lads who'd seen us streaking having a bit of a go about homos and all that.'

'What do you expect if you're both bare-arsed. Please tell me you weren't hugging and kissing and stuff.'

'Course not. Well maybe half a hug. What? Did you expect us to shake hands when we completed the circuit? We *were* all pissed, you know?'

'Including my father?'

'That's what I meant men against boys. He sorted it all out. Alex got a fat lip, but your dad sent one of them flying half over the jukebox, grabbed Alex by the scruff of the neck and faced up to the other two. 'This is my son-in-law – he wouldn't be if he hadn't got my daughter up the duff, so I've got no worries about him.'

'Eric the fucking hero.'

'He is pretty hard your dad, for sure.'

'I don't mean *my* fucking hero – I mean to you and Alex, you pair of dickheads.'

Janet hadn't heard the last of her short skirt that day. She saw Alex looking over at her as he dug her boyfriend in the ribs when they gathered outside the registry office, grinning Jaggered lip and all in her direction.

'You trying to upstage me or what, flashing your knickers at everyone?' Ange grabbed her arm none too gently. Her eyes were red as if she'd been crying on her wedding day – and probably not tears of joy.

'What? Don't tell me you're scared of competing with the Holy Virgin Janet Maria.'

'So that's it, still sulking from last night. You don't have to switch straight from virgin to scrubber. He hardly give me a proper kiss at all – seemed more interested in getting a chance to snog you. Maybe he thinks it's allowed now.'

She was right that Alex had come in prepared to bear the pain of a full lip-crusher on Janet, who was caught by surprise but managed to fend him off. He smelled as if he had bathed in beer then showered in aftershave. His eyes were red too; she guessed he was still (or again) drunk.

Although Ange was certainly not above nursing a grudge, any thoughts she might have had of getting her own back at Janet's wedding when the time came were scuppered by another baby bump – the only reason Ange's skirt was a bit shorter than usual. This time the bride herself was not pregnant; nor was she still a virgin. Janet felt she had grown up a lot since her sister had taken the plunge, as the saying went, though to her it seemed not so much diving headfirst into the water as signalling desperately to all passing vessels until one consented to pluck her out of it.

Her first big decision was to leave school, knowing before the O level results came in she would comfortably outclass Jason, already a sixth-former. If Ange's hurry to adulthood lay in getting married, hers would be through making a living for herself. A good start was not picking strawberries but canning them in a local factory, gobbling up all the extra hours it kept over the seasonal peak. When Jason complained of barely seeing her, she told him briskly he could join her on the line, plucking the stray bits of green from the red fruit and smoothing out its flow as Stephen Smart upstream tipped tray after tray, pallet after pallet onto it.

Jason may have been receiving some cash subsidy from his absentee dad – an offer she would have spurned from hers if it had ever been forthcoming – or just not missing her enough to take a job. She didn't expect him to leave school so the two of them could run away to Gretna Green (which she had been past in Eric's lorry). She considered herself the practical one in the family, and elopements were not very practical. She did, however, feel a wish to get away – she would not call it running – from Washtown.

Cousin Martin had also left school at the earliest opportunity, to work with Henry, doing well enough to keep his family in London and pay his son the pitiful going rate for a formal apprenticeship. While they only had two bedrooms in their upstairs Brockley maisonette, Aunt Joy had become friendly with the landlady, freeholder of the whole converted terrace house in which she now lived alone below them. After one or two day-trips, Edie Brown admitted Jan as a sufficiently polite and responsible tenant for the spare downstairs bedroom.

Jan's eight O levels were plenty to get her into Sovereign Insurance as a personal lines underwriting assistant, geographically if in no other way part of the City. If she completed her probationary six months successfully, she was promised that in three years she would be eligible for a preferential mortgage rate, which seemed a little more relevant than the non-contributory pension she would be entitled to draw from age fifty-eight.

She left no unfinished business in Washtown. She had promised Jason that on her sixteenth birthday, 25 July, she would finally let him go all the way, the principal clause in all their legalistic wranglings over petting privileges. She now chafed to be done with this once comfortably distant commitment – the more so since she had no worries about getting pregnant.

'Oh no, she's a good girl is our Jan,' Nan had said, to her extreme embarrassment, when the doctor prescribing the pill against her incapacitating period pains felt bound to remind Janet that she should not view it as a sexual licence. Nor had she, not telling Jason of it for fear of further pressure from him that might have caved in her increasingly porous defences.

She was touched that he had troubled to equip himself with condoms for the big day. So she assumed, rather than that he had them about him anyway. He had grouched on occasion that she should not expect him to do without sex just because she wasn't up for it. He was welcome to go with other girls if he liked, she would tell him, without believing herself. He was popular enough with them. She by no means monopolised his time. She did not share with him her secret vow to dump him instantly if she ever found out he was having sex with anyone else. On balance, she thought he – or perhaps his so-liberated mother – had bought the pack of three specially for her birthday.

She had no one to tell how it was (beyond her words of reassurance to Jason). Ange was now engrossed in her Adam, seemingly loving being a mum so much her sisters laughed at the fuss she had always made about having to mother them. The days of her depending on and confiding in Jan had largely ended. She had Alex for that job now, except when it came to his own misdemeanours.

The bond apparently forged between Eric and Alex on the eve of Ange's wedding was reinforced whenever Eric came to Washtown, mainly to see his mother rather than making any great effort with his three daughters. Alex was drawing attention as a goalscoring regular in the Town first team. This ranged from the girls who felt their lives would be enhanced by that tiny amount of celebrity, to the town boys who felt he needed taking down a peg or two. He met both sexes head-on, with or without his father-in-law as wingman.

No one seemed to notice that Jan would never sleep in the house when her father was staying. She was always casually accepted by Jessica if she spent the night at Jason's in one of what his mother called the guest bedrooms. Her own mum was now apparently out of hospital and living in the world again, albeit under constant council vigilance as she tried to get Karen and Billy back to live with her.

Lucy pursued her courtship with Tommy along strictly conventional lines, not innocent of sex but with no overnight stays at either Uncle Pete's or the Williamses. They were at the Olly almost every Friday night, where Lucy liked to think she had developed her own standing rather than being just one of them Roper girls (a minor one at that). They would go to the pictures on Saturdays, meeting up two or three nights in the week to sit in their front rooms, watching telly with Aunt Shirley or Tommy's parents. Neither of the young pair let homework detain them unduly.

With no regularity, Jan would receive twenty-page letters from Karen, leaping from topic to topic without any discernible link. Their mother's 'boyfriends' were a favourite, a sub-Dickensian catalogue of grotesques described with remote malice. Billy's slow progress at school always got an honourable mention, the books she was helping him read merging into a much longer and deeper list of those she was enjoying herself. She wrote nothing of her own day-to-day school and home – as in 'the home' – life. Unless it was the arrival of a new man in their mother's life, it was almost impossible to discern what prompted her to write. She showed no interest in her sisters' Washtown lives, never responding to any of the news Jan felt obliged to include if only to eke out a modest two sides when she dutifully replied to Karen's wodges.

Their new status as lovers was not something that made Jan reconsider her decision to leave Jason behind for London as the summer ended. She had thought she would feel much more *different* than she did once she was no longer a virgin, a difference people could not fail to remark. Having nobody to tell, she was still a bit miffed that no one thought to ask, unless she counted Alex and his insinuations.

'What have you been blabbing about to my brother-in-law?' she confronted Jason.

'Hold on, babe, what you talking about?'

'Don't "babe" me – you know very well what I'm talking about. I'm beginning to think I wasn't the only virgin in your bed on my birthday. Did you feel you had to brag about it to everyone, impress your mates with what a big man you are? It's hardly likely to impress someone like Alex, let me tell you.'

'What did he say to you? Has he been coming on to you?'

'And what would you do about it? Says he's heard, he's heard I'm a "bit of a wild one" nowadays. He's soooo cheesy. Let me get it right. He said, "Let me know if you ever fancy a proper walk on the wild side." Yeah, that was it. Are you going to put up with that about your girlfriend?'

'Well maybe he was only—'

'Don't shit yourself, Jason – I know you're not going to go up against your precious Alex for little old me. I don't expect you to take a hiding for me. Peace and love, that's what we stand for, not fighting, right? If just once you could get off your arse and *do* something. And if you want to keep on doing what we do now, you better not talk about it to anyone. Got it?'

'Maybe if you hadn't kept me waiting so long it wouldn't have been such a big deal. I mean you're not the only woman in the world with that thing between your legs.'

'No, Jason.' She sensed in his sulky tone her own uncertainty, fears of inadequacy, even shame. 'It's exactly the opposite. We've all got one. Maybe you need to get out a bit more.'

Despite everything, she missed having a boyfriend when she went to London, not allowed to leave him without repeated reassurances that it was not in search of romance. When she eventually realised he was angling for some kind of blessing to see other girls while she was away, she grandly told him to do what he had to do, before claiming the moral high ground. 'As far as I'm concerned, Jase, I still love you. I won't be going out with anyone else unless that changes and I have the guts to tell you first.'

She soon realised insurance was every bit as boring as everyone else assumed. Double periods at school dragged nothing like the afternoons when all she had to do was copy-type schedules of household valuables into the policy documentation for all-risks cover.

She had little or no social life in the week. Mrs Brown – she never presumed to call her Edie (and was never invited to) – was game enough to read out articles from the *Express* for her to practise her shorthand, and kind enough to offer to do her ironing for her, but she wasn't family.

Although she did have family just up the stairs, she soon developed a reluctance to spend her evenings with them. She felt uneasy in one of the armchairs of their three-piece while her cousin sat with his dad and mum on the settee, often as not between them. She started to tell Karen in one letter she found that a bit creepy, before crossing out the phrase as mean and disloyal. She wrote instead that it was sweet to see such a happy family ('not like ours, hey sis???!!!').

While Mrs Brown had made it clear the room she offered was for a single girl, she could hardly object to a weekend visit from Jason, ostensibly staying upstairs and bunking with Martin. He made the effort to come up once; they went to find Carnaby Street and got drunk there together. He told her how much he missed her. It wasn't until she returned home for Christmas that they recaptured something of their earlier intimacy and ease with each other.

Lucy remained snug at Uncle Pete's, while spinning a similar cocoon in the Williams household with her Tommy. Ange did not seem entirely happy to be still living at the Reeds' with Adam already walking. Flush with an extra week's wages as a year-end bonus from her benevolent employers, Janet treated her to a Christmas Eve lunch at the Blackfriars in town, the toddler asleep between them in his stroller.

'I mean Gwen loves the little one, I'd never lack for a babysitter, and Simon, Mr Reed, you'd never believe how he gets down on the floor and roughhouses with him. Alex says he never remembers him being like that with him or Jimmy, but then they don't get on.'

'Who don't?'

'Alex and his dad. Especially not since he gave up the job in his office – "article clark" was it? You remember how Nan always used to say about someone she didn't like he's a proper article? It made me laugh when Alex said that's what he was. Not that he was bragging – he couldn't stand it really.'

'I wouldn't say office life is all that great myself now I've had a taste of it.'

'It got him out of the house. You know he done his cruciate playing for the Town a couple of weeks back? He'll be out for the rest of the season. He expects me to wait on him totally now, he's *so* selfish. I don't know if it's just he's bored – honestly it seems more like he wants to humiliate me. He'll unzip his trousers right there on the settee and expect me to go down on him. He won't even let me get on top in case I jar his precious knee – makes me feel like a slave or one of them women in a harem.'

'Perhaps he just doesn't want any more kids for now?'

'Are you kidding me? You must know there are plenty of ways of preventing that. Surely you and Jason must, unless he really is a botty-basher.

They say his house is getting to be drug central now.'

'Shit's not so bad, Ange – better than getting out of your head drunk. I know Jason's probably too laid-back for his own good, but he's really pleased to have me back home till New Year.'

The only sibling missing from Aunt Shirley's Christmas table was Ange, at the Reeds' but coming round in the afternoon. Jan, invited to join Jason and his mother for their customary Christmas dinner at the Railway Hotel in town, found her own fragmented-family affair less sad than that. Eric was no miss as far as she was concerned. He had brought Grace down with Karen and Billy the eve of Christmas Eve, spent most of his 36 hours up town drinking and left before they got to the presents.

Karen had distributed their father's gifts to her siblings, in the form of envelopes at each of their places at the dinner table except for her own and Billy's. Their little brother would not be separated from a pistol, fed with potato pellets he'd begged from the dinner makings. It could give you quite a painful ping on the ear. He was only persuaded to holster it when Nan and Aunt Shirley were dishing up.

'You're lucky,' Karen said, laughing, 'he really wanted an air gun.' She had grown into a teenager with the looks and, more importantly, the self-confidence to pass easily as sixteen. She wore her blonde hair short, but there was no longer anything boyish about her figure. The combination of fair skin and her dark-brown eyes was striking, though she seemed largely unconscious of the impression her looks might make on others. 'The vouchers were my idea. I've already spent mine. You've also got Lil to thank – she was the one went and got them from Smith's.'

'I hope you can use them for other things, not just books,' Lucy said. 'I mean, I'm thinking about Ange really – when did you ever see her read anything except *The Sun*?'

'Didn't know you were such a big reader yourself, Luce. I knew it was a waste of time for Billy, like tits on a fish, but I wish already I hadn't got him that bloody gun.'

'Language, Karen! You might be able to get away with that in Northampton, but not here.' Nan punished her with an extra ladleful of sprouts.

'Does he live with Lil now then?' Janet would not for the world have asked the question, yet when Lucy did, she found herself anxiously awaiting the answer.

'Yeah, you know that song "Wherever I Lay My Hat" – your hero Marvin

Gaye wasn't it, Jan? That's Dad. You didn't think he'd be looking after himself, did you? Or us? No danger.'

The women had seated Grace with her children, as if she was just one more of them, the quietest at that for all the third glass of sherry had put some colour in her cheeks. 'She's welcome to him. Believe it or not, I get on all right with Lil now. She's got no side to her. Her eyes are well and truly opened, without doing half the time I did.'

'Nor half the kids, Mum. She's probably left it too late to catch up altogether with you now.'

'What do you mean "altogether", Miss Karen Chatterbox?' Nan demanded. 'Pete, are you sure them bottles of apple cider you brought home from the Service are all right for kids? That's the third one she's had already. What's she mean about your brother and that woman?'

Uncle Pete was not given the chance to answer, even if he could have. 'She means he's got her pregnant, Liz, starting off on a new family now that he thinks he can have done with this one. A few envelopes at Christmas... He doesn't know how we're going after him for proper child support in the New Year.'

'Hold on, Grace, *you* don't know what he might send us here for the girls, and from what I hear, you're not exactly looking after Karen and Billy yourself anyway. And who's this "we"? Found yourself some other support with our Eric out the way?'

'Mum, can we have our dinner in peace?' It was about the first time Pete had raised his head from the plate. 'Shirl, go after Grace and see if you can get her back to the table. Kids, how about we pull crackers right now – no need to wait till pudding. Come on Tedge, Billy, you two big boys, let's see what colour hats we can get you.'

'Welcome to your first Roper family Christmas, Tommy.' Karen smiled at him, and then it all kicked off between her and Lucy too.

'Family Christmases,' Aunt Joy said when Janet returned to London in the New Year. 'I don't think your Grandad Cecil misses them – it was all we could do to get him round here for his dinner.'

'How is he? Is he sad being all on his own now?' Jan wasn't as aware as the other girls of how much their grandad had sought his own company when all but she were living in the same home as him. She asked from politeness more than any real feeling for the old man.

89

'Not so's you'd notice,' Uncle Henry carried on. You never got the feeling that he and Joy were interrupting each other. The mainly silent Martin was also something of a relief after the bustle and jostle of her siblings over the holidays. 'You were lucky to miss having to try his home brew, I'll tell you that – he expected us to get through a dozen bottles of it on the day so he could take the empties back to make some more.'

'It's a shame you thought to get your son to help. Ruined his Boxing Day.'

Henry only chuckled at his wife's scolding. 'If he wants to be a proper drinker he'll have to learn to neck the odd bad pint – he knows that, don't you Marty? At least they were free. And we did manage it between us, Jan, in case you're interested.'

'Of course she's not interested. And if you think I drank mine you're wrong – it went straight down the sink once I'd pretended to take a drop. You shouldn't really have driven him home afterwards you know.'

'I wish I hadn't. Only just made it back to our bog in time myself. I know you've done your best to brighten his place up, sweetie, but it's not much is it, two rented rooms?'

'Let's not go through all that again, Henry. I know we might have found him something better in Northampton, but unless we move back there, I'd rather have him at least a bit closer. He's got nobody now apart from us.'

'Poor old bugger. Maybe we should have set him up with Edie instead of bringing Jan in. Only joking, girl – he always did prefer to be locked away on his own, hours at a stretch. I know we owe him a lot, I'm not moaning, but you've been a good daughter to him – better than your sister for sure.'

'Grace has been very ill.' Joy's tone made it clear this was far from the first time she had said as much. 'Jan says she seemed much better over the holidays, didn't you, love? What does she think of your young man? That would be the first time she met Jason, wouldn't it?'

'Yeah. They didn't exactly hit it off.'

It had been at Jessica's insistence that Janet dragged her mother, already fortified by a morning sherry or two, round to their house on Boxing Day. 'They've got plenty of drink, Mum, you don't have to get sloshed before we go.'

'I hope you never get like me, Janet. Do you realise I can hardly talk to anyone I don't know? I can see it's stupid, but I just can't. I don't care what they call the people at the corner shop, I keep going there all the time mainly cos I've got comfortable with Mr Patel and his wife, not just cos they're always open.'

She knew from the two hours it had taken her mother to get ready for their minor excursion to the Tylers, and any other she had been persuaded to make during the holidays, how meticulous – neurotic obsessive was probably nearer the mark – her preparation was to leave the house. She imagined her in contrast slopping down to the Patels' in a bathrobe and fluffy slippers at all hours of the night when she happened to run out of fags or vodka.

Not that Jessica or Jason were in pristine condition when Grace and Jan arrived at their big house. A bottle of white wine was already open; between them the two older women finished another through the afternoon. Jason seemed a bit out of it, greeting Grace slackly, keen to take Jan to his bedroom at the earliest opportunity. Jessica excused them both with a would-be regal wave. 'Off you go then, darlings – one foot on the floor at all times, remember. We have no locked doors in this house, Grace, but I trust implicitly – implicitly, I trust your Jan to keep my wild gypsy boy on the straight and narrow.'

'Wild gypsy boy? Since when?' Jan sat down on his bed while he went to the record player.

'I know. They're horrendous, aren't they?'

'What's horrendous about my mum?'

'Well, you...' He half-turned. The look on her face made him change tack, holding up both hands. 'Nothing, forget it – my mum's the only horrendous one. Listen to this – it's a bonus Christmas box. I want you to hear the track I bought you the whole album for. I read he wrote it for the same woman as "Let's Get It On".'

The only thing she could think of to say less than three minutes later was, 'Well my name's Janet not Janice, but I'll let you off.' She threw her arms around him, moving in close so he wouldn't see the tears in her eyes. It wasn't so much the song – not one of Marvin's best – but the romance she never knew he had in him, the *thoughtfulness* of it, just for her.

After his carefully planned set-up, she would have welcomed something spontaneous. Instead of starting to undress her, as she wanted even with their mothers cackling away downstairs, he gently moved her aside, shifted the needle from 'Jan' to 'Please Stay' and set to rooting about under his bed.

He came out with a little square package, fancy-wrapped. 'This isn't exactly for Christmas – I was going to give it you New Year's Eve, but today suddenly seemed more right.'

'There's no world without my loving baby' he crooned horribly. 'Jan, will you marry me?'

'Don't be daft, come on, get up.'

'Is it the ring? You can change it. I never meant you'd have to stick with it. I didn't know what you'd like or if it would fit your finger, but I wanted you to have one.'

'The ring looks fine. It's just I'm not…I'm not quite ready to wear it yet.'

'Why not? I thought we could ask your Mum's permission as well, long as she's here.'

'What do you mean, as well? You've already asked your mum's permission then, have you? Was that when you were smoking shit together this morning?'

'Jan, why are you being like this?'

'I'm sorry Jase, I don't mean to be a bitch. It's a really sweet gesture, honest it is. I just wasn't expecting it.' She pulled him upright – there was something too ridiculous about him still being down on one knee in front of her, his back to the bed she realised they would not now be using.

On their way home, arms linked with Grace more from fear she might stumble off the pavement into traffic than from daughterly affection, she almost rushed straight back to accept Jason's proposal when her mother warned her off him. She made the mistake of asking for her opinion of Jason, to hear he looked 'a bit of a nancy boy', didn't sound as if he'd ever done a day's work or ever meant to, and was 'not really our kind'.

'Not really our kind? What, you mean I'm not good enough for him, is that what you're saying?'

'I'm saying you're *too* good for him. You don't know how I admire you getting off your backside and going down to London. I talk to your Aunt Joy. I know it can't have been easy, but you did it. Don't follow my example, nor your sister Ange, cos you can't tell me she's happy. Don't make the mistake of rushing into life with a man – or a boy really – before you've had a bit of it to yourself. Or are you trying to tell me something? Sweet Jesus, don't tell me he's put you in the club?' She stopped them both sharply and turned to scan her daughter from face to waist.

'If you'd been there for me, you'd know I've been on the pill for quite some little time, and maybe if you'd given Ange the same advice she wouldn't be where *she* is now. You know what, Jason's mum may be a bit pretentious, and she says herself she's a lush – I'd never heard the word but I soon realised I knew what it meant. She may not care much one way or another about me, but I *do* look up to her – there's something makes me think I'm *not* good enough for her or her fucking wild gypsy boy. If he was a real gyppo I might be! Anyway, thanks for your input. I'll bear it in mind before I take any decision.'

'You'll have to, my girl. Cos until you're eighteen, you won't be able to get married or anything without my say-so – or your father's if you want to ask him.'

'You what? You don't seriously expect me to believe that?'

'Believe it or not, don't think I would have allowed Ange, for all the mess she was in. We would have found a way – your dad did that without me knowing. Are you going to ask him to do the same? I know you all think he's so bloody marvellous and I'm such a basket case, so why don't you? I'm sure he'd say yes, and probably for the same reason he said yes to Ange – so you're not his dependant when I get the CSA on him.'

'I won't ask him for anything. I'm not dependent on him now and I never will be. What's the CSA when it's at home?'

'Child Support Agency. Henry – not Joy's Henry, someone I know in Northampton – says it can make him pay up for you all. Maybe even backdated. So we could all be together again. All except him, of course.'

'Of course. I'm glad we can agree on something. Thanks for telling me that you can still just pop into my life and ruin it whenever you want. I don't suppose it occurred to you that I might love Jason.'

'That's exactly what did occur to me, Jan.'

Grace made her think, for the first time really, if she *was* in love with Jason. She was adamant that she would not accept his ring before she returned to London, nor any deadline to give him an answer. 'Jesus wept, Jason, where did all the free love and stuff go? Does that James Taylor and all your hippie heroes think about putting a sparkler on a woman's finger to tie her to them for life?'

'As a matter of fact James *is* married, to Carly Simon. I knew your mum didn't like me. She turned you against me, didn't she?'

'You think I'd trust her taste in men? Really? It's not about her, or fucking James Taylor for that matter. There's no for or against, no turning – I feel the same as I did when I first moved. I want to give London a proper go before I commit to anything else. I don't know if it will work or not, but I'm not coming home with my tail between my legs to marry you or anyone else.'

Through a January made more dismal by disruption from industrial action on London Transport than its usual foul weather and abbreviated, sunless daylight hours could manage alone, Jan acknowledged to herself, if no one else, that she did not feel the same as she had before Christmas. Then there was that holiday to look forward to. What now? The end of her probation at Sovereign in March, the date from which all those mortgage and pension benefits would start to accrue?

She was surprised to get a call at the office one day in February from Mr Reed – the more so when that turned out to be Alex rather than his father.

'What's happened? Is Ange all right? Or is it Adam?'

'Hello to you too. Yeah, they're fine, both of 'em, thanks for asking, and I'm not too bad myself. Can't I call you without something being wrong?'

'Well seeing as you never have called me in my life, you can understand I might be a bit worried. You haven't gone and left her, have you?'

'No, you'll have to wait a bit longer for that. I am down in the Smoke though, working at ICL. Putney to be exact – that's where their head office is.'

'Whose?'

'ICL, I just said. International Computers Limited. My new career. Anyway, long as I'm down here, I thought I might invite you out for a drink?'

'Oh, did you? And does my sister know?'

'For Christ's sake, Jan, I'm not asking to take you outside the Olly for a snog. Aren't we supposed to be adults now? Who do you think gave me your number?'

He met her from the station where she went straight from work – careful that morning to make no special effort to dress up for him – and took her straight to a pub, one of those massive London ones heavy with woodwork and a piano camped in one corner. Alex caught her looking at it as he ordered up their first round. 'I do go home most weekends – the one cockney wankers' knees-up singalong on the old joanna I was here for was more than enough.'

'How is Ange coping with you being away then? How long is it for? You really haven't left her, have you?' He'd shown her no mercy at the pool table, which oddly relaxed her a little bit.

'On my life, no. You would have heard from her if I had. I was going crazy stuck in Washtown without even the football till the knee clears up. If it does…' He tapped his forehead. 'You never did see me play, did you?'

'I saw you enough at the Olly. Come on – there's still time. I promise to watch when you make it big down here, on your debut for Chelsea.'

'Fuck off, Chelsea. United till I die. That Jason's a bad influence on you, making you support a crap team like that. I told him not to go sniffing round Ange while I'm away – he's got his own Roper girl. She says he's totally besotted with you. Is that right?'

'Besotted, I don't know.' (She would be surprised if Ange had used that word.) 'We've been together a while now.'

Beyond their initial skirmishing, they talked no more about Ange or Jason. She knew nothing about computers, but his interest in them was a side to him she had not appreciated. The idea was to gain a good footing in that industry with ICL, bringing his family to London or moving on wherever there might be better opportunities once he had proved himself in it.

'Have you got a probation at work then, like me?'

He laughed. 'You might call it that. A year, that's how long the old man said he was prepared to sub me before I was out on my own. He still thinks I'll end up back at Braithwaite and Sons, but there's about as much hope of that as him getting his name up there instead of Braithwaite. One way or another, computers are the future. His mob are closer to the fucking quill pen.'

Alex talked more about himself than anything else – you had to expect that with boys. She did with Jason, and it generally suited her as someone who liked to keep her own thoughts to herself. Perhaps it was because he had taken a similar step to her that she was able to talk to Alex about her own office life, in a way she never had to Jason under the excuse that it was all too dull.

While she wasn't wearing a particularly short skirt, she was well aware of Alex's eyes on her legs whenever she crossed or uncrossed them. Typical of boys again, though she wondered if Jason had ever looked at her with quite that greedy appreciation.

She was startled to realise suddenly it was past ten. 'Listen Alex, it's been a good evening but can you point me the right way to the station. I need to be getting off now?'

'Really? I kind of assumed you were going to stay with me.'

'You never change, do you? Just when I was thinking you might have. I'm not one of your football groupies from Washtown. What sort of girl do you think I am?' She was furious with herself the moment she asked that stupid question.

'You're one of them Roper girls, and about my only friend in London at this moment. No need to get worked up, Jan – I only meant to doss down. No, that's put it wrong. You can have the bed obviously, but what with the strike, I didn't see how you could be thinking about getting home.'

'What strike? I thought all that was finished.'

'That's why they call 'em wildcat strikes – come out of the blue. I mean they do give a little bit of notice – not much though, the bastards. I thought you must have seen or heard coming down here there'd be no services after eight o'clock tonight.'

'No, I didn't. It's always the ones in the mornings have caught me out. I'll have to get a taxi.'

'If you've got that sort of dosh, go ahead, and good luck to you. I don't know how much it'd cost to trek across South London, assuming you could find a cab I'd be happy letting you get into. Look, I'm sorry if you thought I was trying it on. I didn't plan the strike myself, you know.'

'But you didn't tell me about it, did you?'

'You're the London veteran – I thought you'd have known. Whatever, it's no use squabbling now. Might as well have another drink before chucking-out time. I've got some shit at home – and music.'

'I didn't know you smoked?'

'Not cigs, not normally. You must know yourself, Miss Mary Jan, it's easy as wink to get dope up here. I know you're well into it. Come and listen to some white working-class music. You ever heard of Bruce Springsteen?'

When they stood up an hour later, she knew she was pretty drunk. Feeling she couldn't stomach another half of lager and lime, when the landlord called last orders she'd agreed to a Bacardi and Coke, which Alex had made a double. She hadn't complained, and it was too late when on the way to his digs she was sick twice – one, two, as if each of the Bacardis was coming up separately. 'I haven't even got a toothbrush with me,' she wailed.

'Never mind, I keep a spare one there for my girlfriends – only joking, come on, easy does it.'

'I've got to get up early in the morning, mind – first train out of here so I can get home and then to work. You can have your own bed. I'll sleep in the chair.'

'I couldn't have that. Let me be a gentleman for once. I'll let you use the bathroom first – try to hit the pan if you're going to puke again.'

'A gentleman wouldn't mention that.'

She took the bed and he the armchair. At some point in the night, he joined her. She was sleeping in her bra and pants under a plain white T-shirt he had lent her.

He moved inch by inch. She could pretend to be still asleep. She could wake up indignant. She could make him back off, she was sure. She could let him continue.

It was the most complicated sex of her life. She had only been with three men: one against her every instinct except that of parental obedience; one where she was able to regain a measure of control; and now one where she knew she didn't want it, felt she did want it, thought of her sister but couldn't keep her thoughts focused on anything, felt sick and felt excited.

She would not turn to face Alex in the bed. Everything else, she allowed him.

In the early morning, she refused to look at him – not easy when climbing over him to get out of bed. Whether or not he understood her embarrassment, perhaps shared a little of it, he again let her use the bathroom first. She was as quick as she could be, emerging fully dressed.

'You don't have to come with me.' She saw from the corner of her eye him scouting out underpants and pulling on a shirt. 'I can find my own way to the station.'

'Don't be daft, course I'll come. Look, Jan, don't shut me out...'

'Leave it, Alex. Nothing happened, all right?'

'Nothing happened? Are you crazy?'

'You never even kissed me.'

'I kissed your shoulders, your back, your neck, and when...you didn't seem to want me to turn you around, there was no need – that was fine, that was great. You didn't stop me, you didn't seem like you wanted to face me was all. And afterwards, you wouldn't let me again, you buried your head in the pillow. I like it that you were a bit shy, honest. Come here and let me kiss you properly right now.'

'No, Alex, no.' She pushed him away. 'You don't understand. You never kissed me.'

'Fucking right I don't understand. I mean I've heard prossies won't let you kiss 'em, but that's all. I thought I might mean a little bit more to you than that.'

She was rummaging in her handbag, head averted, but that snapped it round at him. 'Is that why you insisted on buying all the drinks last night? Thought you were paying for it in advance? I'm not a prostitute, for your information.'

'Jan, I never meant—'

'Nothing happened. Understand that and make it stick. You never even kissed me. And you're not coming to the station with me, so don't try.'

She left him standing in the doorway. But first she did give him a kiss. Just one – one proper kiss.

Two mornings later, a Valentine's Saturday, Jason turned up on her doorstep saying he couldn't live without her.

9

Lucy

Jan's wedding wasn't much like Ange's, except they were both registry office. I made sure to get dressed up nice, even if one more time I wasn't going to be a bridesmaid. I wouldn't cheat anyone out of the chance to be a bridesmaid at my wedding. I knew it would be my turn next. None of us expected Karen ever to get married.

When do you have to be a matron of honour rather than a bridesmaid? Ange must have been still a teenager but you'd never have guessed, looking frumpy as well as lumpy, trying to keep Adam in check most of the time.

With a registry office do there's no walking down the aisle, obviously, but that needn't stop you having bridesmaids or a best man if you want. We'd all assumed that would be Alex for Jason, living in London now with Ange and their growing family, so it was a big surprise when he asked my Tommy to do it. Tommy had to ask me, and I wouldn't let him show the others he was a bit nervous about it. In any case, it wasn't really like a proper best man – no speeches or anything. I kept the ring for him myself till the last minute so all he had to do was hand that over and sign the register as a witness. He nearly balked at that believe it or not, saying his hands were sweaty, frightened he might blot the big book.

'I'll give it six months,' Karen whispered. Well not whispered actually – everyone had to make like we didn't hear her. She was sitting beside me in her jeans and Doc Martens with a tatty old Levi waistcoat. Mum did try to shush her and slapped her on the leg, but she couldn't control her. We all knew that.

Lil was there with Mum. Perhaps it was true what they both said, that they were proper mates now. Dad was in town – he'd brought them down from Northampton without an invitation himself. 'I won't have him at my wedding,' I heard Jan say with my own ears when Mum raised the subject.

'But who'll give you away?'

'It's a registry office, Mum. You don't need someone to give you away.' I tried to help out too late. Jan was already going off on one.

'Shut up, Lucy. If he thinks I'm his property to give away, he might have thought about trying to keep us over all these years. And don't say Grandad can walk with me instead. I don't forget Fang. I won't have any more fuss. We wanted a quiet do, already it's getting out of control, Jessica sorting out some kind of ponced-up garden party. Why can't people leave me the fuck alone?'

'Why bother getting married at all? Aren't you supposed to be hippies?' I couldn't resist asking. She didn't have an answer to that – stomped off when Mum started crying, saying London had changed Jan and when did she get so hard-hearted and what sort of language was that for a bride-to-be.

I don't know so much that London had changed our Jan. If you ask me, she always liked her own way. You could tell she had Jason wrapped round her little finger, for a start. He was older than us, a bit of a hero for Tommy till I discovered he was getting him into dope. I lost any respect I might have had for him when he went running off after my sister with a Valentine's card nearly too big to carry.

For a while it looked like I might be the only one of us left in Washtown, with Jan followed to London not only by her lovesick boyfriend but by Ange when it seemed Alex's thing with computers was taking off. She – Jan I mean – didn't tell me at the time why she came back, but I got the impression from Aunt Joy they were all fed up with Jason hanging around the house without ever showing any signs of finding a job. It was years later Jan told me she came home from work one day to find one of his mates shooting up heroin in their room, without admitting Jason might have been doing the same. I did ask. At least when they moved back into his house – well his mum's house – I suppose you could say he was contributing something in a way.

That was big enough that they could easily have held the reception inside it, but Jessica got her way with a 'marquee' in her garden. I'd seen bigger beer tents at village fairs around Washtown, and we didn't need any shelter against rain as it turned out – more against the sun if anything.

Not many were directly involved in the wedding. Jan, Jason, Jessica and, for the first time I think even Jan had met him, Mr Tyler. He was the only one in a suit, whether in rebellion against his ex-wife who wanted everything to be 'mega informal' or to show he was the money behind it all. He didn't stay long. I saw Karen talking to him. As usual, she was all over the place, running wild.

So were the kids – running wild I mean. Tedge was easily excitable, needing no encouragement from Billy to show off his special talent. Tell him your birthday and he'd tell you what day it would fall that year, like Monday or whatever. You might think nobody would bother to check, but sometimes we did and he was never wrong. It was only when computers were a lot more common and Little Jan could use one, we found his gift went further than that. If you gave him your year and date of birth, he would tell you the day of the week it was – again, never wrong. Maybe it wasn't so very much use to know that. Still, it was something he could do that nobody else could, proved he could make real music on that drum of his. Had a bit of the rain man about him, did Tedge.

It was definitely Jessica's show. She not only had outside caterers in, which left Nana and Aunt Shirley displaced and disgruntled – for all Aunt Joy told them to relax and enjoy themselves – she even had schoolmates of ours primped up in white shirts and black waistcoats to carry around trays of little sandwiches and snacks. I wouldn't waste money on that at my wedding. We were all quite capable of finding our way to a buffet and more so to a bar.

She might have been better paying someone to do the doors than the serving, since apart from her own crowd of theatrical friends – all cravats and overloud voices – the washed-out unwashed crew that normally populated her house with Jason to get high all seemed to find their way in at some point. They stayed mainly indoors. Most of them looked like they had a dislike for sunshine as well as soap if you asked me.

Lil hadn't brought all her kids – that would have been too much, and perhaps they wouldn't have cared to come. We did meet our new half-brother though. Her and Mum were hardly separated all day long, like little Eamon belonged to both of them. Billy treated the toddler like a proper brother too, so I added another number to my own wedding list. I was the only one of us who made any effort with him – Jan seemed to feel the grudging invite to Lil had been enough on her part, while Ange was occupied with her own boy, her pregnancy and waiting for her husband.

I said she was now living in London with Alex, but Ange came home (I bet she still thought of it as home, like it still was and always would be for me) more often than he did, whether to stay at the Reeds', who were always glad to take Adam off her hands, or round at Nan and Grandad's. She was back for a few days before the wedding – not that she had anything more to do towards it than any of us – with Alex due to arrive from London on the day itself.

He came with our dad. When I answered the door to them – I'd gone to the kitchen to get Tommy a Coke, noticing he was going at the beer a bit too hard – Dad seemed to be on the point of leaving.

'Hey Lucy, the sweetest and prettiest of all them Roper girls. Tell your dad he'll be more than welcome to come in on this, the day of his daughter's wedding.' Alex said the last few words in a kind of solemn voice, like he was in *The Godfather*, which everyone was raving about then. He liked to make a bit of a fuss of me did Alex. I always had to tell Tommy he had nothing to worry about.

'More welcome than you'll be with Ange if you're pissed already,' I said. Honestly, they made you talk and behave like parents, they were so childish, those big men.

'It's all right, darling. I only wanted to make sure this one got out of the marketplace pubs and here in one piece. How did it all go? How did Jan look?'

I took a decision. He was our dad, after all. 'Come with me. Never mind if she chucks you straight out, you can see for yourself.'

When I led them through to the tent, Jan was at the bar necking white wine with her new husband. When Jason made as if to come towards us, she held him back. She slung an arm over his shoulders, holding the glass in her other hand with her back now turned full against the bar, so that she was facing the two men directly when they approached her. I suppose she was drunk – or stoned. Her face was red anyway.

Once again, Dad hung slightly back. Alex didn't seem quite so cocksure all of a sudden. He said congratulations and sorry to be a bit late. He looked as if he was going in to kiss my sister, except she made no move in return. It would have been like taking advantage somehow if he'd advanced further, with her arms out either side and her legs slightly ahead of her as she lounged back against the bar. Instead, he turned to a handshake with Jason on her right. He looked relieved when Adam came charging at him, Ange not far behind.

Jan didn't make any move towards Dad either, apart from raising her head a little to look him full in the face. He seemed doubtful of what to say, taking in her white trainers, legs bare (at least she'd shaved them for the occasion – you could see the nicks) to where that awful tweedy shift dress ended around the knee, and what was surely one of Grandad's oldest cardigans, once dark blue with a pocket for her roll-ups and lighter.

'Congratulations, love. You too, young man. I hope you'll both be very happy together. Don't worry, I won't be staying. Have a drink on me is all.' He was dark-suited with a navy tie, his hair perhaps not as thick or black as once but still Brylcreemed to death. He pulled out an envelope from his inside jacket pocket – why do I keep thinking about that film? – while Jan did not take her eyes off him.

No doubt forbidden by the bride to help her make herself look presentable, Jessica had gone overboard on the groom, dolling him up in white trousers of all things, and a maroon blazer. She had him in a boater at one point, but that was too much even for him to wear. Dad drew Jason towards him as if – I thought for one horrible moment, it could happen just as quick as that with him – he was going to headbutt him. Thanks God no, he just stuffed the money into the blazer breast pocket then got himself out of there. Alex started after him, was held back by Uncle Pete but didn't stay much longer. He took Ange home on the pretext that she needed to rest for the baby and all. She said he went straight out again himself, ranting about Jan and how rude she'd been. He was still following Dad, I shouldn't wonder. I hope he had more luck finding him than Mum and Lil did during the rest of that weekend.

Everything worked like clockwork on my own wedding day, from Sainte Marie church onwards. My three bridesmaids (all from Tommy's side of the family because I knew I could count on that) were gorgeous. I had no reason to complain, except it was all over too quickly. Perhaps Tommy and me had just looked forward to it all a bit too long. That wasn't his fault. He was keen as mustard to get married as soon as he got a job at the Metal Box when we both left school. It wasn't for sex. I was realistic about that – didn't expect him to wait. We both loved the thought of being able to spend whole nights together in bed, which I wanted to be in our own place if at all possible, so we had to save up first. Uncle Pete and Aunt Shirley were generous as ever but didn't have much in the way of spare cash, no more than Tommy's parents did. Still, we managed to get a decent mortgage on a bungalow at 61 Sandringham Avenue, a new development then off the Lynn Road.

I got married in white, but I was sensible about that too. We couldn't afford something only to be worn the once, though I must admit my white mini and white knee-length boots didn't get too many outings after our big day (I don't want to be crude, but I was still wearing both when I had sex for the first time as Mrs Tommy Williams). I pretended not to hear Karen's sarky comment about being caught in a time warp back to the sixties. Minis were still in fashion – if you ask me, they've never gone out of it. Actually, I felt sorry for her. As gobby as ever, she wasn't bouncing around quite as much, despite looking like a bloody space hopper. And she was alone, no sign of any father for the bab. She wouldn't tell and I didn't have the time to press her on it. She was still living in Northampton but racketing around in Washtown and London too. Until this happened, everyone said she was nailed on to go to university.

I wondered if I should have Uncle Pete walk me down the aisle. I know he was touched when I asked him. He thought it was Dad's place really, which I agreed with myself in the end. He did beg one favour though, Uncle Pete. Tommy had always been good with Tedge, and was fine about having him as best man – we passed on the speech obviously, but he managed the ring OK.

Dad was happy enough for me that he came over special from Ireland, where he was living now with Lil and their little Eamon. He was apparently doing well with a lorry of his own. So he told me – we all knew Dad could be a bit of a romancer. I don't know how much was in the envelope he gave Jason, but I had no reason to complain about the one I was happy to accept from him. He told me to keep it quiet, as one of the reasons he left England was that Mum was chasing him for child support. I did tell him he should give her what was her due – they were still married as far as I knew – but I must admit, I did as he said and didn't mention anything to her.

If Mum was blaming herself for Karen's situation, she made a good show of hiding it. She had left her in Northampton, or rather Karen had run back there – after that man or boy would be my guess; nobody really knew – when Grace took Billy down to London, to be closer to Aunt Joy.

I don't want to say anything bad about Uncle Henry, who was always good to us, but I think he was a bit racist. Thanks God he didn't say anything outright – and I must admit there were a few other raised eyebrows at our wedding and reception – when Mum came with a black man. I'm not prejudiced myself, and he was polite enough. Norman his name was, but he didn't really look comfortable. He was the only one there, not because we were prejudiced or anything, there just weren't any of his kind in Washtown. Not like London.

Jan and Jase obviously had to show they knew all about London and how liberal they were; Jessica as well (I'd felt bound to invite her after she hosted their wedding). Probably they drove Norman to leave early if anyone did, trying to make conversation with him and not leaving the poor man alone. The reception was at the Service. Uncle Pete wouldn't have it any other way and booked the big back function room out for a private party. He wouldn't hear of charging us anything for it either. Secretly I'd hoped as much since we didn't have the budget. One of his mates did a disco – it was a great night.

Nothing much had changed with Jan and Jason. She was still the one earning all the money, working in King's Lynn, still in insurance I think. After their Denis came along – she got paid time off for the birth so it must have been a good job – she went straight back to the office. Jason was supposed to look after the bab, if he weren't such a dosser – I think he had his mum do most of it. I bet Jan wasn't happy about it, though she was always too proud to admit she might have made a mistake.

Once we were married, we'd agreed I could start a family straight away. We'd done the sums. I knew it would be tight but thought we could just about manage without my job at Shawl's pastry shop off the marketplace. Tommy was never much of a drinker, and I kept him away from Jason's drug den. I let him have his fishing, mind – we always laughed about how I freaked out the first time I opened a Tupperware dish in the fridge to find it full of maggots. He had to get himself a littler one for the utility room where we kept the washing machine, sometimes with a few beers in it as well, or less often a bottle of wine for the two of us to share in front of the telly. I always made him fetch them out of it. As long as I didn't have to go near it, I didn't care what else he kept in that fridge.

The others might say I only wanted kids to catch up with them, but it wasn't that. Everyone makes their own choices, and mine was always to be not only a wife but a mother. I joked this was the first wedding of our three when Ange hadn't been pregnant. I always wondered how she persuaded Alex to call Adam's sister after ours, since he never really seemed to get on with Jan.

10

Karen

Aw diddums, so nobody took any notice of our Lucy. She had her big day just like she planned it and not everybody was ready to kiss her arse, for all it was largely on display in that mini over her chunky thighs. Dirty little mare didn't even take it off then – I knew they'd had sex in the toilets of the Service because I happened to be in there at the same time on business of my own. I guess she felt she had to take the edge off poor Tommy, his tongue hanging out. She had him good and proper, I'll give her that.

She felt sorry for me. Did she, *actually*? I felt sorry for myself, though I wasn't going to give anyone the satisfaction of knowing, especially not anyone at that wedding. Aunt Joy made a point of talking to me on my own, as she always tried to whenever we were in the same postcode. She had the sense not to pump me, and I volunteered nothing.

When asked whose the baby was, I would say mine and that was that. I'm sure many thought I didn't know, including my own sisters. Good luck to them. There was Alex naming his child after his sister-in-law, while Jan named her firstborn after a legendary footballer from a team her husband didn't support. I picked up on these things; I was always watchful. I made a lot of noise without saying very much, and I was always a listener too. Lord, did they give me plenty to listen to, those sisters of mine, whenever we were together. Why couldn't they take a lead from Billy's generally mute (or was it muted?) suffering.

I did do well at school; selectively well I suppose, in that it was only in the subjects I cared about. I was the only girl who didn't hate Latin. It was a point of pride with me to be top in French, especially after Mr Hooper wangled it for me to go to Livarot, our twin town in Normandy. It wasn't a school trip as such, though he tended to go on it every year to help with the language, administration, and supervision of the kids. It wouldn't have occurred to me to put myself forward, since there was a charge I had no means to pay and no one to ask to pay for me. Mr Hooper taught me the word 'bursary' and sorted that side out. Parental permission was never a problem – I could write and sign their names better than either of them.

Mr Hooper also explained that not everyone who stayed with a French kid was forced to invite them back to theirs. How could I invite anyone back to Colditz, as we called our home, after that telly series about the prisoners of war always trying to escape the Germans in World War Two? Anyway, there were do-gooders who were happy to have kids over without benefiting from a trip themselves, and some who might have more than one, as I think our teacher and his wife did. She didn't go with him on the trips though, Mrs Hooper.

I may have gone three times in the end from third year onwards, not every Easter but definitely more than once. We would travel in those holidays, and they would come to us during the summer. I kept up a correspondence beyond our schooldays with Josette, the girl of my own age whose room I shared. There was also a bit of a spark with her two brothers, the older Frank – who barely deigned to notice me on my first visit but I later knew how to make sit up and beg – and the more doggishly devoted, younger Jean-Louis.

All in all I became pretty fluent in oral French – no cracks about those boys please – as well as the written on which most of our schoolwork was based. Mr Hooper had introduced German, an O level course he let me sit in on with younger kids while I was doing my English, French and Latin As. Not many took it up so perhaps he was glad of anyone extra, though that didn't stop bitchy comments from Tracy Bevan about me and him. For once I chose not to react. She was only a fourth former. It was probably just a kiddie crush she had on Sir that made her take the class, certainly no linguistic aptitude I could see.

Of course I discovered boys early. I think we all did at Colditz. Although I've never liked the word 'promiscuous' as I know it has been applied to me – I hear a lot, remember – we were definitely promiscuous in the sense of being jostled and jumbled together, for all there was a segregation of girls' and boys' sleeping quarters, between what the staff called the north and south wings and we knew as Stalags One and Two. As my sister so classily proved at her wedding reception, there were always ways and means, by day or night, outdoors or in, involving free citizens as well as between Stalag inmates. If you think I was a troubled child, you should have seen some of the others.

It's another lie of Lucy's that I ran away from Grace when she moved down to London, let alone ran in pursuit of some putative baby daddy. I never had to chase boys – they knew where to find me, and many would have followed me much further than the sixty miles or whatever it is down the M1. I had no intention of leaving school coming up to my A level exams. While nobody in the family seemed to think much about my education – which I did not forget to compare and contrast with how they made sure Jan got a fair run at her eleven-plus – I had a sentimental view that it would be a way of changing my life, starting it all over at university. I would have stayed in Colditz, but Mum's emancipation from the strictures of the social services and the fact I had turned sixteen somehow made this problematic. I had to find a solution myself, so I did.

I promised to go down to London when Mum was settled there with Billy, the one who did run away if only Lucy knew it. My childhood dream of living in our nation's capital would have to wait, but not forever, as was the case with her.

I knew, and knew of, success stories amongst Colditz escapees as well as others who were living in squats or on the streets. Apart from those options I had another, a kind of family one. Dad and Lil were flitting to Ireland, and Brenda was going with them to find herself a husband (she was disappointed in love locally, on the rebound from an abortion). They were hedging their bets by somehow keeping a hold on Lil's council house, whether or not they were able to transfer its tenancy formally to Eddie and Michael, who apparently cared nothing for the land across the water. Eddie was working for his namesake Stobart, while the dole office was trying to find something for his younger brother, who had similarly left school without any exams.

The idea was that I would earn my keep by keeping house for Lil's boys, who she'd always spoiled from what I'd seen. They were happy enough to have a replacement mum to cook, wash and clean for them, and more besides if I let them. I'm not proud of myself – maybe I did swap favours for favours. At one point they came to blows over me.

The pregnancy was absolutely not my choice, though I had seen it weaponised by other girls to get a husband or a house. Good luck to them, say I. That's always been the case, not something our generation invented. I don't take any credit for never seriously considering the Brenda way out, unless you count getting very drunk on gin once or twice during my first trimester; that was just normal drunk, not swigging from the bottle locked in a lavatory or anything like that.

I don't suppose Mrs Hooper was delighted to see a clearly preggers schoolgirl on her doorstep. As it was school holidays, I had somehow just assumed Charles would be the one to answer the door. Flustered, he invited me into the first study I had ever seen. I wanted his life then.

I wasn't there for anything except advice on the practicalities of my situation. I had achieved three grade As in my main exams, more than good enough to trigger my conditional acceptances at Manchester, Leeds and Durham. He had recommended I apply for Cambridge, where he went himself, but I said I wanted to get further away than that. So much was true, yet I can now admit to myself I probably thought university was a big enough step up without shooting for Oxbridge.

By the time I went to Lucy's wedding, less than a month from full term, I had everything planned. I saw no reason to share with my family, beyond saying that they needn't expect a wedding invitation from me any time soon.

Mum said before I'd asked her she was not 'strong' enough to accompany me at the birth, then volunteered her sister Joy. No, that's not fair – I mustn't play the martyr too much. Joy was glad enough and had always let me know she would provide whatever support she could. Lil too had offered to 'pop over' from Ireland when the time came. The boy would be fatherless – like me – but I hoped to arrange a dad for him. My own dad had enough kids for me not to bother him with another arrival.

Conscientious about attending all my medical appointments, I couldn't face going to any of the antenatal classes the nurses recommended, where I thought I would find smug twats like Lucy with pussy-whipped men like Tommy pretending to share the pain. Nothing makes me feel sicker than hearing them say, men or women, 'we're pregnant'; perhaps that's just bitter and twisted old me because I was on my own at the time.

I shouldn't be so nasty about Lucy I know, my bad – writing about those times makes me feel like lashing out. I wouldn't be doing it, writing I mean, except there's no one else can tell that part of my story. I don't know why Lucy puts my back up so much. It's not even false the way she tries to rub along with everyone – keep us together as a family as she puts it. For all I take pride in my outsider status, I can applaud that as a worthy goal. The best Lassie would struggle to herd cats like us Roper girls – be likely to get her face scratched.

Just as she'd failed to find a bridesmaid's berth at our other sisters' weddings, Lucy had no success in offering to be my 'birthing partner'. I expect she'd already been reading up on pregnancy, always one step ahead. As far as I knew, Ange and Jan, not as close as when the two of them used to try bullying us as kids, had not been notably present for each other as they became mums, so I didn't expect much interest from them. They did not surprise me.

I had always passed the exams I wanted to at school. This one wasn't an optional. I tried to approach giving birth by being as well read and well prepared for it as possible. While that didn't extend to stopping drinking or smoking – people didn't make such a fuss about that in those days, and I would have bridled if they had – the truth was I didn't do as much of either towards the due date as I had been; didn't feel like it somehow. As Lucy observed, I got pretty big-bellied in the later stages of my pregnancy.

I discovered there were some things you can't learn in books. I never had an exam that lasted twenty hours, for starters. Don't they say that if women could remember the pain of childbirth, there would only be only children in this world? I was prepared to gobble whatever drugs they offered me – that was my lifestyle, as it goes – but was no creeping Jesus, meek and mild patient. One of the nurses said without censure she'd never heard such language in ten years on the ward, nor at such volume. As usual, I was channelling rage more than love.

When I held my beautiful baby boy in my arms for the first time, it was all worth it. That's what you're expected to say, isn't it? In fact, that was when I started to get really scared. He was perfect, which meant they would come for him all the sooner, the couples who couldn't have children of their own, the adopters.

A natural birth, probably routine enough for everyone else, it left me pretty knackered. In the end, I hadn't let Aunt Joy know when I went into hospital. You have to remember people weren't connected by phone to everyone else back then like they are now. There was also something of seeing myself through my own mess. Lil was in the Wellingborough Road house when I got home – to check if the bab looked anything like her boys, I thought uncharitably, glad of her support though I was. Eddie and Michael were kind of sweet in a way, but in the main pretty useless.

I had fantasies of changing my mind and keeping him, all the more so when I had named him an unconnotational Gary Wayne. Something specific had to go on the birth certificate in that box. The social lady said I could choose what I wanted – without any guarantees that his future parents would not change it, she explained when I asked if my choice would be legally binding. So then I didn't care. She also kept me up to the mark when I got what she called 'an attack of the wibberly wobberlies – totally natural, dear', reminding me that we had discussed matters exhaustively and had to think what was best for Gary Wayne as well as myself. I snapped that she didn't have to use both his Christian names – I didn't mean them together like the kids in country songs, the Billy Joes or Bobby Jeans (or Frenchies like Jean-Louis); I just didn't want him to go short on that one small thing. She kept talking about my deferred place at uni, which was really the last thing I needed or wanted to hear about at that point.

We had a little mock family, or a mockery of a family, for a couple of months. Lil went back to Ireland, Eddie and Michael to expecting their tea on the table every night and taking minimal interest in Gary, scared to pick him up in case they dropped him (which the great lumps might well have). They were surprisingly prudish about me breastfeeding him anywhere in their vicinity. I'd more expected them to be encouraging it so they could gawp at my swollen tits. That was something else deemed best for Gary – mother's milk. Only later did I wonder whether it was good or bad for me. Didn't it make the bond stronger, the breaking of it all the more painful? It's only my opinion, but I've a right to it, and I say yes. It did.

There was no contact between me and prospective parents. If I was selling a puppy I would have had more say. Once they took him, the separation would be total and final. I was allowed, encouraged even, to write a letter which would be given to his adoptive parents, who might or might not choose to show it to him at some stage. That was the worst – not writing the letter, knowing its delivery was not guaranteed. The prisoners in Colditz, the WW2 one I mean, had the right to send and receive mail, didn't they?

'This little piggy went to market' came into my head every time I took him into what they then called a 'home for unmarried mothers' – another home, at least I was spared living in that one – where he would be put on display with the other babies, to be cooed at, mauled and petted by strangers. I tried to persuade myself it was for the best that I would never know who took him. I knew I was being totally selfish when I would brood on it as being an abortion at twelve months' term.

The first serious indication of interest came on 24 December. Our one

Christmas was a small affair – what gifts could I buy him? – with Eddie and Michael mainly pissed around us. I had insisted on keeping Gary to myself as far as my own family was concerned, preferring they should not get to know him at all. I did not want my memories contaminated by their recollections, I told myself. The truth was I couldn't have borne their pity. None of them objected strongly. None of them met him. I dreamed, awake and asleep, of another outcome, a family unit of father/Dad and Gary completed by me as Mum.

He was gone by mid-February, was Gary Wayne Roper. The milk in my breasts dried up quicker than the tears from my eyes – or is that just a hackneyed literary conceit? Turns out I'm not really capable of writing about it after all.

Part Three:
Eighties and Nineties

11

Munsley

Lucy told Ange over the phone of her deal on a house almost on the beach at the Norfolk seaside town of Munsley, owned by the boss at Shawl's where she'd returned to work when Louise started school the previous autumn. 'If you book soon enough you can get the one right next door. You'll have to pay full whack, but I suppose Alex can afford that.'

'He should be able to. Everybody says he was right about computers being the thing. I don't know how much I see of his wages. And you wouldn't believe how expensive London is. Plus, we didn't exactly plan for another addition to the family when Janette was nearly finishing primary school.'

'You should count your blessings. You know you wouldn't be without Suzette. Three lovely kids! We'd die to have another one, Tommy and me. I thought once Louise came along, God love her, it would be like opening a gate, but you know how it's been.'

'If you both died we'd have to bring up Lou, so that would hardly work.' Ange knew only too well how her sister had to wait almost seven years after marrying Tommy to give birth, while Jan had brought off the trick successfully with successive husbands Jason and Ray, and Karen had given a baby away. She had no wish to hear again about Lucy's 'misses' and false alarms either side of Louise, the longing to provide her with a sibling almost becoming an obsession since she became godmother to Suzette. Much as Ange loved her Jan and Suzie, she sometimes felt she could have been equally happy if they had left it at Adam. She was nervous of any pill, and Alex refused to put a rubber on. For her, it was more like a struggle to keep floodgates closed than the endless fiddly and frustrating negotiation of locks Lucy endured.

'Maybe the sea air will put some lead in Tommy's pencil,' she continued tactlessly. 'What dates are you talking about? Jan and Ray are supposed to be coming to see us when they're home from Hong Kong.'

'I'm glad she keeps in touch with one of us. If the dates fit, why not all come down together? The Boat up the road does rooms if a rented cottage isn't good enough for Ray. I expect he's loaded as well?'

'Hush up. You and Tommy do all right, without uprooting yourselves like we have. From what Jan says, they're not as well off as you might think. How's Nan and Grandad?'

'I did ask if they wanted to come with us – we're taking Tedge anyway – but Grandad won't budge. Sits in the room every day in front of the racing with the sound up high as it'll go, fire full on while Nan's there in the kitchen with the back door open. Come down – they love to see the kids, and I know you enjoy it too.'

'I do, but I can't always get Alex to bring us. He has his football weekends, and the Tube and train's a nightmare with all the kids and their belongings.'

'He's not still following football all over the country, is he?'

'No, he seems to be done with that. The aggro's died down a lot so maybe that's why. When Kar was studying in Manchester, or supposed to be, he said she was one of the worst in her bovver boots at matches – it used to make him laugh when they saw each other. Getting arrested that time put the mockers on it for him. I'd rather have him playing again, however much he moans it's not the same level as before.'

'No news of her I suppose – Karen?'

'What do you think? I see her when she turns up on our doorstep, which may not be every time she's in London. I think she goes to Joy's sometimes. She appeared at Grandad Sess's place once – Joy told me he didn't recognise her.'

'I'm not surprised. He probably hadn't seen her since we were kids. I struggle myself sometimes – her hair's always a different colour and normally cut short like a boy's. You don't think she's gone...you know...do you?'

'Thin Lizzie? Wouldn't blame her if she did, but I think if she had, she would be turning up with a different woman hanging off her every time, not a man or a boy like it used to be, so you never knew what colour or nationality to expect. If she could do anything to get a rise out of any of us, I think she'd love it.'

'Could we invite her down as well? Staying in your house mind, not ours. She hasn't had a steady job since she left uni, has she?'

'I think she works – something to do with languages, but that's all beyond me. She talks sometimes about going back to finish her degree, but only when she's had a few.'

'Which is most of the time, isn't it?'

'I couldn't say. I'm not with her most of the time. Wouldn't blame her for that either. Just about to have my own first tipple of the day if you must know.'

'For elevenses? All right Ange, I'll leave you to it. See you soon. Bye. Love you.'

When had that closing 'love you' crept into Lucy's conversation? It may have been OK for Tommy, but for her sisters? She never waited to hear it said back, perhaps fearing she would wait in vain. Ange wasn't going to mother her now they were all adults. She dreaded becoming their own mum enough as it was. She hadn't been joking about the drink, even if Lucy thought she was. She had nobody to talk to about it, and sometimes she was grateful for that, being as how her mum and Grandma Alice had only dragged each other down rather than helping themselves to get better. As she unscrewed the wine, she cheered herself that at the seaside, everybody would be at it. She wouldn't have to drink alone.

'Remember we've got Kimberley in the back, Ray.'

His eyes flickered from the A47 to Jan beside him. 'I know that. Why do you think I'm sticking to eighty? I did say we'd be there for a dinner-time bevvy with Reedy.'

'We should have left earlier then, if you hadn't had to have that massive fry-up at your mum's.'

'Least I could do for the old dear, being as we didn't get there till gone teatime last night, thanks to visiting your fucking ex.'

'I'd hardly call it a visit, dropping off Denis while you sat and sulked in the car. Jason wouldn't bite you.'

'I'm not worried about him biting me. I'd as soon smack him as not.'

At least he restrained himself about Jason in front of Denis, the only legacy she treasured from her first marriage. It was already in trouble when she got slapdash about birth control. Jason was delighted to have a son, or at the idea of it. Maternity leave gave her an unwelcome insight into her husband's lifestyle, or rather confirmed what she had long known it to be without caring to admit it.

She had slackened her attention to contraception because it seemed redundant. While she would defend Jason to the death against any hint of the homosexuality something about him led people to infer, and sometimes imply – the only bent she would allow him was a theatrical one like his mother – Jan had realised, not without some dismay, that her sex drive was greater than his, as was her drive in every other aspect of life.

When Karen had her meltdown, it had seemed to spur their mother to get her own act back together. Norman was abandoned in London as Grace moved back to Northampton, at first to Lil's house then, when Karen took up her place at Manchester University after a gap year that would mark her for life without her ever caring to recall it (there was no foreign travel involved), into a flat of her own. It wasn't ideal for Denis to be on the eighth floor, but Jan did now feel she could trust her mother to look after him while she went to work.

She had made it clear to Jason that he must not follow her this time. It was over. She did not tell him about her thing with Bob Austin, one of his so-called mates, one who seemed to have some little interest in her as well as getting high. The interest proved not great enough for him to visit her more than a couple of times in Northampton. She had liked him well enough without ever liking the thought of herself as a cheat. She never tried to look him up – didn't actually know where he lived – when she returned to Washtown every other week to let Jason see Denis.

The element of destiny between her and Ray Roden – as seen through rose-tinted glasses at any rate – was their discovery during the People and Places round at the Racehorse that both were born in Washtown's Whitefriars Maternity Hospital. They were in the quiz team of the Sovereign Insurance Northampton office, where their paths had rarely crossed since the day of Ray's arrival, when he'd been walked around it by the branch manager's secretary. Jan would not match his subsequent protestations of falling under her spell from the start, nor go so far towards the truth as to admit she had been distinctly unimpressed by him. He was a graduate trainee in his first substantive role, while she was a section head in commercial underwriting. Although not viewed as career staff, she had a good enough track record to have continued to find jobs with Sovereign in different towns.

Ray had grown up in Feltwell, the village where she and her sisters had gone summer fruit-picking, where they had left his mother that bright morning, their shades functional enough if less tinted. Their courtship had been rushed towards a tipping point when Ray successfully applied for a job in Hong Kong, entailing first a short-term transfer to SID (Sovereign International Division) in London. He took a bedsit in Clapham for the few months before his posting.

While he was too young to have come within the magnetic field of attraction of the Roper girls at school, Jan was resigned to learn that Ray looked up to his now brother-in-law Alex as a one-time local hero footballer and still someone to keep on the right side of about town at night. He had been more than willing to go on holiday with his new family, sharing one of the houses, though he did not jib at staying in the Boat when Jan had stated that as her preference. 'It's likely to be a madhouse down there with all the kids running about. I'd rather try to keep Kim to her bedtime routine if possible.'

'Shame we couldn't bring Den as well – he'd probably have enjoyed the seaside more than staying with Twathead,' Ray resumed their conversation as they bypassed Norwich.

'Maybe.' She ignored the ugly name for Jason – not Ray's ugliest by any means – knowing he used it mainly to get at her, as if fearful and jealous of her past. 'I think it's only fair to let Jason have him this week. I hope he doesn't refer to you as his dad.'

'Tough titty if he does. You know I haven't forced him or anything.'

'I know. Anyway, that and the hotel will give us a little bit more privacy, a bit of time together.'

'A few early nights, hey? Wink wink, nudge nudge.'

She swatted his hand away from her thigh, not entirely discouraging, though she was looking forward at least as much to seeing her sisters again as to a holiday romance with her husband. She was surprised at the extent to which she missed her family while abroad, despite having a nuclear one of her own. At times she told herself she had just exchanged one high-rise for another, then reproached herself for being negative. There was really no comparison between Grace's flat and what Sovereign had sorted for Ray and her in Hong Kong. She hoped the same was true of what her mother had with Eric and she with Ray, who had been frank enough about a populous sexual past in those early days when the convention is to share everything.

Such sharing was always a qualified option for Jan. She felt guilty sometimes at perhaps adding to Ray's antagonism by representing Jason as her one-and-only, childhood sweetheart and all the rest of it – in short, as her ex no doubt saw it himself. If anyone disabused either of them, it would not be her. At least she had always known where Jason was, always been able to trust in his fidelity, though again she told herself such comparisons would do her no good at all.

'So how's your second go around suiting you, Jan?' Ange took the head off her lager and lime and offered an Embassy Regal before lighting up herself. They were the first customers in the Boat's garden, with its unrestricted view out to sea.

'If something's broke, better chuck it away than keep fiddling with it.'

'You talking about me and Alex by any chance?'

'Not at all. Well, maybe I was having a bit of a dig, but I meant really just me and Jason.'

'Ray seems to have a bit more get-up-and-go than him, I'll give him that.'

'He's been got-up-and-gone all this holiday. The way he trails after Alex reminds me how Alex used to after Dad, you remember?'

'The one makes me laugh is Tommy – he's like a puppy not knowing who to follow. You can see he wants to be off with the men as well, then Lucy calls him to heel and he has to be straight back there, to service her or look after Louise or help keep Tedge amused.'

'Fair play to her on that, Ange. I'm glad she brought him along. He seems a bit better nowadays – I almost had a proper little conversation with him.'

'Who, Tommy or Tedge? No, she seems to understand him OK, but then they practically grew up together. I still struggle, to be honest. He gets some funny looks on the beach as well, a great big feller playing around with the kids. No harm in him – we know that, but maybe others don't. I suppose we should get back, so as not to be accused of leaving her all the kids to look after like Alex had the cheek to tell me we've been doing yesterday. They think if they take 'em to the park for a kickaround or a game of crazy golf while they're waiting for the pubs to open, that's them done.'

'Yeah, we should get down there and see about some lunch. Are you feeling calmer now?'

'What do you mean?' The older sister was instantly on the alert.

'I'm not being a snoop or anything, but like we all do I remember Mum, and apart from her I've seen some addictive behaviour up close.'

'You'd know more about drugs than I do.'

'You can have that one, but I'm not just talking about drugs. I mean it's great to have this half hour just the two of us before we go down the beach with the rest of them, but it's every morning. I do sometimes wonder if it's me you're really here for or what Ray calls a livener, the first drink of the day.'

'Jesus Jan, lighten up, we're on holiday. I've seen you knocking it back too. What's that in front of you right now, Scotch mist?'

'All right, forget I said anything. I just wonder – I know we were kids and everything – I wonder if we could have done more for Mum and Gran, and I think we should be there for each other.'

'What you tearing up for? That's not you at all. I would have expected it from Lucy maybe, except all she can think of is getting pregnant. I know what men are like, but I can understand Tommy wanting to get away with the boys now and then. Lucky he's got his fishing, poor sod, otherwise she'd probably have him at it every night.'

'I think it's kind of sweet the way he dotes on her.'

'You had the same with Jason, didn't you? Obviously wasn't enough. Talking of getting pregnant, you've not done so bad yourself. I never did ask you at the time, was little Kim your plane ticket to escape from Mum?'

Jan blushed. 'No need to have a go at me, Ange, I wasn't trying to be nasty to you. For your information – because I don't have to tell you this – I *was* pregnant, but I would have looked after myself if necessary. Ray didn't know when he asked me to go to Hong Kong with him.'

'And it didn't make him change his mind?'

'You can see it didn't, can't you? "More the merrier" he said. He's been really good with Denis. Sometimes I do worry a little bit that we've never had a time together without kids being involved. Like he might think at some point we've missed out.'

'Me and Alex seem to have had kids running around forever. I started a lot younger than you, and we didn't exactly plan Suzie. My nightmare is falling again. I don't think he's ever felt like he's missing out – he's still all over me. Funny how it seems to be a bit different for poor Luce.'

Although Jan suspected that Alex had no reason to feel he was missing out on female company, she always bit her tongue rather than talk about her brother-in-law. She also tried to avoid being alone with him, which wasn't difficult in their current group. 'I know, you'd think we'd all be fertile if we take after Mum. It took Luce forever to fall with Louise. I can see her going in for that treatment if Tommy doesn't give her another one before too long. What are you smirking at?'

121

'She's ahead of you there. Maybe I shouldn't say, but what the heck, we're all sisters. She's already made Tommy go for the tests, in case he's the problem. What do they call it? Not quite a jaffa – low sperm count or whatever.'

'That's it. I bet she'll get it organised one way or another. Look, I don't want to keep on, and I promise not to mention it again for the rest of the time we're here, but that's what worries me in a way. That we might all take after Mum. And don't forget our father. I mean it's not exactly a surprise that we all like a drink – I'm not saying it's just you, Ange – but we've seen what can come of it. I know I might sound sentimental – maybe it's being halfway across the world making me think a bit more about family – but I'd like to hope we can stand up for each other, help each other out, remember how close we used to be, especially me and you.'

'You was the one that moved away, Jan. I don't know why, and I'm not talking about now you've moved right across the world, like you say. Do we really want to go back to our childhood, any of us? And for *your* information, it wasn't the drink that killed Grandma Alice, it was the pills. The pills was what drove Mum nuts for a while, not the drink.'

'All right, Ange. Let's enjoy our holiday.' Her sister didn't resist when Jan took her arm on the way down to the beach, walking linked and needling each other just like they used to on the way to the Olly.

The Philpotts Painting and Decorating van was owned and driven by Les, for whom apparently No Job was Too Small. Billy had failed to bag shotgun, Karen made him sit with her, leaving Grace in the front to enjoy her current boyfriend's company on the long drive from Northampton. The siblings emerged from the double back doors as eagerly as from a burning house, though the smoke clouds accompanying them were of their own making.

They found the girls on the beach, Lucy presiding, Ange and Jan enlivened, Little Jan in her early teens caught somewhere between the adults and her cousins jockeying to make their three (Kimberley) and two (Louise) years on pre-school Suzette count enough to mother her.

'Nice welcome! Nobody there to roll out the red carpet for us at your luxurious coastal residences.' Karen and Grace had gone down to the sea, Les and Billy up to the Boat.

'What are you doing here?' – 'I didn't know you were in England' – 'Hello Mum, how are you?' – 'How did you get here?' – 'You might have let us know, Kar' were among the volleyed exchanges of the older ones as the

122

preteen Roper girls instinctively sheltered behind Lucy, or in Suzie's case stuck doggedly to battering a sandcastle with a spade.

'How could we – didn't decide to come till late last night and on the road since stupid o'clock? What is this, a hen party? Am I not the only one without a man then? Even Mum's pulled – all I've got's that excuse for a brother of ours up at the pub.'

'The men have all gone to play football on the green. They wouldn't let us go with them,' Janette complained to her aunt, as she already had to all the other adults.

'Is that right, JJ? We'll see about the football in a few. Your dad will have to let me play – me and Alex were in the Red Army together. Let me just say hello to your namesake I haven't seen in yonks and her little girl. She doesn't look like a Roper, Jan, so that's a good start in life.'

'Talk about motormouth,' Lucy niggled, walking up from the beach with all their belongings after Karen had hauled Little Jan, Kim and Lou off to play football with the men and boys. Her mother had seemed surprised and a little disappointed at Louise's defection, once reassured by Ange that she could cope with Suzie on her own for a little while.

'Looks like she's on speed to me – she'll never last the whole day at that pace.'

'Leave it out, Jan – everyone's always on something according to you.' Ange was slightly ahead of them beside Grace, who asked her what speed was.

'Never mind, Mum, it's only Jan having a pop.'

'Whatever it is, I wouldn't mind some if it would give me the energy that girl's got. She just can't sit still.'

Little Jan was outraged when they reached the council playing fields a couple of streets back from the front, behind the Co-op, to find females in the kickabout of a dozen or more people, a mixture of visitors and local kids. Alex and Tommy were on one side, Ray and Adam on the other, which boasted the only other adult in the group – a game slaphead grandad in the goals. They had discovered on their first day that Tedge, without any malice, was clumsy and enthusiastic enough to hurt some of the smaller kids when challenging for the ball. He seemed happy enough to run the line, doing his best to keep up with play and flagging imaginary offsides with his filthy once-white handkerchief. Alex was always careful to acknowledge his calls with a raised palm and 'Thanks, linoe.'

'Hey, skinny little Gerry Daly.' Alex tried to greet Karen with a bear hug.

'Big Gordon, you out of shape or what?' She instantly disengaged herself. 'You're soaked.'

'It's a hot day case you hadn't noticed – don't need to break a sweat to keep up with these amateurs. Right, we'll have you Kar, and you're responsible for the littluns by the way – you brought 'em. Jan, you can go on your brother's side.'

'Why do I have to be on Adam's team? And you said there were no girls allowed.'

'That's what I thought, baby, but you see that man in goal there, he's the big boss at the council and he said it was OK as long as he's here to supervise. And I can't have you on the opposite team from Adam or you'll be kicking lumps out of each other, then I'll get in trouble with your mum.'

Billy followed United as a matter of course, but wasn't a footballer. He worked most weekends, his only sporting hobby motorbike scrambling. Les's van had come in handy recently to load the bike into and head to the countryside, sometimes with Grace along for the ride and a few drinks. Billy was as glad as his sister to get out of it after their long drive, and more than ready for a pint of lager dash. Not a big lad or a big drinker, he could occasionally be bullied into what Alex called a proper session by his brother-in-law.

Les *was* a big lad, a steady beer drinker. He and Billy were comfortable enough together without the aptitude or appetite for much conversation, choosing to stay on at their Boat table rather than join Karen and her ragtag squad on their way to the playing field. 'Please yourselves – you'll soon meet the noisy Roper girls, Les. I'm the shy and retiring one.' She necked half of her brother's drink without asking permission, berated him for the lemonade top and was gone.

Only the older man was at the table when the beach contingent appeared, carefully levering himself to his feet. There was much fluttering of Grace's hands before they came to rest, failing to meet around his upper arm, leaving the girls to make their own introductions. He had a speech pat for when Lucy asked him where he was from.

'Rugby originally. Warwickshire born, Warwickshire bred, strong in the arm, thick in the head. Been in Northampton for years now though. My dad's business originally. He died a couple of years back, but I'm struggling along, keeping it going. It's good to meet you all at last – your mum's always talking about her girls. I've seen photos but not too many recent ones.'

'No, we don't see as much of each other as we should, and it's not as if we live that far away, except Jan of course. Hey, Billy, did you know our globetrotting sister was back in England?' Lucy continued to their brother, appearing from the bar with a pint in each hand.

'Well yeah – I was at her wedding last week.'

'Her what? You got married again? Did you know about this, Ange? Mum, you must of – why didn't you say anything? Where was it? I'm glad for Kimmie, but you might have told us. Especially if Billy was there. What about Karen, was she? If you were there, Ange...'

'Calm down, Lucy. Ange didn't know about it any more than you did. There were no bridesmaids, if that's what you're getting worked up about.'

'Never mind that,' Angela spoke for herself. 'Luce is right – you might have told us. Not a word to me about it all week. So much for being close like we used to – was all that bullshit then?'

'It's not a big secret, Ange, don't be like that. Nor you, Luce. It was a quiet do, not like the circus when I got married to Jason.'

'That wouldn't have stopped you inviting us like before. Apart from the tent, that was only a registry-office do.'

'I couldn't face Washtown registry office again – they'd be offering me a bloody season ticket. Look, I didn't need to get married. We were a couple already. It was the bureaucracy of Sovereign or Hong Kong finally caught up with us – made things a lot simpler my so-romantic new husband said.'

'So where *did* you get married then?'

'London – Clapham to be exact. If we'd tried Northampton, Ray's mum would have kicked up, probably tried to get us into Feltwell church, so we went for neutral ground. Ray had to be in the office for a couple of days anyway. Nobody there but Agnes and an old mate of Ray's with his girlfriend. Mum was too nervous on her own so Billy come down on a day return with her.'

'Excuse my language but who the *fuck* is Agnes? What about Aunt Joy? She lives in London.'

'Agnes is Ray's mum, Lucy. Aunt Joy, yes I mean she's always been good to me...'

'Oh so it was just you and Ray and Denis and Kim and Mum and Billy and Ray's mum, Ray's mate and his sodding girlfriend and Aunt Joy and I suppose Henry and Martin. You'll be telling us Grandad Sess was there next. And your sisters didn't know about it, or have you forgotten to mention Karen as well?'

'Karen didn't know. Still doesn't, unless Billy Big Gob told her on their way down here. I don't know why you're getting so worked up, Luce. We were going to tell you at that dinner out Ray promised you all on our last night here. I mean we didn't have a honeymoon or anything. One night in a London hotel, and believe me it wasn't the Ritz.'

'Er, let me go and get the drinks in. What you all having?'

'And I suppose he was there too,' Lucy shrieked at Les's intervention, almost sprawling to the grass when she caught her foot in the crossbeam fixing the bench seat to their table. She skittered off towards her house – or to check Tommy hadn't been involved in the conspiracy against her.

'I'll go get a place at the bar – you come and shout 'em up, Billy.' Les had already emptied his glass. 'I thought Karen was joking about her sisters being the noisy ones.'

Despite that shaky start, the day turned out a good one. The footballers returned, led by Alex and Karen, who toasted their victory with pints accompanied by shots of vodka. Lucy didn't object when her sisters and mother joined her with the children on the beach that afternoon. Tommy was liberated to snooker and more boozing at the Workers' when Billy cried off, making up the four with Alex, Ray and Les.

'Did you put your trunks on under your kecks like I told you, Billy?' Karen asked him. 'If not, you can borrow a pair of Adam's to go in the water.'

Shucking out of her sawn-off jeans and T-shirt to reveal a lime bikini, she grabbed his hand and, laughing, pulled him to the water's edge. 'Never mind how disappointed we get in luv, bruv, we'll always have each other. However cold the sea is, it can't be any worse than that poxy pool we used to go in out of Colditz.'

They swam out far enough together that no other bathers were disturbed when Billy puked up a couple of pints of Carlsberg. 'Lightweight,' Karen tried to duck his head into the vomit before it dispersed.

It was still plenty warm enough to eat outside the Boat when they all reassembled there that evening for the wedding party/celebration they had brought forward to allow the newcomers to share (and, though Jan would not admit it, in part to mollify Lucy). Once the kids had finished their meals – Adam and Little Jan long since in the adult section of the menu – and grown tired of running around the garden area, they were allowed back to Lucy's house. Little Jan was bribed to keep an ear open for the smaller girls, not so much settled to sleep by their mothers as falling asleep in their arms.

Lucy had told Tedge he was the one really in charge of the kids. Seeing her mistake as his face creased up at the responsibility involved, she reassured him that didn't mean he had to stay awake if he felt tired – she would be popping in from time to time and keep them all safe.

'You can stay here all night if you like, Tommy, but I'm about done in. It must be nearly closing time anyway.'

Tommy's protest that it was barely half ten received back-up from an unexpected quarter. The effect on Les of comfortably outdrinking Alex on pints of mild all day had been an occasional verbal confusion and a much more relaxed attitude around the Roper girls. 'Just wait a minute, me duck – we don't want to make the same mistake… No, now's a good as time as ever, Grace …this lady and I, we've got an announcement to make.'

'Don't tell us you're pregnant again Mum, please.' Ange spoke more loudly than she had meant to. She had enjoyed her day, quietly at Grace's side with the conversations going on all around them, both drinking unobtrusively – they never had to request one – yet steadily. Ange always found she didn't need it so much once she was out in company; her thirst was greatest before having to join others, or if she was left too long on her own.

'That would be some announcement.' Jan smiled, only hoping her sister was joking rather than regressing to their childhood. She was herself far from sober.

Les laughed. 'It would be a fucking miracle, pardon my French. No more kids between us – I'm happy enough with just your mum. It's been a pleasure to meet youse of tho I didn't know till today. I hope you will *all* be able to attend our wedding. No date yet, only a small do, but meantime go to the van for us, will you Billy mate? I've got a bottle of Grouse in there – a full one unless you and Karen found it on the way down. If the guvnor won't let us drink it here, we can polish it off on the beach.'

12
Lucy

They might have been the happiest years we had. For a while it looked as if everything would work out. I mean the years we used to go down to Munsley on holiday – there were several of them for us, and we were sometimes joined by different members of the family. The one everyone remembers is when Mum announced her engagement, or rather let Les do it for her. The landlord of the pub let us drink our own whisky there in his garden then chipped in a bottle of his own after we invited him and his wife to join us. Everyone remembers that, but there were other holidays, just as good.

Karen was still wild – you could tell that. She was living back in England by then, doing something at last with her education and her languages. Billy had been a bit of a handful as a boy, we knew without knowing the full story. She had helped him out and they were still close. He had a steady girlfriend, a bit younger than him, saving for a house together they were. He didn't have a great education, but he was a marvel with motors and stuff – like Dad, which is funny when you think how little they really knew each other. He worked in a garage in Northampton, could always get a car going, then went into something more specialised in the engineering line. Big industrial machinery – don't ask me for details.

We all knew Alex was an arsehole, always had been. Still, he was earning good money in London, and Ange shouldn't really have much to complain about. Jan looked as if she'd landed on her feet as well, although we didn't see much of her nowadays or her new husband. It would have been nice to get to know him before they got wed, but that was her choice. I know things must have been hard for her when she first left Jason. Whether or not he was any real help with Denis, it's not the same trying to bring a kid up on your own, is it?

I know I did get a little bit obsessed about a brother or sister – I really didn't mind which – for our Louise. You'd have thought Tommy would be delighted at the amount of sex I needed from him – and without using anything, which always pleases boys. He never did complain, but maybe it put a bit of pressure on him. As you get older, you get more perspective. It seems comical I let that get to me so much when there are far worse things that can happen. I thought I could always find a way to get what I wanted. Now I know I can't because nobody can.

Karen always said things started to go downhill – or tits up as she put it – when our dad died, over in Ireland. It wasn't illness or anything, just a stupid car accident. Possibly drink was involved – nobody liked to ask. They managed to cut him out, but Lil always said it would have been better if he'd died on the spot. He was in that much agony at the end.

We took the car across on the ferry from Holyhead, leaving Louise at home with Aunt Shirley and Tedge, picking up Mum from Northampton on the way. Uncle Pete flew with Nana, straight in and out more or less. They were both broken up. Grandad was practically housebound by then. I think he would have gone otherwise, even if Eric wasn't his actual son.

We understood why Les wouldn't want to go. He had never met our father, and perhaps that was just as well. I liked him from the start – a good, solid bloke for Mum. We were always nervous about her well-being and mental stability. At least I was. I don't know why really, because I must have been the only one of us who didn't go running to her with dramas and problems of my own. We hadn't heard so much about Les lately though – no further mention of a wedding from Mum.

I doubt if Jan would have crossed the road never mind the sea to Ireland. She always did blame Dad. It was no use talking to her. You could never make her admit Fang was only a dog. Anyway, she had the excuse of being abroad as usual. Karen got a ride over there with Ange and Alex, who surprised me. I swear he was crying at the graveside. Billy drove Lil's boys, Eddie and Michael.

There was no drama at the funeral or wake. Mum and Lil weren't best mates anymore, living in separate countries. I did wonder if they ever really were. Karen said they had to present a united front to keep all Dad's girlfriends from coming and bawling over his coffin. I never knew where she got all her ideas from. A lot just weren't funny if you ask me.

Eamon, the boy Lil and Dad had together, must have been eleven or twelve. Although he was our half-brother, he didn't show any interest in getting to know us, wanting to hang out more with Eddie and Michael who, when you think about it, were only his half-brothers too. Lil's oldest Brenda had several kids running around. It's funny how some people have no problems at all. If only I'd known how things would turn out, I might have asked to adopt Karen's bab, me and Tommy. I don't know it would have been that weird – stranger things happen. She was obviously fertile. I doubt very much if she was living like a nun, but there were no more kids or any serious boyfriends we heard about. Not that lack of a steady fellow stopped her the first time.

It was in the ferry bar on the way home Mum started to cry and talk more about Dad than I'd ever heard her. She didn't stop till we'd stayed an extra night with her in Northampton – that's how worried I was despite Tommy needing to get back to work. How Eric was the absolute love of her life, she never thought they'd ever part, all that romantic sort of stuff, then the next minute how she would have killed him herself if she could.

There were some strange stories in there. I couldn't picture him with a convertible car back then, but she said he'd had one and she'd slashed its roof to shreds before pouring paint all over the seats, rather than see him run about in it with other women.

She was suddenly bitter about Lil, how she'd not only stolen the man but our inheritance, never a penny in support for any of us and, for all we'd heard of him doing well in Ireland, nothing coming to us from his death. 'I asked her and she said they'd been struggling to keep his business going, didn't know how she was going to manage herself, might have to come back to England. I don't know what she was hinting, Luce. I had to tell her, told her straight not to come crying to me – we've got nothing for her.'

I must have been mad to say I'd try to find out if Dad had left any money, and if he had to get our fair share. We could have used it, me and Tommy, more than Ange and Jan for sure, but it ended up stressing us both worse than ever. It put me on the outs not only with Lil, which I didn't care about, but Karen when she said I was taking things too far. I may not understand all her fancy words but let her know I didn't like 'money-grubbing' being applied to me, especially when I was only trying to do the best for all of us. Including

Mum, who may not have been entitled to anything legally but couldn't let it go – couldn't let him go I suppose. She stayed married to Dad all the years when they were living apart, then soon as she takes the big step of divorce, planning to marry again, he goes and dies. She made it sound as if he'd done it just to spite her. I wonder if her and Les was partly to spite Dad – some hope.

We never got anything, which I didn't give a shit about, not once I lost my Tommy within twelve months of Dad. A heart attack when he was out all-night fishing, only thirty-three he was, same age as Jesus, no sign of it in advance or nothing. They came to me the next morning before I was even worried. They might have found him in the river, but it was not a drowning. I always knew it was a heart attack, whatever some people said.

13

Karen

Meltdown, breakdown, use whichever word you like, it's true I had a bad time of it for a while after they took Gary away. I schooled myself to say it like that: 'they' took him away, 'they' wouldn't let me keep him; took the 'I' out of it whenever one could.

It wasn't like a bereavement for anyone else because of course he was still alive. They could give you all the consolatory guff – Eddie and Michael in their rough way, Mum, my sisters, Aunt Joy when I let them come near me now he had gone and there was no reason not to, all wanted me to put the Pollyanna spectacles on and believe it would all work out for the best in the end, you'll see. All that type of bullshit. Charles, whom there was no reason to call Mr Hooper now I'd left school, kept mentioning university and the open place for me, determined not to mention the open wound. I eventually told him straight to fuck off – there was no reason I couldn't do that either now.

Billy's bother did the trick of getting me out of bed. I was showing signs of turning into Grandma Alice; apart from making sure the boys had their dinner of an evening I wasn't contributing much to the household, and their good-heartedness had its limits. It was typical of Billy not to show the slightest curiosity about me. I'm not sure he even acknowledged my pregnancy, so why would he want to ask about its outcome?

When I'd try to cheer him up at Colditz by saying we'd find a way to bust out of there, go make a home of our own together, it took me a while to realise it was only myself I had any chance of cheering up. Perhaps the poor kid didn't have enough memories of life outside to miss it.

Precocious is a better word than promiscuous. I don't doubt Billy was involved in the fumblings between boys and girls at an earlier age than he might have been in a conventional family outside Colditz – perhaps not the Roper family; we could hardly point ourselves out as a shining beacon of morality in the community. I didn't want to know about that side of his life – there were limits.

What I hadn't realised was, the daft little sod had fallen in love.

When he left school, Alex had tried to help out by getting him a job in ICL. He was on the right track, but our brother would turn out to be more one for the nuts-and-bolts, get-your-hands-dirty type of machinery than computers, gigantic things in those days that had to be cosseted in temperature-controlled rooms, access authorised nerds only. As far as I could gather, his starting job was a glorified night watchman, making sure it carried on churning out its reams of poor-quality paper, calling someone who knew what was what if any red lights started flashing.

Not that he spoke more about his work than he did about anything. Eddie and Michael were glad enough to see him when he came up on his bike supposedly for a week's holiday, especially as Michael was still at a loose end jobwise. I was hardly in holiday mood, but it made no difference to put out another plate of dinner. In a way Billy's lack of interest in my condition was refreshing, better than the sympathy others dished out, which I knew was genuine enough but could not for the life of me accept with any grace.

It might have passed off without any rumpus if they hadn't been on opposite sides of the magic age of sixteen, or if Caroline Matthews hadn't panicked when they were caught and started screaming. He was in her bed shagging her for Christ's sake, in a dormitory – the time to start screaming was a bit sooner if he was really unwelcome. They had history together it would not have suited Colditz to bring up, since it went back to the days they were both under its care.

I do wonder since the staff let him get that far, having been tipped off in advance by another girl, a jealous one (or so we pieced together), if there wasn't a degree of prurience in their tardy intervention, not just wanting to have him bang to rights as it were.

Billy clearly wasn't a child anymore, but Mum had always babied him and came running up at the mention of statutory rape charges. I had been trying to deal with the school myself – as I said, it did drag me out of the house, and it turned out my aggression hadn't been extirpated; I was well up for the fight. Whatever we'd become, they'd played a large part in making us.

We both got away with a probation order, suspended sentence or whatever you want to call it. Caroline didn't want to make too big a fuss once she'd recovered her composure. She had no family to make a big fuss on her behalf, and perhaps I shouldn't have taken out on her Billy's unwillingness to understand how serious the situation remained. Mum wasn't shy of bringing Gary into things as mitigating circumstances on my behalf, which disgusted me as I let her know. Something in me wouldn't have minded being locked up; maybe Billy wasn't the only one who had a secret nostalgia for grey prison walls.

I hardly touched her; the assault charge was ridiculous. I only spoke when I saw her by the clock tower to give her sound advice. I said I hoped she was taking precautions, kept my temper when she said I was hardly one to talk – she fancied herself a bit of a hard case did young Caroline, a lot of them/us did in Colditz. When she started talking about getting pregnant being no big deal I only shook her about a bit. As luck would have it, plod was around – you did occasionally see one on the streets in those distant days.

Billy might have been better advised to go back to London with Mum, except despite all that happened he retained some stupid fantasy about being in love with the little slapper – always a bit of a romantic was our Billy. Mum never had much of a problem finding men and, except for Dad, never much of a problem leaving them either. After ditching Norman (or possibly a successor), she returned to Northampton and soon had her hooks in poor old Les.

I was glad to move out of the Sheridans' house. Eddie had brought in a girlfriend by then. For just a few months, we saw what we might have missed as Billy and I lived with Mum. Frankly, it was nothing like my no doubt idealised memories of childhood when she and Dad were still together. I was happy enough to take up my books again and my place at Manchester University.

It was a wonder I survived the years of following United without being caught in breach of my probation. The coppers were even more sexist back then – probably couldn't believe that a little girl like me could really be a threat to hairy-arsed opposition fans, plus they had plenty of scope around football matches to make their arrest quotas without bother. Alex was one of them, but that was his lookout.

University saw many people finding for the first time the kind of life that was already nothing new to me in terms of freedom from restraints. I did well at Manchester, three years of my four-year course completed if you count the third abroad where I stayed a lot longer than a year. I went to Evreux University in France until Christmas, then Cologne for the rest of the academic year, improving my French and German to (I don't want to boast) a high degree of fluency. I looked up my sometime hosts in Livarot, though the longer relationship, the one that kept me out of England for nearly five years in all, was with a German Lothar – no Lothario but he had me at *Hände hoch*.

And somewhere as I careered through my twenties and thirties, they changed the adoption laws.

14

Angela

Alex would always blame me for ruining our marriage by insisting we leave London. The arguments are long over now – don't think I carry a torch for him like Mum did for Dad. He never liked country music like I did, all that yeehaw shit he used to call it. Well now I can listen to it as much as I like – Paddy and I both love Dolly, and Taylor too whether you call her country or say she's more poppy. Alex and me are never ever, ever getting back together. Yeehaw.

Alex always wanted to be right. If I'd had the energy to fight, I might have said moving out of London kept us going for many more years than we would have done staying.

I'm not blaming him for everything. He always said us Roper girls were more than a handful, and he should know because I think he fancied all of us – even Mum, the way she used to flirt with him in our early years together. I don't know what it was about London that did for me. Maybe it was just when Suzie started school there I had too much time at home on my own – not enough to want another bab, mind. I might have adjusted sooner or later, but I think it's more likely, as I feared then, it would have been downhill all the way.

I knew very well I was being silly in so many ways. For a start I could have spent time with Aunt Joy – she would have liked that, and me too. Only I could never work out the bus routes, and the Underground…well that's it. I think it was partly because of it being underground. Don't think I don't know how stupid *that* sounds. Whatever it was, I just didn't dare go on it. Course I *did* go on it if I was going out somewhere with Alex, but you wouldn't believe how I clung to him. He would joke about it, say was I that desperate for his body when we were only heading to some boring old office do – anything made him think I was after sex.

I wasn't totally unreasonable. I said we could move back to Washtown to be near his family if he'd prefer that. The Reeds would have loved to have their grandkids back in town, and I would've given it a good go. I'd come to get on all right with them, Gwen especially. I had some of my own family there as well. But Alex said it was too far for him to commute to London, so that was that.

Northampton then, where Alex could get to work from and I did have family – not just running back to mummy like he said. Billy had a place of his own there, living with a young girlfriend Sally-Anne. Jan and Ray had bought a house as an investment while they were living abroad. They got at it big time later, blaming each other for not putting their money into London instead.

Aunt Joy was the only one to stick it out in the big city. Karen was there again teaching English at a place for foreign students, from what she told us. Nan and Grandad would obviously never move from Washtown, the same with Uncle Pete and Shirley. Tedge would be with them forever. Any change wouldn't be fair on him they always said, but I don't think they were the type to want to move either.

Lucy was still in Washtown, still close to them, thank God she was when Tommy died so suddenly. I could forgive her a lot for having to go through that. It was a Saturday morning we heard, and Alex made no bones about us going over there straight away to be with my sister. He probably knew Tommy a lot better than I did – always quiet, but he seemed decent and totally devoted to Lucy. The other men used to take the mickey out of him for it, calling him henpecked and worse, which he just had to put up with. I thought it was sweet. It doesn't make you a weak person, wanting to please your partner.

At some point over that first weekend we all got to Washtown – except Jan, who was abroad, and Billy, who didn't want to know. It was true he had been mainly brought up apart from the family, except for Karen, but she said he was just the same with her. She didn't use the word selfish, so I won't either. He didn't feel he had to pretend to care, whether it was weddings, christenings or, unfortunately, funerals, the things that normally do most to bring families together.

Nobody ever said Lucy wasn't strong, and she had to keep herself together for the sake of Louise. That's what she said. Nobody mentioned how Mum had failed to hold it together for the rest of us. She invited them both to come and stay in Northampton – everyone could see it was a half-hearted offer and she probably meant to stay with us rather than at hers. One thing about moving out of London, and this was before the prices there went through the roof, was that we had a much bigger house where we were now.

Poor Tedge was pitiful to see that weekend. He loved Lucy. Not in any creepy sort of way, not sexual. I don't want to belittle him either by saying it was like a dog. He might have his issues, but he was human as any of us. That weekend he *was* like a dog though, always in everyone's way as they tried to pass their condolences on to Lucy and spend time with her. He never left her side, however many little errands people kept trying to find him. Uncle Pete was bad too. He'd lost his brother less than a year before, spent more time with Tommy than most of the rest of us, and I'd be prepared to bet he was more distressed for Lucy than Dad, God rest him, would have been.

It wasn't from our family that Alex heard that nasty rumour. I'm so slow he had to explain what it meant when he said the word around Washtown was they found Tommy with rocks in his pockets. People can be horrible at times. I never doubted Lucy when she said it was a heart attack. I said I never wanted to hear Alex repeat that sort of talk again. He was drunk when he told me it. He did sort of say the next day it was just a bad joke. I don't know why men think about making jokes like that. I wish I'd heard it. I would have punished them the same I did that lad at the New Year's Eve disco for his, short enough for me to hear the whole thing as we moved through the crowd past their table to our own. Tommy and Lucy were with us as it happened.

'What's the smallest pub in England? The Thalidomide Arms.'

I wasn't dumb enough to repeat it to Alex. He might have laughed himself. I started flirting a tiny bit with the kid when I saw him looking at me and Lucy dancing together – that was the one thing she could never get Tommy to do. He mustn't have known who I was, cos he showed a bit of interest right back. I'd had a few before we went out, because I always did – that wasn't why the joke upset me, but it may have been why I did something about it. All it took was one word to Alex that the boy was trying it on, and he was bouncing him off the walls, never mind the muscles the little idiot had been showing off in a T-shirt for all, like I said, it was New Year's Eve so freezing cold. There were plenty of other pubs we could go to afterwards anyway, and Alex would be fine back in the Tappers on New Year's Day.

It wasn't surprising that Lucy couldn't face up to Munsley, where they used to go every year. They always had more of a thing for that place than the rest of us, but then they were the ones getting the half-price deal. I thought it was a good idea to invite them to join us on holiday for a change, whether it came from me or, as I later wondered, Alex.

I didn't like the cramped roads of Cornwall any more than I did Norfolk's wide open spaces. Alex always said it was his dream to retire down there. I don't know why – he had no family connection. Maybe it was to get away from all us Ropers and the Reeds. His relationship with his dad never got easier. He made a point of telling me when he knew he was earning more than Simon, as if to prove he'd been right not to follow his career advice, so maybe he rubbed it in with the old man as well.

We didn't really expect Lucy to take us up on the offer, but she said it would do Louise good, and then she was never one to mope for long. All the Cornish houses are a bit poky, so they ended up staying in a caravan in some old farmer's field, above the pub where we would end up each evening after days mainly on the beach. When Alex was around, he was as good with Lou as I have to admit he always was with our own kids, at least when they were small, and when he took Adam off fishing she got on well with our Jan and Suzie. I mean kids are pretty strong, aren't they? Although Jan hated it when her dad would do something with Adam, boys only, I was glad of it. I didn't want them to end up like him with his own dad.

This was before official twenty-four-hour drinking, but the landlord at the Tinners was never in any rush to chuck us out. Alex always said they had to make most of their money off mugs like us in the summer – what is it they call us, grockles? I wasn't so keen on them either. They could have been polite about us if we were supporting them, and the ones in the village looked a rough lot. It was only right and proper that Alex would see Lucy and Louise back to the van when they went home after dark (which wasn't till quite late). I'd usually wait in the Tinners so we could maybe have a last one before walking back to our place down towards the sea.

It was the last night of their stay – we were there for another week – so it can't have spoiled their holiday as much as it did mine, her accusation. They had live music on in the bar, not the sort to interest the kids, so it was agreed that Lou would stay at our place, with no pressure on them to go to bed any earlier but leaving them all together and letting us for once have an adult night out. One or two of the locals had taken a shine to Lucy and tried to get her to dance. She was having none of it, so though she didn't lack other offers it was better that Alex walked her when she insisted she wanted to go before the end. We had said she could come down ours that night, but she said no.

'Are you and Alex OK, Ange?' she asked me out of the blue the next morning when I went to help her clear up the van, Lou happy enough to stay at ours until her mum came to fetch her.

'Yeah, experienced boozers us. Are you feeling it a bit then? One too many Malibu and lemonades last night?'

'I don't mean hungover – I mean between you, like.'

'He's always been a good provider, Alex, at least since he got going in computers, and then we've got the kids…I'm sorry, Luce, I don't mean it's all about that, I know you and Tommy were trying for more. It's not all plain sailing in any marriage. You've seen for yourself this week we're not exactly lovey-dovey anymore. We weren't just restraining ourselves so you didn't miss Tommy all the worse, believe me.'

'I never thought you were. What would you do if you thought he was cheating on you?'

And I *still* didn't see what was coming. How dumb can you get?

'Luce, come on, surely you're not thinking there was any of that with Tommy. I mean he worshipped the ground you walk on. If he said he was out fishing, I bet that's just where he was, nothing else. I might not trust Alex if he suddenly started being out all night long, but there's no comparison between them two. He gets bored fishing taking Adam out for an afternoon at it.'

'I'm not talking about Tommy. He hasn't been dead three months so it's the disrespect as much as anything – not only to him, God rest his soul, to me, *and* to you.'

'I'm sorry, Luce, you've lost me.'

She'd been busy folding the beds away but turned to look right at me, all serious. 'I don't want to hurt you, Ange. I really appreciated the invitation to come down here, thought Alex was being great about having us along, but he was bang out of order if he thought I was going to have sex with him.'

'You what? He wanted to have sex with you? Come on Luce, he must have been joking if he said anything like that. I mean he's no angel, but—'

'Come on yourself, Ange. Haven't we all been propositioned enough in our time to know when it's for real and when it's not? I don't know what it is about us Roper girls. You think at first it's nice that men find you sexy. It's not as if any of us – not even Karen I bet – tries to attract men for the sake of it, just because we can. There's nothing special to that anyway. Any old slag can get a man, like that Juliet Ramsdale who was mooing after Tommy at the Metal Box till I stopped her gallop.

'Sometimes I used to wonder if I'd missed out, being with him since school. I'm not sorry now, when it turns out we had so little time anyway. Don't think I didn't have chances. I'm not a silly little kid. Alex may say it was a joke, I expect he will, but I know what's what. He was serious.'

'What are you talking about, on the way back from the pub? Or in the caravan? Christ, is that why you were in such a hurry to strip the bed and put your sheets away? Let me go have a look at 'em.' I really would of too, but she kind of got me in a bear hug.

'What do you take me for? You don't seriously think I would have said yes, do you, even if he weren't my brother-in-law? You're my sister, Ange – don't you think I'm a little bit better than that?'

I pushed her away. She must have banged her bum on the table but I didn't care.

'I'm not saying he was aggressive. He might find a way to put a different slant on it, and if you want to believe him that's your lookout. All I'll say again is he didn't get anything, but I knew exactly what he was after.'

I was already heading out the door. I'd had half a thought of a cosy drink with my sister on the way back, but went in the Tinners on my own, something I'd never normally dare do. I had to wait until Ron behind the bar looked away after serving me because I wasn't sure I'd be able to pick up my wine without spilling it. I managed it two-handed, stumbled outside to the beer garden and got it down me.

I was wondering whether to go back inside for a second one when she pulled up on the road beside the pub. Had to drop the keys to the van off there. I'd forgotten that.

'Come on Ange don't be silly. I know I was right so I can't say I'm sorry. Let me drive you back down – let's not upset the kids.'

I suppose I knew she was right as well. 'I think they're made different from us, men. It's a bit of a shock. Can you give me a chance to think about it?'

She grabbed my hand. 'Sorry if I've upset you. I know it's none of your fault – we all know what Alex is like. If you can live with it, that's up to you. I just had to get it off my chest. I thought you had to know.'

Why is it only bad stuff people think you *have* to know, never in such a rush to bring you any good news? Whatever everyone thought about Alex he was still my husband, so she lost me again right there. My mood was changing every few seconds. I wasn't joking when I said I was in shock. I nearly said something about Tommy and his rocks, but I was always glad afterwards I didn't.

I said nothing to Alex either, not at the time. We'd made love the night before, and I hadn't noticed anything different with him. Lucy left as planned, pretending to be in a great rush after she drove us down in her little Beetle, although Alex wasn't there – probably already down the club. I didn't think that was fair on our kids, because the girls at least would have liked a proper goodbye hug from their aunt. I didn't say anything though. Let her go. We made love that night as well, and had a good second week. Whatever else might have gone on, our sex life was about the last thing to break down in our marriage.

That was the end of joint family holidays. For years Lucy and me were not close. I made a point of asking Karen if he'd ever tried anything on with her. I knew they'd seen a fair bit of each other when they were both chasing all over the country after United, and it wasn't as if she was always choosy. She laughed and said they were nothing more than mates – too busy fighting the opposition fans to think about fucking each other was the way she put it. I didn't need to ask Jan. She'd never had much time for Alex right back to the Olly Street days and always made that very clear. If I'd gone to her about Lucy, she would only have said I told you so, and I didn't need that. I wonder if Lucy put the poison in anyway. Maybe I was paranoid, but Jan seemed to choose to spend more of the times they were in England with her – especially later when Lucy moved to Chelmsford, which didn't exactly help us make things up.

There was no way I was going to confide in Mum. That would most likely have only got her off about Dad and Lil and all his other supposed women again. I say 'supposed', but that may be just me sticking up for him again. I *suppose* there wasn't any doubt about it. Don't think I was blind to all the rumours about Alex either, especially around Washtown when he was a little bit of a local hero for a while. Did you ever see that sex film with Tom Cruise? That's what I was like – *Eyes Wide Shut.*

Then I had the kids, where I was determined to do a better job than Mum. We would have our tea together at half past five, me saving some of mine for later in case Alex came home. He was never back before seven, which was fair enough travelling from London. One or two nights a week it would be much later – he would just bolt down whatever I'd made him after shoving it in the microwave.

I couldn't go to bed or even get undressed properly since however late

– and it might be well after midnight if he overslept and went on to Rugby, or Birmingham at least once – he always expected me to pick him up from the station, just as I dropped him off every morning. He did most of his socialising in London, just as I did most of my drinking at home. I don't know how he could get up, togged into his suit and back again to the office after only a couple of hours' sleep some nights, but he always did. It didn't improve his temper, mind. I think it was around then he hit me for the first time – I mean seriously hit me.

I would think he had to behave himself in London as he got to be more important in his job, not with women necessarily but avoiding fights in the street. There was still the odd time he came home with blood on his clothes, always making a big thing of saying it wasn't his. If I complained about the stains not coming out, he'd tell me to do a better job of washing the shirts and be grateful it wasn't lipstick on them.

I'd been a fool when we first got married to put the iron on every morning he was going to the office and help him put on his shirt, crisp and still warm from it. You can get into a routine for everything. In some ways, it was worse when now he expected that only on certain mornings. I'd never know which, and he would get nasty if I didn't give in and do it.

It wasn't that I was scared of him, like a lot of men were. I wouldn't have stood for one of them blokes who the only person they can beat up is their wife, so they do. There were times I hit him. I don't deny it. In the early days it was more play-fighting than anything, or maybe the signs were always there and the force involved just grew naturally. Alex wasn't a bully like that – the reason he took a few hidings was that he would go after men much bigger than him if he thought he had cause. Mainly he liked to get his own way. If his charm didn't work he got frustrated and might lash out. He would always apologise, always come back to it being me that forced him into the commute that was killing him. The station was crowded every day for the trains to London and I didn't think it could be killing everybody, but there you are.

I did feel a little bit guilty, because I was now drinking every morning without letting on about it. I got nervous about driving him to the station first thing. The traffic around it was unbelievable and he had to be dropped off right at the entrance. It was all I could do not to make a slug of whisky in my wake-up coffee a regular thing (I'd tried vodka but found that mix spoiled both drinks). Funnily enough, the ironing helped in that, so it was on the mornings I was feeling most vulnerable he'd sometimes get the surprise of me putting his arms in the sleeves of his shirt. I didn't have to be careful about him smelling anything on my breath in a goodbye kiss. They'd long gone by the board.

I thought about going to see a doctor but that frightened me as well – not only going but what they might say. I was more terrified of being put on pills than anything, anything except not being able to get off them. I didn't think drink would kill you, but I knew very well tablets could.

I hope I wasn't a bully myself either, even if the kids probably saw as much of my temper as Alex did. I honestly wasn't scared of him, but generally I gave in to his demands. Knowing these were sometimes just to be awkward didn't help, because once he got an idea into his head he would keep on and on about it. The kids could get round me that way too. I was a bit of a soft touch really.

I don't know if it was mixing with a different crowd in London or just that we'd been together so long now he wanted a bit of variety. I might not have minded *that* much if I did find lipstick on his collar. When everyone started using mobile phones, he called me one night and said he wanted me to meet him at the station with no knickers on. I was used to him trying to grope me on the way home when he was drunk, and when he was late he was always drunk. Unless he wanted his dinner more, once we got in it would sometimes end in sex.

I thought he was joking – turned out he wasn't. He got real sulky when I refused to go commando and kept turning up as usual. I mean it was the middle of winter. I don't know whether he'd somehow planted a seed in my own mind to try it, but eventually one night I did. You would laugh at what a botch I made of it – he wouldn't have been able to tell unless he got frisky because I was still wearing trousers. As it happened, that was one of the nights when he was more drunk than usual, the sort when he would often miss our stop the first time by it, and he let me drive, falling back to sleep on the short ride home.

I didn't start doing it every night after that or anything – I was never a sex maniac. Maybe he'd already nearly given up on the idea, except next time he mentioned it, I made the mistake of saying he'd had his chance and blown it. He said trousers were cheating anyway, then he kept coming at it stronger. I was perhaps getting a bit of a kick out of it all myself now. In for a penny in for a pound, one night I put on a super-short leather skirt I hadn't worn in years – I could hardly get into it tell you the truth, I'd looked it out but hadn't tried it on – and a smart full-length coat to protect myself from any other eyes in getting out of the car or while I was smoking, waiting for him to appear.

As usual he was too drunk to drive, but I didn't think I could have concentrated on it so I let him. I'd had an extra drink myself to tell you the truth. If he was surprised at seeing me in the overcoat – I had an old parka for the station run – he didn't say anything. He soon noticed when I undid it. He ran a hand up my leg, me telling him to keep his eyes on the road and not wanting him to take the hand away. We lived a bit outside town, so when he pulled off the road into a turning down to a farm we weren't likely to be disturbed.

After all that fuss, it was a let-down. It was years since we'd done it in a car, and then usually in the back seat. He couldn't wait for that but got me on his lap in the front passenger one. Then he couldn't get properly hard. I had to finish him off with my mouth once we got home – I didn't complain cos I could tell he felt ashamed of himself.

Although the leather skirt never came out of the wardrobe again, all in all I don't think he had much to complain about from me on that front. Could I have showed a bit more interest in his job? What did I know about computers? I knew he switched companies from time to time, always moving upwards, which he may have regretted bragging about because I made sure then I got a rise in my housekeeping money. Karen was totally indignant when I mentioned once that was how it was. Not that she didn't think I deserved it. She meant we should have a joint bank account, so I could take whatever I needed whenever. She was always a bit of a feminist, Kar. I didn't ask if she practised what she preached because I thought she was never with any man long enough to get round to having a joint account. I expect she might have been glad of regular housekeeping money at times, though she was careful only to mix with us when she was in funds.

Alex started travelling more, or further anyway, abroad rather than in England. I would always be packing a suitcase for him. At least I could iron his shirts in batches. If he had someone to put fresh ones still warm on his back mornings when he was away, good luck to him and more fool her.

Then one night he told me he had a chance to work in the Gulf.

'It won't be forever, Ange. I got in touch with Ray for the scoop on working abroad. A mate of his went to Saudi, said you go out there and the minute you touch down, you have to imagine you got a bucket in each hand. One will start filling up with shit, and the other with money. Whenever one of the buckets is full, whichever one it is, that's the time to come home.'

It looked as if he'd already made up his mind, after talking to our brother -in-law. He obviously didn't feel I might have anything worth him hearing.

15

Janet

From: Janet Roden <janmro@hotmail.co.uk>
To: Ange; Karen; Lucy
Subject: MERRY CHRISTMAS AND HAPPY NEW YEAR

Dear All,
Well I never thought I'd be sending out one of these Christmas messages. Round robins I think they call them. Don't know why but it sounds seasonal. It's a big blow we're not coming home this year, but Ray's boss wants him to be here, and since it's his first in the new job Ray wants to show willing (for once).

I know I've always thought when I get a message like this addressed to lots of people it's mainly so they can brag about all their holidays during the year or their perfect lifestyle and family. I won't go that far. Me and Ray have had our ups and downs for sure (don't get me started on Hong Kong!), but we're both trying to treat Puerto Rico as a new start. We haven't got a swimming pool of our own like Ray's boss has, but there's several at the club where we might be going on Christmas Day for our dinner – no cooking, yippee.

Denis seems to be enjoying himself at school, too

146

much so if anything. The company pays for them both to go to a private one. Kim took a bit longer to settle in. She was making herself sick with worry the first few days but is much better now, already correcting her brother's Spanish – as if he could give a damn.

The other thing I always think about these multiple emails is that they're just a lazy way to avoid writing to individuals separately. On that my conscience is clear. I've sent you all emails, personal ones not just describing the delights of San Juan, without much success and none in some cases. You know who you are – naming and shaming will follow next Christmas if things don't improve.

Anyway this message isn't sent to all my vast circle of friends and acquaintances, only my three dear sisters (I can see you, Karen, putting your fingers down your throat!). No point in writing to Billy – it's hard enough to get a word out of him when you're sitting across the same table. Is he still with that Sally-Anne, and has she left school yet if that's not too bitchy a question? I suppose he might be a bigger catch with his own house, even if he'll always be a little (s)prat to us.

I've sent Mum a separate Christmas card – this is it for you I'm afraid, girls – but I don't expect to hear back from her. I'm guessing Les may have gone the way of many others by now. I get the impression the death of our father knocked some of the go out of her. I'll be surprised if she marries anyone again now. Is that cough of hers any better? Luce, you're the only one who can really have a word with her about it while all the rest of us are still smoking – unless Ange or Karen surprise me WHEN they write back? Maybe we should all make a New Year resolution. I'm worried over the example to Denis all the more when I hear schoolkids nowadays might smoke something a bit stronger than Benson & Hedges. Fair cop, I can hear you all laughing from here – yes it's true, the old hippie has changed her tune.

I'm not working, unless you count a bit of volunteering at a charity library – that was very welcome since I haven't found a proper public one and for once in my life I have time to read.

Not as much as you might think though. I spend a lot of time ferrying the kids around, not to mention Ray to work. I'm sorry now I used to take the P out of Ange doing that for Alex. I've turned out just as soft or just as generous, whichever way you want to look at it.

Must close for now as I'm on parade in a few minutes, heading off to the airport to meet Agnes – you know, Ray's mum. I did say our life wasn't perfect! Only joking, the kids are really looking forward to it, funnily enough Denis almost more than Kimberley, whose real nan she is. It will be strange not to be in England for the holidays, even when we haven't necessarily spent Christmas Day together – and counting the ones we did which were a disaster – we've always managed to get together at some point and have a good giggle.

I hope we'll get home in the summer and next Christmas as well. If Ray can't make it, I may bring the kids. Jason has kicked up a bit about not seeing Den this year (without wanting to make any effort when we are home, natch). Apart from that, why don't you all think about visiting us? It's a bit closer than Hong Kong, and trust me at times you wouldn't have wanted to be around us there anyway. Come out to San Juan and we can have a great time. It may not be Munsley or Cornwall, but it does have the worldwide headquarters of Bacardi AND they do free guided tours. Right up your street, Ange.

I miss you all. PLEASE write and let me have all your latest news and family gossip but remember not to press 'reply all' if you're going to slag off one of the others (as if us Roper girls would ever do that, ha ha). Look forward to hearing from you each and every one, no excuses. Merry Christmas and Happy New Year.

Love, Jan xx

From: Janet Roden <janmro@hotmail.co.uk>
To: Lucy <tommysluce@hotmail.co.uk>
Subject: HAPPY NEW YEAR

Dear Luce,

Many thanks for your Christmas card which arrived through the normal post – snail mail I heard someone call that the other day – and better still your long email. You won't be surprised to hear you're the first one to answer mine. I did get a card from Ange, nothing yet from Kar and I'm not holding my breath.

Don't worry, you obviously weren't the one I was talking about when I said some of my sisters don't keep in touch regularly. I only wish I could have been there in person for you in the terrible time you've had since the death of Tommy.

As I said before, it was a real shame that Alex went over the top during your holiday in Cornwall. I know you'd been looking forward to it (as far as you could look forward to anything at that time). He can be a real dickhead, we all know that. It was totally inappropriate behaviour at any time and especially that time, but how often have we seen him do stupid things?

Don't think I'm sticking up for him – I'm just thinking of my sisters if I say you've got to try to put it behind you. It has been a while now. Knowing him, I bet he hardly remembers it. I haven't heard anything about Ange giving him a hard time for it, but I'm worried that you're letting it get you down too much. Brothers-in-law come and go (example, do you ever see Jason nowadays?) so don't let him get inside your head. We don't have so many sisters that we can afford to be on the outs with each other too long. Ange may have seemed a bit unsympathetic, but she was probably hurting too. And if you think back to Tommy – he was definitely one of a kind, no doubt about that – wouldn't you have stuck up for him against the whole world, whatever he'd done and whether he was right or wrong?

I'm sorry Lou isn't her old bubbly self and that it may be dragging her down at school. It's natural she'll still be grieving for her dad (not that you're not, I know). It wasn't the same thing for Denis when I left Jason, nothing like, but I know for a fact he suffered from it. I understand your concern. I tend to worry more about Kimberley than him. Maybe we think about Mum and Grandma Alice and forget that if they were weak (I'm trying to put it kindly), we've been strong enough to make our own life, all of us in our own ways.

I'm glad the endowment policy came through for you, to take the financial pressure off a bit. I think you're right to go back to Shawl's though. You must know enough about that business to set up on your own if you ever wanted! When I get back to England maybe we should open our own shop, or how about a pub? We could call it the Ropers Return. It's things like *Corrie* I miss out here. It drives Ray mad we can't get Premier League, only American sports channels. I'm sure you can get away when you like, so why not come out here for a holiday? I get it that things must be too raw for Munsley. I guess that's why Cornwall seemed such a good idea till Alex put his size tens in it.

Seriously Luce, it doesn't have to be the summer holidays, in fact the weather's better if anything here in the first half of the year (and no risk of hurricanes!). Why not bring Lou over when she's off school for Easter – you know Kim and her love each other, and that may give her confidence a bit of a boost as well?

Don't think I'm overlooking your mention of this Greg Brewington either, you sly dog, just slipping it in. I can't wait to hear all about him over a cuppa, or better yet a Bacardi Breezer. I've always fancied being an agony aunt even if I can't claim any better record with men than Ange or Kar. It may do you good to think of him from a bit of a distance too. As you say, it's early days yet. For what it's worth, my opinion about 'moving on' is the time for that – whatever it means, it doesn't necessarily mean leaving Tommy behind – is whenever you think the time for it is right.

I've got myself excited now about the idea of you and Lou (and a dog named Boo? Remember that one?) coming over here, so please do think hard about it and let me know. It will only cost you the airfare, and whether in the Easter or summer holidays, both would be fine.

Love, Jan xx

PS: Remind our sisters I still exist when you next speak to them.

From: Janet Roden <janmro@hotmail.co.uk>
To: Ange <angela.grace.reed@hotmail.co.uk>
Subject: Hello

Dear Ange,

Glad to see you venturing at last into using emails. It's great that Alex's Arab friends are paying him enough that he can stay in touch by phone whenever he wants to. We're not at that pay grade here so this is definitely the best way for us until we can sit down again together, hopefully later this summer.

We can argue by email too, you'll see. I really don't know why you should be annoyed about Lucy and Louise coming to visit us. I did say you would ALL be welcome – even including Alex at a push. Honestly Ange, you'd complain if you was hung with a new rope. If he's earning that much money that they call him Golden Alex when he comes home, then why doesn't he bring you all out here? Better still, from my point of view, SEND you all out here while he's busy in the desert.

And I'm NOT taking her side against you at all – there's no sides to take. She doesn't blame you for whatever nonsense your husband got up to in Cornwall, and by the way, that's almost getting to be ancient history. Would it hurt to call on her when you next take the kids to see their grandparents (and ours – you don't say how they're getting on)? I feel jealous of you able to meet up whenever you like. I wish I'd taken more advantage of it when I could.

You did make me laugh about the swimming pools when you went out to visit Alex that one time, finding something to moan about on what was supposed to be a romantic break. I think we're getting too old for romance, sis. Ray took me to St Croix on one of his trips and I just found the people so RUDE. Everyone says the Gulf is no good for women. I'm not sticking

151

up for Alex, but it may not be all that fantastic for him out there either despite the money. Beer brewed in the bath sounds like that horrible stuff Grandad Sess used to make, remember? Does anyone ever hear of him? Lucy didn't have any news, but I suppose Mum should?

So Les is officially dumped and she's thinking about going back to London then Mum, is she? I wonder if she'll ever really settle down again. Ray's got his faults, plenty of them believe me, but I'm not sure I could go through all that again. Better the arsehole you know…well, you would know that with Alex.

I know the doctors tell everyone now to lay off the fags, there's no argument against it EXCEPT for people like Mum – if smoking helps her relax and keep off the pills, then I'd have to say puff on. And what about you, Ange? This is the bit where I really need to be able to look you in the eye. You can't hide anything from me then. You don't say anything about that side of things.

I never expected Billy would turn to the drink – thought he was too tight for one thing. Men do go a bit mad when they haven't got a woman to keep them on track, and sometimes when they do. I can understand Sally-Anne – not that I ever really liked her much, it must be ok to say that now – wanting to have kids, her being what was it ten years younger than him. If he wanted to hang on to her so much, why didn't he just agree to it? He could have seen from the other men in our family it wouldn't have meant much extra effort for him, only the fun bits. I hope you'll be able to keep him coming round yours for his tea – company for you and also he won't be going out on an empty stomach. You don't suppose he'll move down to London if Mum does? He was always closer to Karen too.

I could hardly believe it when you wrote that Adam is having a twenty-first birthday party later this year. Let me know as soon as you've fixed the exact date and we'll do our very best to be there. I think it's great that he stands up for himself to Alex, stands up for you too. It might cause extra tension in the house, but why should that man get his own way all his life? And you say Jan is set on uni next year. Let her know her favourite aunt is cheering her on from afar – wish I'd done it myself. If Suzie's the quiet one, watch out! Keep a hawk eye on her these next few years. It may have worked out for us – more or less – but I know I made mistakes, big ones sometimes, and I want to think I'll be there to help our Kim avoid them. I'm sure you feel the same about your girls – and Adam, even if he can look after himself.

Conversations to have over a livener sometime, or if you would prefer a coffee I think I'd be glad of that too. Anyway, you look after yourself until we meet again, try and keep all your ducks in a row, whatever that means. Remember the ones Grandma Alice used to have on her bedroom wall? Wonder what happened to them. Please do write again. Don't worry about, as you put it, having nothing interesting to say. Maybe our lives aren't interesting anymore, neither of us. Just write whatever comes into your head, like you were talking to me face to face as I hope we will be before too long.

See you soon,

Your ever-loving twin, Jan xx

From: Janet Roden <janmro@hotmail.co.uk>
To: Kar <UNITED.tillidiekar@hotmail.co.uk>
Subject: Wow!

Dear Kar,
I was just about to send our Christmas newsletter. Who knew it would become a habit? This year we're hoping to get away for a few days around New Year, slumming it in St Lucia, but I wish we were in England now I've heard your news. It's not true I would rather have waited till you had something interesting to bring to the table, as you put it, than hear from you more often, but I can't deny you've come up with something REALLY exciting this time.

I never knew about the register for people who have

children adopted to put their names on so they can make contact when they grow up. You say it's only been something done in the last few years. I think it's a great idea and that they should have made a bit more publicity about it, including for people like me without the direct experience, but if I'd heard of it I would definitely have wanted to make sure you knew. Obviously you were well in touch with developments anyway. I should have known you would be.

Without rehashing old spuds, I hope you didn't think we were cold when you went through the adoption in the first place. I know Lucy especially tried to reach out, but you were very definite that you didn't want us involved. I was only trying to respect that. We all have our secrets – not ideal between sisters maybe, but there it is, and I did understand (perhaps more than the others). You were one of us Roper girls even if the rumours about Eric not being your biological father were true and not a figment of Mum's imagination. Everything was all about him, to love him or hate him, for so long with her, never thinking of the damage it might have caused any of us, so I wouldn't necessarily take it as gospel. Remember, for all his faults, he never denied you. I admit I don't think of his and Lil's Eamon as any relation at all, and he is our half-brother when you think of it, so I reckon it's more about who you're brought up with than any blood thing.

Sorry I'm wittering on. I'm not just trying to match your impressive word count honest, double honest, triple honest, or avoid giving you the advice you asked for. When you say you always felt a bit of an outsider, are you sure you're not just saying you felt unhappy? You were always very funny about Colditz as you called it, but I knew that couldn't be the whole story. I guess we all had our different times of trouble. Don't forget I was left alone in Washtown when you all went to Northampton that first time. Let's not make it a competition in who had the worst childhood like that Monty Python sketch. I know you used to love them when none of the rest of us did (and speaking for myself still don't), so I'll grant you were an outsider in that.

Since you make no mention of him, never have to my knowledge, I assume there's no question of involving the birth father of Gary – are you pleased his adoptive parents chose to keep the name you gave him? Gary Michael Pemberton, sounds distinguished already. Go ahead with giving him my contact details – only sorry I won't be able to meet him for a little while yet.

That brings me to your toughest question. Backing up a bit, I think you should be proud he took the trouble to sign up on the adoptee side of that register, so the social services people could give you the option of arranging a meeting. I don't believe for one minute you'd forgotten even putting yourself on it. I bet you were secretly counting the days until his eighteenth birthday – we don't know the exact date, his aunts, but never mind!

I think you've done the hardest bit now. You were taking a risk as he might never have tried to make contact at all. Wouldn't that have been far worse than him doing it? I'm flattered you thought of me to be the initial point of contact with him. Are you expecting him to have two heads or something? If you want to get a fix on him before meeting up, I'd suggest Lucy. Nothing against Ange, and I know she's the oldest – Lord, will she ever let any of us forget it? – but I can imagine her terrified at the responsibility. I wouldn't consider Mum. Lucy would be good for it and love to be involved. I sometimes think she's got the strongest sense of family out of us all. I get the impression she feels a bit isolated since she moved to Chelmsford with Greg, however much I tell her she's only just down the road from you all compared to me.

I'm sure Gary will turn out to be a good lad, and if he's not too much like a Roper that may not be such a bad thing. He's obviously bright like you if you say he's up for university. Has he got your gift for languages? There must be a bit of trepidation, mixed feelings, whatever you want to call it, but I've never known you back off a challenge yet.

I'm so glad you've got this opportunity, Kar. Worst case, you're still better off than you were because you know he reached adulthood safe, which you can never guarantee, AND you know he grew up wanting to see you. On the counselling beforehand, I know what you mean about not wanting anyone 'poking around inside your head'. I'd feel the same way, but I would seriously consider it. I do think us Ropers tend to keep things bottled up too much sometimes. So WHEN you meet young Gary, make sure you take photos and let me know right away how it goes.

As I said at the start, you'll be getting my robin redbreast message with all the others in a few days now. I'm including Billy this year. Ange says he spends a lot of time on his computer, not just at porn or playing the stupid video games – he'd have a good mate there in Denis (the games anyway, or I hope it's only the games) – but something about astronomy, or is it cosmology? Studying the universe sounds kind of grand. She says he's got a telescope set up in his bedroom. Maybe we should all be pleased if he's developing a new interest. It just sounded a bit weird to me – what do you say?

All the talk of your Gary somehow made me think of Billy as a lost little boy in our family, even if he is over thirty now. You were like a second mum to him, though I also hear he's been making up for lost time hanging out with our first and only one, so if she does move to London that might hit him hard. Give him my special love for Christmas, and let me know he's all right if you can.

Good luck one more time with Gary. May the reunion be everything you hope for. Don't let the butterflies put you off – I'm sure he's more scared of meeting you than you are of him!

Your ever-loving sister, Jan

16

Karen

From: Karen Roper <UNITED.tillidiekar@hotmail.co.uk>
To: Janet Roden <janmro@hotmail.co.uk>
Subject: Ouch!

Dear Jan,

Funny how we still begin emails just the same semi-formal way we always used to with handwritten letters. Why is that? Not saying you're not dear to me and all that – take this as a little Valentine card if you like since I'm writing on that day. I won't be sending one out to anyone else, believe me, not even a cod one to my firstborn. I expect you're keen to hear how my meeting with Gary went. All in good time. I haven't discussed it with the others yet except to laugh it off as a total disaster.

I did appreciate the concern in your emails. No doubt Ange told you how I was caning it when I was up there over Christmas, the same as I was down here in London, on my Twixtmas visit to see Nan and Grandad in Washtown and especially on my day trip to Chelmsford. Between you and me, this Greg is a merchant banker by profession and rhyming slang both. I would have preferred a natter round their kitchen table to the lunch at Chelmsford's finest French joint. Lou was about as bored as I was there, but Lucy says she's doing well at school again, which for her is the main thing. I think she has an exaggerated respect for schoolwork, university and all that bullshit. I know I'm unfair to her – I should give her more credit for the way she's built herself a second home. Built it from the same prototype, mind. Greg must be ten years older than her, but he's just as much under that dainty thumb of steel as poor, dumb Tommy ever was.

Enough of the malicious gossip. You asked me to run the rule over our little bruvver, in whose company I spent many wasted hours. I may have unburdened myself of certain things to him, but whether then or at our most soberest (education is important but vodka is importanter) I never had to worry that he would show an unseemly – indeed any – interest in my life.

His interest in the cosmos, on the other hand, does appear to be genuine. I hope it helps him keep a sense of perspective rather than the feeling it inspired in me – what's the point of it all? We're more insignificant little specks of shit than we ever thought we were, might as well just wipe ourselves off and out. He had to bore me to tears about it to prove he doesn't have the telescope set up to spy on the school playground you can see from his bedroom window. I'd rather he set it up in the loft to look out the skylight, but on the plus side it is a secondary school not a primary.

I took your advice about a bit of counselling, post rather than pre reunion, as might have been more desirable. I don't need to be told by anyone it's unhealthy thinking that me and Billy will somehow be stuck in Colditz all our lives. I've read Primo Levi (the jeans magnate, as Lucy would probably think him), though of course I'm not comparing our Colditz in any way with the real prison, much less the industrial horrors of the concentration camps.

I'm talking about Billy more than myself now. I mean fine to go out with schoolkids when you're one yourself, fine to go out with nubile teenagers when you're in your early twenties, fine to go out with sexy young widows when you're a tosser pushing fifty in Chelmsford, but not so good if you get fixated at a certain point and stick there (der, Karen, that's what being fixated is).

I'm not saying our Billy is a wrong'un, nothing like. That suspended sentence back in the day did its job of putting a scare in him; I believe it when he says it was him that had to hold Sally-Anne off till she turned sixteen – one second after midnight, apparently. We all know he's not into the niceties of civilised social intercourse – with women it's only the sexual kind he cares for, doesn't have any grasp of the world of adult relationships. If it *is* only sex you're after, I suppose logically the younger and more physically attractive the better, the porn fantasy men seem to live with, another substitute for the real thing. (He doesn't bother to hide his search history on the computer. I checked that out as well – nothing too deviant unless you count a bit of a thing for 'Asian Babes'.)

He assures me he's still holding it together at work, still as tight as ever but on decent money, better than many of his pub mates anyway. Do you remember that dive the Criterion? Used to be where the real scrubbers – I mean proper prostitutes – hung out. That's his local now. Let's put it this way, the type of girls he'll meet there make Sally-Anne seem more like Princess Anne.

Not that my own milieu back in London is any more salubrious. I haven't hit the big four oh like you have, sis, but I'm a lot closer to it than I am thirty. At the language school – my only current source of regular income – the students are mainly around twenty, the teachers mainly under thirty, so come to think of it – and I don't *like* to think of it – maybe I'm not so far off a female Billy myself.

I certainly get no income, regular or otherwise, from my attempts at fiction. That's an occupational hazard of the arty-farty set I move in, émigrés from Eastern Europe and Latin America scratching a living in London now Paris is not as cheap as it was for the likes of Hemingway and Joyce, with bigger ambitions beyond teaching others their own language. My writing may not be very good, but it's one of my saner and more harmless pursuits.

And now I find the best way I can talk to you about the meeting with my long-lost son is by sharing a short story about it. If it's ever published, then we'll know it worked as such. At a private level, you, Jan, were the ideal reader I had in mind. It is a tale, I insist, but you can take it that all the worst bits are true.

Let me know what you think, your loving sister Karen (no need to look for a nom de plume as a published writer any time soon)

FAMILY REUNION

Mary did not sleep at all well before the big day. Maybe her mistake was going to bed early, without having taken so much as a single drink. She tried to tell herself when she finally gave up and got up, before six on the Saturday morning, it was excitement she felt, butterflies it was only a matter of getting to fly in formation, or at worst the stomach-cramping pains of period, not just plain old fear.

She called to mind the advice Isabel Allende found helpful: the others are more afraid than you are. They – or he in this case – must be really bricking it then. Neither of Mary's grandads were benevolent and wise old fool counsellors like Isabel's, so she might do better with one of her dad's sayings: a Croker never backs down.

While she would give private classes at weekends, this one was free. Having already devoted more time to cleaning and tidying her flat over the last two days than in the previous three months, she was determined not to go over it again. That would be bordering on OCD. She had made an effort, which she did not begrudge. She was not, however, going to be conned into cooking. There were peanuts and crisps in the cupboard, a bottle of Stoli in the freezer and one of Diet Coke in the fridge if anyone wanted a mixer.

Her brother arrived around eleven, choosing to crack open a can of wife-beater from the sixteen he'd lugged in rather than accept a coffee. She was tempted to join him, yet more determined to greet Geoffrey alcohol-free. She briefly considered a shot of vodka, before deciding the principle was the important thing; he might not realise, but she would know. Would they greet closely enough for him to get a whiff of her breath?

*

'I still don't know why we couldn't take him to the OB. No need to pretend to be better than we are.'

'Nobody's pretending anything,' Mary snapped. 'We may end up there later if you can't bear to go twenty-four hours without a visit. I just wanted to have a bit of time first, somewhere we won't be pestered every five minutes by your mates wanting us to go outside for a smoke or play pool or whatever.'

'Your mates an all, Mare. If I'd of known, I wouldn't have said I'd come. They were all dying to. Still don't get why you picked me.'

'I wish I hadn't. Stop whingeing for fuck's sake. I wanted a chance to have a proper conversation, thought I could trust you not to cut in like they would, Jane especially. Didn't realise you'd wake up chattier than any of our sisters. You haven't taken something already this morning, Sammy, have you?'

'I wish.'

For all they had been waiting twenty minutes for a Southern Rail train to come in, Geoffrey took them by surprise.

'Mary? Mary Croker?' That was one question answered then – how he would address her. She hadn't expected to be approached by two young men, or rather not by the black and white pair that had alighted joshing and jostling each other a couple of carriages down the platform.

'That's right. Are you Geoffrey?'

'That's where the smart money would go in a two-horse race, Ms Croker.' The other youth broke the moment of silence, the holding back from an embrace, a handshake, a touch of any kind, then offered his own right hand. 'I'm Joe's roomie, Charlie.'

'Joe's?'

'Yeah, sorry, that's just a thing we have. Started off as Geo then somehow got corrupted, like we all do in the end. This is Geoffrey Wayne Prendergast all right, even if he is a bit shy of introducing himself properly. And you, sir, do I detect a family resemblance?'

'Don't stand there gawping like a wide-mouthed frog – give the boy your hand. Samuel William Croker, my brother.'

'Sammy,' her brother said.

Everyone else getting off the train had dispersed by the time they left the platform, Charlie trying to engage Sammy in conversation, leaving the other two trailing behind them; awkwardly side by side, not speaking but sneaking glances at each other as if they were both teenagers.

'Hope you haven't had to come too far?' Mary managed at last.

'Not too far – a doddle down the Northern line.' He almost talked over her in his haste to answer.

'You dared venture south of the river then?' She risked a sideways smile at him.

He smiled back at her. 'Only with Charlie as my bodyguard.'

'You ought to be ashamed of yourself letting our guests buy the first round, Sammy, and them not working yet.'

'That's no bother at all, Ms Croker, or Mary if I may. Your brother had to stop to tie his shoelace up when we got to the front door.' He clapped a bemused Sammy on the back. 'He said a pint of cider for you – hope that was right. Joe, I got us two pints of the dark stuff. Geoffrey likes that, Sammy. Guinness,' he added after a moment.

The pool table was unoccupied until Charlie offered to take on Sammy. 'I'll put your name up, Joe. You on for it, Mary?'

'You bet. Ladies first – I'll take on the winner of you two.'

Left at the table together, Mary thought it behoved her to try to take some control of the situation. 'Felt the need to bring some moral support with you then?'

'Charlie might laugh at being called moral anything, but I suppose so, fair enough. Truth is I was nervous. Reading up on this sort of thing will do that to you. They say these first meetings can end up anywhere between the mother and son fighting and never speaking again to them having sex with each other.'

'Well that's obviously not on the agenda, sonny boy – the sex I mean. We'll have to wait and see about the fighting if you should beat me at pool.'

'And that's it, a one-bedroom rented place in an only moderately shitty part of South London, teaching English to foreigners and Spanish to anyone who needs it,' Mary concluded the one-minute tour of her flat. She and Geoffrey had gone there when the pub closed for the afternoon, as Charlie and Sammy set off for the snooker hall.

'It's a nice place, and you certainly seem to have all the essentials in.' He gave a half-gallon grin at the melting Stoli bottle on the coffee table between them. He was taking his with Coke, Mary too, but with markedly more vodka than he'd allowed her to pour him before diluting it.

'I had so many things I wanted to ask you I nearly brought a tape recorder or a notepad, but I thought that might seem a bit creepy.'

'Good call. Especially the tape recorder, but I can see why you're knocking on the door of uni if you're that conscientious a student. I had plenty of questions myself. Let's start with an easy one. What do you plan to study?'

'Not so easy, as it happens. For a long time I thought it would be architecture. I'm on the right track for that with maths and physics A levels – touch wood, not got them yet. It's normally a five-year course, but Dad said he would support me through that. I don't know if that still holds since he left Mum, or if it holds that I want to go the same way he did.'

It wasn't so much that he spoke of Mum and Dad, it was how naturally he did so. It came home to Mary that whatever romantic place she thought she might occupy in Geoffrey's affections (obviously not romantic in any sexual sense, the filthy little perv) it certainly wasn't as a mum. She tried to keep it light.

'So you've got two abandoned mothers then, but I'm sure not all architects leave their wives if that's what you're worried about.'

'What? Oh, going the same way, no, I didn't mean that. I meant him being an architect. And actually Mum threw him out – she kept the house and everything.'

'Good for her, but I'm sorry you had to go through all that. My own parents divorced.' Despite her pause, he didn't give her the opening to tell war stories of Ernie and Ruby. 'How is she now? Doing OK?'

'I'd rather not talk about her if you don't mind. I knew your parents had split – thanks for the letter you left me with that little bit about your family circumstances and why you couldn't keep me.'

'They gave you that then. I'm glad. It was so long ago I've forgotten what I wrote.'

He was plainly not going to remind her. 'I knew I was adopted from as soon as I knew anything. They let me read it when I was twelve. I'm grateful they did it like that.'

'And is your mum…'

'I'm sorry, Mary, I'd rather not talk about Mum. It may sound funny to you, but I already feel bad for her about being here at all. She didn't try to stop me, but I know it hurt her. She was crying when I set out.'

Didn't try to stop you indeed, Mary thought. *You've got a lot to learn about women yet.* 'That's OK, Geoff…Is that what you prefer by the way, or Geoffrey, or even Joe as your…as Charlie calls you. I want to call you what you like.'

'Stick with Joe please. I kind of like that – a name I was actually involved in choosing for myself. I'm having a bit of the same issue with you as well to tell you the truth, Mary…Mother…whatever.'

They talked for two hours, freely enough (Mary thought the vodka was helping), though they both put up off-limits signs at certain points. While Mary was happy enough to talk about her family – he said he would like to 'do the rounds' of her sisters – she gave him no satisfaction about his own biological father.

'That's a complicated one,' she told him gently. 'I suppose if your stepdad – I mean your adopted dad' – she couldn't quite bring herself to say just 'your dad'; he sounded a bastard anyway – 'let you all down, you maybe want to know more about him now – your blood father I mean. I can't talk about that. Give me a little time if you can.' She feared he would ask how much longer than twenty years she could want.

'There's no need to cry. I know it's early days yet and I don't want to rush things. Can I leave you a book that helped me to understand a lot?' He rummaged in the rucksack she'd been wondering about all day and put a paperback on the table between them.

Wiping her eyes, she patted the book as if it were his hand. 'God I'm sorry. I'm never like this. You can ask Sammy – I bet he's never seen me howling. Maybe it's time to rejoin the gentlemen. We might introduce you to the delights of the Holly Bush.'

It must have been worse than she thought, bad enough as that was, if Sammy had come round on a Sunday morning to check she was still alive. Barefoot in just a T-shirt and jeans hastily pulled on, she let him in. Again he opted for a can of Stella over a coffee. There was some left then. She couldn't remember how many of them had come back to the flat.

While Sammy seemed to accept alcoholic amnesia as routine and rarely returned to the scene of the crime, she always liked to try somehow to reconstruct the missing hours, if only to know how hard to flog herself. She knew already it was awful.

'Did Geoffrey get home all right?' she tried.

'How would I know?' Her brother seemed almost offended to be asked. 'He was pretty shitfaced when I put him on the night bus. Not called you then?'

'No. I doubt I'll be hearing from him again. Look, can you do me a big favour, Sammy?'

'What's that?'

'Stay here for a little while – you can hoover up whatever's left in the fridge – just to let Charlie out when he surfaces.'

'Where you going then?'

'Down to the river, throw myself in. No, I don't know, expect I'll be knocking on the door of the OB soon as it opens. See you there. Don't bring him under any circumstances.'

'I thought he was queer – thought they both were at first, tell you the truth.'

'No such luck. Just don't bring him, all right.'

'All right, got you. Where is he?'

'Where do you think? Christ, Sammy, make me spell it out. He's in my bed.'

She snatched up the book her son had left – *The Primal Wound* – and hurried out.

THE END

Part Four:
Nineties through Teenies

17

Lucy

I saw Greg a hundred times before I looked at him twice. He wasn't hiding I wouldn't say. It was me, I wasn't seeking.

Shawl's was an old-fashioned shop in many ways. Mr Shawl – as even I called him, who knew his real name was Shallini – was the baker and left the serving mainly to his wife and family. I never knew his first name, though they and some of the more confident customers both addressed and referred to him as Pop.

Most of the sausage rolls, bakes, cakes and sweet pastries – what the older generation called 'fancies' – were sold over the counter for people's teas. Between the window showcasing the day's most scrumptious creations and the counter were a few little tables where people could eat in.

Pop would make a point of personally taking out the orders for certain of his longest-standing clients. Mrs Brewington was one of those. She always reminded me of that Ena Sharples from *Coronation Street* when I was a kid, right down to having two female sidekicks. She was the only one ever to expand their group with members of her own family – a couple with two children.

Just as Ena's cronies left the Rovers for the Big Upstairs snug, Mrs Brewington's supporting cast fell away. The man who would be my Greg also gradually lost his entourage. It became him with the kids for a while – chucked dad's weekend treat for them. I absorbed, without ever needing to ask anyone, let alone speak to the man, that he was 'a good boy', great to Mrs B, who 'wasn't the easiest'.

All this time he must have gathered something about me. He said he had his eye on me right from the start, or would have if he hadn't known I was already married, but I know flannel when I hear it. He offered personal condolences on my return to the shop after Tommy, without pushing it at all during that period when I was all over the place.

I didn't know till later he planned it that way, one Saturday I was leaving work, heading through the market as they were starting to pack up the stalls, when we met outside Bennett's paper shop. I kept it to myself that Louise would be fine at Shirley's, kept it to one drink that first time, couldn't appear too eager. Besides, he'd picked the biggest dive on the square, the Globe. You couldn't see the ceiling for the fag smoke a foot or more thick, like a stinky cloudy sky.

It suited me fine that he wasn't familiar with the Washtown pub scene. I took over our dating arrangements. He was more than happy to let me after that disaster when we both got a lot more than we expected from *The Crying Game*. He was mortified. I would have laughed in the pub afterwards, except we hadn't quite got to that stage yet.

I liked it that he still kept in touch with his mum, even more when I realised he was coming to Washtown to see me as much as her – and with more excitement, for sure. I know Kar was a bit sarky about him being a few years older than me, but Kar was sarky about everything. She wasn't one to be giving anyone lessons on how to manage their love lives.

It was also good that Greg kept in touch with his now grown-up kids, Paul and Genette. It soon seemed pointless him paying for a hotel room – a B & B actually, but still – when he could stay with me, at first in our spare bedroom. I was very careful introducing him to the house for Lou's sake. Maybe having brought up a daughter of his own helped him get on with her. If he hadn't, the whole relationship would have been a non-starter. I think he would have come back to Washtown to live with us if I'd asked – he said he would do anything for me, and without bigging myself up too much I don't think that was flannel – but the money he earned was too good to throw over. So in the end we moved to Chelmsford, from where he was commuting to London.

Tedge was broken-hearted, there was no getting around that. He worked as potman for his dad at the Service – I suppose he got some kind of disability benefits to help Pete and Shirley keep him. They weren't getting any younger themselves, so I helped as much as I could with Nan and Grandad. She suffered from angina and at last her energy seemed to be running out, probably drained by him sitting still as a battery charging in front of the telly all day. I can't deny I was thinking they would all fall on me to look after before too long if I was still around in Washtown, the only one of us girls who was. Adding into that Tommy's parents, who still treated me like a daughter, and Mrs Brewington, I admit I was thinking about having somebody look after me for once rather than having to be on the lookout for so many other people all the while. Call me selfish if you like.

Mum at last seemed to have found someone she was prepared to let take care of her as well, living in Blackheath, a real swanky part of London it seemed the few times we went there. Her husband – maybe they didn't get married, but how much longer could we keep talking about boyfriends for her? – worked in the City, like Greg. David (he said to call him Dave, but he never felt like a Dave to me) might have been at a slightly higher level than Greg, not that much older but he definitely *was* older, not younger like Ange said Karen told her he was. David wasn't a toy boy at all, though to be honest he wouldn't have been the first of them Mum had either. He lost confidence – Greg I mean – when he got made redundant the first time after we set up home together, talked about going back to Washtown. I convinced him to stick it out till he found something else. He moved around a bit after that, different jobs but always in the City.

I didn't begrudge Mum her comforts one bit, but the light and fire seemed to have left her, unless you count the cigarette she always had on the go. The others always say I was the lucky one never to start smoking, as if that's all it was, luck. Didn't it have something to do with willpower too? Something to do with being sensible?

I would always be grateful to Jan for having me and Louise out to Puerto Rico that time, and Ray treated us very well there too. I don't know what went wrong between the two of them – they always came to see us as part of their grand tour when they were home on holidays (she used to call it leave like they were in the army or something). They would also visit Mum in London and it was Jan told me how bad she'd got – you can put on a front for a short visit, but when people are with you for a few days it's not so easy. She had emphysema (I think they call it COPD now, probably to make it sound less frightening). Even with breathing apparatus she struggled. Jan said they had to call an ambulance out one time – found her keeled over on the floor in front of the telly still hooked up to the machine, David already in bed.

I knew once you had emphysema it never went away, that was the scary thing about it. Mum was also claiming the angina her mother-in-law had. I wouldn't say she was a drama queen. She could still be great company and look good when she made an extra effort to get dressed up. You could see then how she'd landed David, and he was proud to show her off. But apart from the fags, I think there was still daytime drinking. I wouldn't be at all surprised if there were still tablets too.

She never went the way of her own mum, never got fat like Grandma Alice. I know they had some help in David's house, so she could have taken to her bed like that, or armchair like Grandad (he always stayed lean and mean, mind). Mum would get dressed and put make-up on, however bad things got. My theory – and you can laugh as much as you like – is that deep inside she was still hoping Eric Roper might come back for her one day, all smart in his captain's uniform.

It wasn't easy for Greg and me, having to bury both our mothers within a month of each other. Mrs Brewington was much older, pushing eighty, but I'd thought she would still outlast Mum. She *did* pile on the pounds, never giving up on her Shawl's fancies to the end when his ex or Genette had to fetch them to her at home. Pop was no longer around to serve her anyway – we attended his funeral and got quite drunk and sentimental after it.

I tried to suggest to Greg it was a release for him as well as her when the heart attack took his mum, quickly, the only thing she never made a fuss about. He wasn't in the mood to be consoled, though he never turned his nose up at bereavement sex.

David was very formal, stiff on the phone when he told me about Mum. I thought he was trying to be funny when I was asking the how and why and he said she just stopped breathing. I suppose he must have been upset himself, probably wasn't thinking straight. Unlike Mrs Brewington, Mum was taken kicking and screaming – so I like to think anyhow, she might actually have been unconscious – to the hospital where they couldn't bring her back. Just like Dad, she never got a chance to say goodbye to any of us.

As if I didn't have enough on my plate looking after Greg's side of the family, it was muggins who David asked to let the rest of our family know about Mum. I think he would have had me take over the body, funeral arrangements and everything if I'd let him, but I drew the line at that. He must have had people he could get to do it, and it wouldn't hurt him. He may not have seen her at her best, but he was still punching above his weight in what turned out to be her last years, and I would have told him so if he'd kicked up. I was in a funny mood at that time. Not surprising really with all the stress.

David suggested Blackheath for a quiet cremation, probably planning a plaque in a wall never again to be visited. I had to do all the ringing round my sisters, leaving Ange to let Billy know. I couldn't cope with him as well, always Mum's favourite. Ange agreed with me that her secret wish would probably have been to lay with Eric again. Jan said we were just being silly – it would mean trekking over to Ireland and anyway Lil probably had her own berth reserved there. I thought Karen was drunk or drugged. I wasn't going to keep ringing her back. She just didn't seem to care, let alone offer any practical help. And she was probably the one best placed to do it all, living in London.

In the end, the best we could come up with was Northampton, the same graveyard as Grandma Alice. She had a double plot, paid for by a life insurance Grandad Sess had taken out on the both of them, but of course he was still alive and would be wanting that. I did know he was still alive, he might have died long since as far as my sisters were concerned. Aunt Joy was a brick, as always, offering to do anything she could, but I didn't really think it was her place.

Although he'd been with Mum for years not months, it was clear at the funeral how little David was part of our family. He did a short reading, something out of the Bible, dry-eyed and not likely to wet anyone else's either. I will give him credit for the good spread afterwards at the whole upstairs of the Crown and Garter. It was a soulless place, I heard Karen say. I bit my tongue rather than saying if she wanted soul she could have suggested somewhere else. None of us were religious anyway.

I bit my tongue as well because she looked really awful, Karen. You could tell she wasn't right – not dressed to shock like normal, just in standard black funeral gear, right down to black tights. Her legs were like pipe cleaners, and her face was so haggard you'd have thought she was more Aunt Joy's generation than ours.

As per usual the men all clustered around the bar, apart from Grandad, who hadn't bothered to get up from his telly to come. Pete and Shirley brought Nana with Tedge, who always enjoyed family get-togethers under whatever circumstances. He was quick to quiz David on his birthday.

So there was Alex holding court, managing the kitty once the first drink paid for by David had gone (in about five minutes flat). He hardly spoke to me now, which was fine. Billy was at his shoulder, hardly up to his shoulder,

173

supping more than talking. It brought home to me how Uncle Pete was ageing too, thinking back to the days when he and Dad had to look out for Alex in scrapes around town. You could see it would be more the other way round nowadays. If Billy looked up to Alex, it was nothing like Martin to Uncle Henry – two billiard balls in a bag. They were skinheads now Henry had started going bald and was making the best of a bad job, while Martin of course had to shave his. They looked like Peggy Mitchell's boys at the Queen Vic in *EastEnders*, you'd have thought they should be doing the doors rather than necking pints at the bar. Martin was married with three kids, but there was no sign of them.

My Greg knew enough not to get involved in that round, or the card school it would become as soon as they thought they could decently get away with it. He ended up babysitting David, who caught a train back to London long before the rest of the party broke up. I didn't think we'd see much more of him, and I was right.

Grandad Sess was as anti-social as ever. For someone who made his own beer you'd think he would have been a bit more keen on company – most men like nothing more than to gab away once they've got a pint in them. It was his daughter's funeral, and he was in his own world as usual. Aunt Joy managed him at a table with Nan, two people I'd imagine would hardly ever have spoken before that day and didn't look in a hurry to make up for lost time.

Karen started off at the bar. I'd always wondered if there was something between her and Alex at some point. Although they always seemed more like mates than boyfriend and girlfriend, men always want one thing from women at the end of the day. She had a pint, like a man again, but she didn't swill it down her, wasn't anything like as boisterous as usual.

Us women outnumbered the men nowadays. On the Irish side, Lil had come not only with Eamon (who looked like he would be no taller than Billy) but her eldest Brenda – there for the buffet that one, Jan said, which reminded me she could be just as catty as Kar when she wanted. Eamon was the only boy there that day from the younger generation, which the funeral made me sad to think wasn't us anymore. Ange was vague about Adam's absence. I got the impression him and his dad didn't get on. It was the opposite if anything with Denis and Ray, who wasn't his real dad. Jan said it would have been too expensive for all four of them to come back, so it was just her and Kimberley, who was Louise's best friend since our time in Puerto Rico when she taught her to dance merengue and speak Spanish. She was a very pretty girl, fretting at first if her sky-blue outfit was quite appropriate for the occasion.

It did Lou good to see her cousins I always thought. We had Martin and that was about it in our childhood, when he was already like a little old man anyway. It didn't matter because we had each other – we were enough as sisters. I had Tedge too. Shirl was keeping an eye on him like I always did, almost unconsciously. He was used to being around drink nowadays, but you never knew what might send him off on one. He was a strange mixture, built like a bull but docile as a lamb, until suddenly he wasn't, and you might never find out what had flicked the switch. He showed the same kind of protectiveness towards Lou as he had to me. I'm not saying the other girls, Ange's Little Jan and Suzette, would tease him or anything, but I remember their mother could be unkind to Tedge – a touch afraid of him I shouldn't wonder – so maybe that made them a bit leery around him.

Unable to keep up with Alex and the Mitchell brothers at the bar because he was driving, Pete was talking about getting back to the Service not long after David left. Tedge wasn't happy until Louise promised to come and see him the next day on our way back to Chelmsford. We were staying the night at Jan's. That should have been the clue she was heading towards a split from Ray, now I think of it – the fact they hadn't tried to replace their last tenants so had the house, when she always used to bunk up at Ange's.

Lil didn't seem in any hurry to leave, drinking her vodka tonics while big Brenda was polishing off pints of Guinness. It wasn't for me to invite her back to one of my sisters' houses. I suppose her sons were still living in town. I saw the one who was close to Billy hand her some keys when he turned up at the do.

For all she looked nothing like her normal self, I was surprised when Karen came back to Ange's with us as the men set off for some other pub or club, not bothering to change or anything, just pocketing their neckties. I let Greg go with Alex, Billy and his mate (Aunt Joy had dragged her menfolk away with Grandad Sess) – they would have made his life unbearable else, he always told me when I could see he wanted to carry on with them, which was only once in a while. They'd call him pussy-whipped, that horrible term Alex would use on Tommy as well. I was fed up explaining it didn't matter what they thought. It was just their own insecurities when they said nasty stuff like that. They were probably jealous of what we had, though of course I never told Greg about how Alex came on to me that time.

Our girls were perfectly old enough to go out themselves if they wanted – another sign of the passing years – but seemed happy enough hanging out together upstairs at Ange's, including Janette, who was already living with her boyfriend. I was glad to know they were at home – they were welcome to have another drink or two.

Nobody asked if it was wise for someone we all thought had a drink problem to be quite so stocked with such a variety of booze, laid in by Alex no doubt to show off to his mates and hangers-on. Ange had been quiet all day. She would usually hide behind Mum at family occasions, piggybacking on her drinking so no one would notice. She had managed for herself well enough today. I noticed she soon trained Tedge to keep her glass topped up, not that we weren't all having a few. It's not every day you bury your mother, is it? Ange was instantly more relaxed back in her own house, plonking a bottle of red on the big old wooden chest they had in the middle of their front room – full of the kids' toys at one time – to keep us going while she sorted out vodka drinks.

'Did you hear what Nan said to Grandad Sess at the end? "I expect the next time they're all together it'll be for one of us."' I don't know what made me repeat that. It had gone quiet, and I like to keep a conversation going, otherwise you just sit there and drink, and before you know it everyone's sloshed.

'I hope she outlives Jack. She deserves a time for herself after waiting on him all these years.' I wasn't surprised at Jan's sharpness. She had a bit of a down on the old man, nearly as bad as on *our* old man.

'She may be wrong.' Karen did not say it in her argumentative voice.

'Wrong about what? Who?' Ange came back in with two glasses chocka with ice and almost to the brim with clear liquid. I hoped some of it was tonic water.

'Nan, about who's oven-ready next. Ta, Ange. I'm not feeling too well myself.'

I laughed. I admit I laughed. I thought it was one of Karen's jokes, usually bad-taste jokes. She didn't have to look at me as if I was laughing at her unkindly – that wasn't what I meant at all.

Jan, sitting nearest, put a hand on Karen's knee. 'What's up, sis? I thought you weren't looking yourself.'

'Chronic lymphocytic leukaemia is what's up – CLL to its mates.'

We always just called it leukaemia once it had been introduced to us. I only know the full name because I asked Karen to write it down for us before the night was done.

'Going to start looking for a cure?' she asked.

I could understand how it might have made her bitter, so I didn't say anything. I did look it up online, me and Jan together as it happens, but mostly I just wanted to know what was wrong with my sister so I could say it properly if anyone else asked.

That was later. When she first dropped the name, none of us knew what to say. Ange went down like a sack of spuds into her chair, swirling the ice cubes around with a swizzle stick, obviously wondering if she was allowed to take a swig yet. It hardly seemed right to say cheers. Karen did the talking for us – she could always do that, but tonight it wasn't with her usual energy. It was more like the reading David done at the church.

'We've all heard of leukaemia. Blood disease, basically a cancer. No need to be afraid of the word. I never knew there were so many types of it. This one was developing inside me a good while before I knew it was there.'

'Didn't you feel ill or anything?' Ange was already halfway down her VAT.

'I've felt ill forever. No, I swore I'd be calm when I told you all – I only wanted to have to do it once – and now I'm just being melodramatic, playing for sympathy. What I mean is, between drinking and…and the rest, not eating properly, not sleeping enough, I know it's all my own fault, you get to a point where you never feel great. I just thought I was getting old. We've all had a reminder today how that goes. Trouble down below, night sweats, I thought I might be starting the change early till it came to not wanting to get up in the mornings.'

'You what? You were feeling suicidal and you didn't think to tell us?' Jan had already grabbed one of Karen's hands, and for once our bolshie sister didn't shake her off.

'No. Not suicidal. I think we're all a bit obsessed with that after Grandma Alice. Not exactly *feeling* suicidal. How can I put it better? I was more *thinking* about suicide. Don't tell me none of you thought that might have been Mum's way out of living with that desiccated old fart call-me-Dave – it was the first thing that occurred to me. I never had any intention of doing it. If I had, I would have gone to the quacks a lot sooner – they're the ones to give you the tools for the job.'

'But you went in the end. I mean don't a lot of kids get over leukaemia, probably older people too, except that's not such a good story?'

'That's right, Ange. I don't want to exaggerate – they're not measuring me for the baking tray yet. Sorry if I shocked you all. I wanted to get your attention while we're together and didn't know how best to bring it up. I know you all think I'm a bloody show-off at the best of times, but I don't particularly want to be the centre of attention like this, believe me.'

'So what do the doctors say?' I asked.

'It's not a stone-cold killer. They talk about five-year survival rates, and overall most people make it that far. Overall, averages is about all you'll find on the internet Luce. I'm lucky in some ways. Women tend to last longer than men – well there's a surprise for us all – and generally the younger you are, the stronger you are. You're unlucky to get it as young as I have, and I've been unlucky to get a particular sort, more aggressive than most, won't answer to chemo.

'I suppose what you really want to know is the prognosis. Thanks for not being as blunt about it as Billy was. All he could say was "How long you got?"'

Ange put her hand over her mouth.

'The little shit,' Jan said, and then it went quiet as we all wondered what Karen had answered.

She laughed. 'Don't worry, I don't hold it against him. That's our little brother – we all know he's a social moron, as well as a moron in general. He just says the first thing that comes into his head. I told him I'd outlast him if he keeps on drinking the way he is now, and not to worry, I won't be going to him for a transplant.'

'A transplant? Is that the only cure then? A blood transplant?'

'It's the shit or bust option, that's right. They can put it into remission sometimes with chemo, and that can do you for years, before the whole thing starts again. There's a German saying – basically if you get cancer, you die of cancer. I've always thought there's a lot of truth in it, the times you hear about it coming back. You never know, but it looks as if transplants are the nearest thing to a cure – not exactly blood but stem cells, bone marrow.'

'I don't know if my blood would work for you, Kar. Remember I had hepatitis that time, they wouldn't let me be a donor when Alex wanted us to do it together with the whole Town team as a publicity stunt.' You could hear Ange was plain scared of the thought. And if Billy's blood was a bit heavy on the alcohol content, hers might have been just as bad. Before I could offer myself, Karen answered Ange.

'I won't ask any of you to do what you don't want. There's a risk for the donor as well as for me. It's not just popping in, giving an armful, cuppa, choccie bic and job's a good'un. I may have to take my chances, but you don't, especially as you've all got kids. We can look for a match outside the family – that may do.'

She left a little pause none of us filled. 'I know what you're all thinking.

I'm ahead of you. You may not be great matches in any case, if it's true I'm not really Eric's daughter. I was going to put Mum's feet to the fire and get the fucking truth out of her on that once and for all, one way or another, but it's too late now.'

'Worst case, we've got to be halfway there,' Jan said. 'What do we need to do? And when?'

'I have to decide first what *I'm* going to do. The quacks are all very well, but trying to get a bit of definite guidance, God forbid a recommendation, out of them is like trying to get a round out of Billy. All worried about covering their arses in case anything goes wrong.'

'Look, I wasn't going to bring this up today, but I don't necessarily have to rush back to Puerto Rico. I know you've heard it all before from me with Ray – we'll save that for later. All I want to say is, unless the operation has to be done in London for some reason, why don't you come up here? Me and Ange can help you through it better then, and I'll be happy to take the tests to see if we're compatible – is that the word they use?'

'Yeah, that or a match, like a fucking dating agency. I don't really want a blind date, that's true. We'll need to make sure everyone understands the risks involved. I won't be too proud to ask for help. I promised myself, and I promise you that. Whatever happens, I won't be able to earn for a good while, and I've got no savings.'

'You could stay with us at Chelmsford as well, Kar. Greg and me maybe aren't doing as well as the others money-wise, but I know I can speak for him that we'll contribute whatever we can, however best we can. Count on me for a transplant if it will work for you.'

It was the first in a long time any of us had seen Karen cry. We all kind of crowded round her, a hug between the four of us like I could never remember. I do remember the daughters coming down to fetch drinks or something just at that point and Little Jan saying, 'Looks like the old dears are at the kissing stage now – that means they'll be trying to kill each other before you know it.'

That wasn't true. We ended the evening friends, despite finishing the bottle of vodka between us and then some. Back at Jan's, Greg was up and down like a yo-yo all night, pissing and puking. I had no sympathy – it was easier to let him sleep on while we dealt with our own hangovers as best we could with morning coffee.

'Jan, didn't you think it was funny Karen never mentioned Gary once?'

It had come to me sometime in my own troubled night. Greg was hardly considerate as he blundered about in the dark, and I must admit I had to get up for a pee myself a couple of times.

'Gary who? Oh *her* Gary. No, it didn't cross my mind. It was hard enough to take in what she was telling us. I can't believe she hasn't thought of him – you're right.'

'Did you ever get the story of what happened when they met up that time, must be a few years back now?'

'I got *a* story,' Jan replied. 'Never did get a chance to quiz her face to face, and I never met him, so I don't know if it was what really happened. If it was, it was pretty bad.'

'However bad, he's still got a right to know. He did come and visit me at the time – very polite, shy even, not too la-di-da. I tried to pump him on how it had gone with Kar, but he wasn't giving it up either. He said he didn't wish her any ill – I remember because it's a strange way of putting it when you've just seen your long-lost mum. Who knows? Remember how she went all them years hardly mentioning him at all, and to my knowledge she hasn't done it since.'

'That doesn't mean she hasn't thought about him. And he might be the best transplant option for her.'

That had been my big idea. I was disappointed in a way she'd got there without me. In giving me his contact details and keeping in touch with Christmas cards, Gary had luckily left the door on the latch. I was all for talking to Karen about it that morning before she left Ange's to return to London. Jan was more cunning.

'She's liable to say "don't you dare" if we suggest bringing him into it. She might already have done it herself, and he knocked her back. If she hasn't, I wouldn't want to raise her hopes up in case he doesn't want to know. That would be too cruel on top of everything else. Why don't you get in touch with him on the quiet, sound him out?'

It was only on our way back to East Anglia that I realised once again it was me had been left to do all the running around. I didn't mind. I was sincere about wanting to help Karen. Who wouldn't between sisters? Except I couldn't help wondering where she'd been when Tommy died.

I found Gary much more self-assured when I saw him this time, but then he was through uni and working, a mechanical engineer he said. I didn't know there were different kinds. I offered to go to see Karen with him, even though she might get a strop on with me for not having told her what I was doing. What *we* were doing rather – I made sure Jan was involved every step of the way. He said he thought it would be better if he went on his own, which I respected.

We perhaps agreed as well that he might not mention us having talked about her illness, so that might be why I never got any thanks from Karen for putting them in touch. Gary was more than willing to go through the donation process – he insisted on it by all accounts. It's only human to want to be thanked I would say, but I know she was very poorly, so perhaps I should have been more understanding.

If I appeared to withdraw or stay away from her during the weeks leading up to the transplant, it wasn't at all because I was jealous of Ange and Jan being the sisters on the spot when she moved up to Northampton. Let them do some of the heavy lifting, Greg said to me, and I tended to agree. He and I had grown closer than ever during that difficult period of losing both our mums. I knew how much he really loved Mrs Brewington – someone had to.

We had agreed to disagree about having a brother or sister for Louise. He thought he was too old – as if the work would have fallen on him! – and I had almost grown accustomed over the years with Tommy to thinking that Lou was our little miracle, a one-off. If Greg wanted to use contraception, that was up to him. I wasn't going to bother. Maybe it was a little childish of me never to take up his hints about putting the rubber johnnies on for him as I knew he would have liked, though he never asked again after the time I reminded him I wasn't his ex.

I suppose he came to think there wasn't any danger, like I was coming to think there wasn't any hope. I waited until I was absolutely sure, had the stick ready to show Greg if necessary. I would have got a bigger stick out if he hadn't at least pretended to be delighted, let me tell you. He wasn't too old at all. I actually think it made him feel a lot younger, proud of himself in a way he hadn't been for a while after the knockbacks in his career.

I know you don't catch cancer like a cold – I'm not that daft. Still I didn't want to be in contact with it during those early months, or driving or getting on trains to go and visit my sisters when I wasn't feeling so great. I knew this would be my last chance to have another baby, and I wasn't going to do anything to blow it. I'm sorry if that sounds harsh, but I think most mothers will understand. Even Karen – she was a mother too.

18

Angela

Alex must have told me the name of the Arab bank he went to. It didn't sound that foreign really, but I still can't remember it. He worked for them properly at first then set up as a consultant to do it. He'd said that's where the money was for a long time – consultancy and the Gulf as well.

It wasn't so much good riddance to bad rubbish as his being in the house was making things tense. I had threatened to chuck him out or leave myself if I had to with the kids, that time he hit Adam when the boy was only trying to stick up for me.

'Don't be stupid, Ange, it was only a slap. He needs to learn to mind his own business. It won't do him any harm – he'd be taking harder knocks than that every week if he'd kept the football up.'

'I know what it was, and I'm telling you I won't have it. I'll kill you first.'

'Hysterical bitch.' He didn't shout, so I knew he was half-ashamed. I knew I'd got my point across.

Adam was more shocked than hurt – Alex was right, it was only a back-hander. He wasn't a fighter our boy, which made me all the prouder that he'd tried to get in between us when Alex grabbed me. He always thought he could grab me, by any part of the body according to what his intentions were. I didn't find it exciting or funny anymore.

I must be fair to Alex, he had tried – the fishing, the trips to Old Trafford from a time when Adam was far too young. The one time I went, with all the pop before the match he couldn't wait till half-time for a pee. His dad was furious when I made him go with him and miss a few minutes. How was I to know United would score right then? You wouldn't believe he could see the goal later on telly the way he carried on. It was horrible anyway – the crush, beery-breathed men swearing all around you. I put my foot down for him until Adam was older, and by then he didn't want to go anyway. Alex had more luck getting Janette there. She reminded me a bit of Jan pestering Dad to take her with him in the lorry.

Adam left school as soon as he could, got a place to live before he found a job – a rented house with three other lads. From the time he started off as an office boy at Brereton's estate agents he was always smart in a suit and tie. Once he left home, I don't remember him once bringing his laundry back, not a single shirt (which I wouldn't have minded ironing). His smartness – I don't just mean looking smart, he was no fool either – probably helped them decide to get him out selling properties before long, and he turned out to be good at it. He may have inherited the Roper lack of height, but he had to put in the hours at bodybuilding before he put on some muscle like his Grandad Eric. He had a bit of his swagger too, unless that came from Alex. I wondered how long it would be before Adam was telling his dad he earned more than him now.

Janette would have been in her element growing up today when women's football is all the thing. Back then there was no scope for it, not even for tomboys like her. She took after her namesake aunt in that – she was more likely to be called Little John than Jan at primary school, when she was still allowed to get involved in the playground football matches with the boys. Nobody dares stop her, Miss Kerridge said at one parents' evening I'd managed to drag Alex along to.

She would have gone everywhere with her dad if he'd let her. She was definitely his favourite. The unexpected arrival of Suzie, who was the sweetest little girl, didn't put a dent in that. Janette was the only one to show any interest in his career he would sometimes grumble (like he ever told us anything about it), the first to get to grips with computers and still the one we all go to for that sort of thing.

My sister Jan was a bit funny about the name thing, when I thought she'd be pleased. I'm still waiting for anyone to be called Angela. It was harder for the kids to get to know her when she moved abroad with Ray for so long. I felt that separation myself. Not that Karen was around much either. Their Aunt

Lucy was the only one they could absolutely count on for a birthday card every year with a fiver in it – from the other two it might sometimes be a tenner, but it seemed like just as often nothing.

It was the same ending for Janette as Jan with the sporty thing. Like Jan dropped the table tennis from one day to the next without any regrets, Little Jan packed up the proper tennis and hockey as soon as she discovered boys.

It was different than in our day, when it was like a battle with boys, them always trying to get the upper hand, sometimes using force to get what they wanted. 'Get what they wanted' is probably out of date as well, unless girls use it about themselves – high time if they do. I'm not a feminist like Karen, for me it was just a fact of life. You know how they used to say about boys who could fight 'he can look after himself'? That was what I thought about us girls. You had to stick up for yourself when necessary. Mostly they were so surprised they'd back down. I know Luce understood that. Karen was more downright aggressive, which can put them off altogether, and you don't always want that. Jan was the one who seemed a bit more naïve if that's the right word. Luckily she never had anything to worry about with that drip Jason, and I didn't hear of Ray mistreating her like that.

I think there was proper friendship between some of the boys and girls in Janette's group, not only the ones supposed to be boyfriend and girlfriend. That was no guarantee friendship would follow in my day, when it was nearly unheard of for the friendship to come first. That was our experience. Maybe it was different for ugly girls. Not blowing just my own trumpet, everyone knew about us Roper girls, but it wasn't always a good thing either. Alex would never trust me, which was sort of flattering at first. Lucy once said she never had a man beat someone up for her, like Alex did pulling Tony Marsden out of his car at the lights that time and kicking him all over the pavement just because someone see him talking to me in the street. She sounded envious, but it soon got old. He said the same thing himself one time about Janette, with Suzie still to reach that stage. 'I can't go another round of beating up all the kids who start messing with another generation of Roper girls. I'm too fucking old for one thing.'

I didn't remind him it was a different town as well. In Northampton he didn't have the reputation he did in Washtown, earned partly because he had Dad and his mates to stand behind him when he was coming up.

I wasn't soft on my girls, though I could hardly be a prude with our family history – they'd soon have let me have it if I'd tried. I wanted to make sure they could talk to me about anything, but I did always try to resist dragging them straight into conversation when they came home from school, to give myself a bit of company apart from the bottle.

Billy was no help on that. He'd started coming round for his tea every night when Mum moved back to London. I made sure he gave me some housekeeping for it, tight little sod. Alex wouldn't have thought of that, but then he wasn't normally there to eat with us. When I complained about him cluttering up my fridge with beers, Billy went and bought a little one to put in our garage. I got to keeping a reserve white in there, and we both knew there was a fun-sized vodka bottle in the little freezer space at the top.

While he was happy enough to sit at the kitchen table and drink with me, you can't say Billy had any real conversation bless him. He would occasionally stay round to watch football with the kids – Alex had splashed out on all the channels in the days before we could really afford it, which we could now. I knew he went without fail to that dump of a pub, the Criterion, on his way home every night. I didn't begrudge him the nightcap – it was the place I didn't like.

I think Alex would have smacked Billy if he'd ever found out Janette had been seeing Jamie, the first serious boyfriend we knew about, round at his house. She was very matter of fact when she told us she was sixteen and had no plans to leave school, but if he wasn't allowed to come round ours and stay in her room sometimes, then she would have to think about moving out.

Janette had a key to Billy's house because she was doing some cleaning for him to earn herself a bit of pocket money. I'd noticed it was getting to be a bit of a tip after Mum left for London. Don't think I was too proud to do a bit of cleaning myself. It was more I didn't like leaving the house on my own. I don't suppose he noticed whether she did a good job or not. He never complained anyway.

She may have asked him if she could have friends round there. I can imagine him not giving a toss either way, but I did have a word when it started to be a regular thing and there was talk he was getting involved with them himself. Remembering the situation with my sister and that crowd at Jason's house, I always thought it was a bit strange his mum being there with all the teenagers. There would be a lot more talk about an older man hanging around young women, girls really.

With Janette it was too late to change anything, so we made the best of it. Things were different nowadays. Boys weren't coming home with a black eye or a bloody nose – there were knives about, and one of her friends took a glassing for nothing more than wrong place wrong time. Everyone said she got over it well, but the scar was still there. She'd been pretty till then. I didn't mind at all if Janette and Jamie preferred to stay in, or go to the Oak up the road. We lived in a decent area – the town centre was the roughest part, like everywhere.

With Billy it was probably already too late as well. You could say what you liked, he never took offence, but then he never did anything to change his ways either. I had hopes he might settle down with a single mum he was seeing for a while, more like his own age was Jennie. He always said she was fine but he didn't love her, and couldn't imagine himself as a dad to her little boy or anyone else. I think Billy's problem wasn't that he was heartless, more the other way round – if anything, he was too much of a romantic.

It wasn't easy being the oldest one in the family, supposed to be responsible for all the other girls and with an eye on our kid brother as well. It wasn't as if I had any real friends outside the family to talk to. The closest I came to a conversation with anyone was my hairdresser, believe it or not. Does that sound too pathetic?

At first I would just let Paddy rabbit on about everything and nothing while I was in the chair, but gradually I started putting in a few words of my own. I know they're being paid to attend to you and all that, but it was amazing to have someone listen to me and appear to be interested. Paddy even laughed sometimes at things I would say, and not because they were stupid. I got to going at least once a month rather than every six weeks or more. Alex could easily afford it – not that he ever noticed anything I did to my hair as long as I looked smart enough still to turn the occasional head in the street.

Even before Mum and all the stuff with Karen, I was wondering if I should ask Alex to come back home. He was always telling me he didn't really enjoy it out there. It wasn't like I could have gone to him. It was no place for a woman to enjoy life, for all he said it wouldn't be much different for me to stay on the compound like I sat on my arse at home all day in Northampton. I said I wasn't prepared to drink beer out of a bath and that was that.

I'd gone once. I did make the effort, for a long weekend (their weekends were different – Friday and Saturday then working Sunday) not to Saudi but Bahrain. He said it was a lot more relaxed there, we could get drinks and decent food and everything, but sorry it wasn't for me. The heat was unbelievable, like being smothered with an electric blanket whenever you went outside. We might complain about getting in the water in England for that freezing feeling until you get used to it, but when they have to have machinery to *cool* the water in the open-air pool at the hotel, you know there's something wrong.

I was planning to ask him if one of his stupid buckets wasn't full by now when he came home for Mum's funeral. At first he'd been home a lot of weekends, then that dropped off. Perhaps he got fed up with showing off his bling – gold rings like golf balls, chains round his neck, bracelets I would never have expected since he'd always said they looked poofy on a man. I got plenty of gold jewellery off him for myself as well, I won't deny that. I made no complaints generally about the amount of cash he arranged to go into our bank every month – that joint account I don't think I ever did tell Karen I'd got at last – or about the load of shit that came with it.

I don't know why, but I had a bad feeling about her illness right from the start. I knew the minute she mentioned a transplant I'd be the best match, just knew it. And I hated hospitals. Call me a coward if you like, I couldn't help it. The thought of going into one to visit someone else made my skin creep, never mind for an operation that might kill me. I hoped Alex would step in and say I shouldn't do it, that we had the kids to think of after all, but no such luck. He wanted to be tested himself, like he was as much one of the family as any of us. He must have thought I'd be only too happy to do the same, which goes to show how little he knew me.

I was right as well – I was the closest match. Thank God Jan remembered Karen's son she'd had adopted. I'd never met him so it wasn't surprising he hadn't occurred to me. Good of him to do it. I don't know if I would have myself in his position, abandoned at birth – not that I'm blaming her, nor saying what I'd done the first time I got pregnant was any better. Please don't think that.

And Luce pregnant again, what a turn up for the books that was. It would have been all good, except she could have been a big help around Karen if she weren't so frightened something might go wrong she kept herself in Chelmsford all the time. Course she had a husband on the spot to support her, lucky cow.

Karen was so weak she finally gave in and come up to Northampton. She moved in with Jan, who did most of the running around for her to be fair, in and out of hospital all the while as they started to make whatever preparations they had to for the operation. I don't remember what her problem was that morning, when Jan rang and asked could I take her there for an appointment because she couldn't manage it. Well, she didn't ask – she pretty much told me and had hung up before I could think of a good enough excuse to get out of it.

I was still driving Alex's car, though never far outside Northampton. It would have made more sense for Adam to have it really, except he wouldn't have been able to afford the insurance. I would have been more comfortable driving his old crock than Alex's pride and joy, a Mercedes (that's all I know, don't ask me what make or model).

Wouldn't you just know it? The red light for petrol would have to come on that morning. I always panic then, have to fill up straight away. I wasn't tanked up myself or anything – admittedly I'd had a drink before Jan's call, never thinking I would have to go out. All right, it was stupid to have another one to help me get out the door. I should have phoned Jan back, me and Karen could always get a taxi or something, but then I would have to organise that as well.

Whether from the rush – there should be enough time but I have to get dressed and made-up – the nerves or what, it's only when I've got the petrol already pouring I suddenly know I've come out without my bag – no money, no cards, nothing. I click the catch to make it carry on working without me holding the pump then go back to look in through the driver's door, hoping the bag will be right there on the passenger seat, knowing it won't.

I can still go in the shop and explain, I've seen my vodka-man through the window, will he believe me, does he even like me? The blood is all rushing to my head, I think I'm going to pass out leaning over the steering wheel, no bag. Next thing I've jumped in and I'm pulling away. There's a horrible tearing sound behind me as the pump rips loose spraying petrol everywhere, turning to see what's going on I hit a big old dustbin and knock it flying then I'm out on the road again heading for home.

19

Janet

When people asked Jan why it took so long for her to get wise to Ray and leave him, she always thought they were asking the wrong question. She'd been onto him all along. Within a couple of years anyway, after what happened in Hong Kong for sure; if it was all along, she told herself not even a Roper girl would have been dumb enough to hook up with him. And then she went and married him into the bargain, wilfully closing her eyes for more than the 'I do' kiss. They had made light of that marriage between themselves as well as to the family, an administrative convenience to help them continue to live abroad, yet later it was surprising how it weighed on her, much heavier than her first; how little she wanted to be someone twice divorced.

It would mean two kids from two different men in her background as well, still some way from that horrible phrase she'd heard men used about certain female celebrities: four-by-fours – there to be driven over all kinds of terrain by anyone who wanted a test ride. You only had to look at male rock stars to see the sexism and double standards in that, which made Jan ashamed she could not help sharing some of the implicit disapproval of the same women. Without four lovers in her whole life, she had no great wish to extend the number.

She had left Jason on a principle, when she came to admit to herself that she did not love him, or perhaps no longer loved him. She would not dwell on the third possibility, that she never had. It had rankled with her that she was the only one of them working – that was natural enough surely? It wasn't as if he was incapacitated or anything, or later that he became a proper househusband looking after Denis (part of her would have thought less of him if he *had* dived delightedly into that role). Just as she knew his idleness was not the main reason, she could give herself equal credit that staying so long with Ray had nothing to do with their comfortable lifestyle, the fact she no longer had to work. She had never thought of herself as either a lackey or a kept woman.

Things were complicated while the kids were growing up. However much she acknowledged the benefits of private education and them seeing something of the world, she felt an element of guilt at moving them from country to country, depriving them of more regular contact with their wider family; this despite knowing that her own hadn't exactly come up trumps during *her* childhood. She always felt herself rather than Karen the odd one out, an only child.

The year focused around the death of her mother, and Karen, brought her back with a vengeance into that extended family, while it seemed her nuclear one might be going into fission. She had indulged Denis by letting him start a degree course in fine arts at the University of Puerto Rico, thinking he could always do a 'proper' degree back in England as and when they returned. Then it turned out he was planning to take advantage of the green card their residence had earned to stay on and make his life out there, whether in Puerto Rico itself or using it as an open door to the States.

She had left him to keep in touch with his father, neither insisting on such contact nor in any way impeding it. If Jason had a problem with their boy's intentions, he could discuss it with him as between adults. Her conscience was clear on her ex. She had never demeaned herself to pursue him for child support, however tight things were at times for Denis and her. She had made Alex swear when he'd forced her to accept a bundle of notes on a couple of occasions that Ange knew all about it, yet somehow never taken the logical next step of also thanking her sister. Alex it was too who had shut down Jason's pathetic attempts to badmouth her around Washtown, as if his word carried any weight outside his own bedroom and with his own mummy.

Kimberley was no more biddable than her brother. She had all the tantrum-throwing capacity of an Ange or a Karen, all the stubborn persistence in getting her own way of a Lucy – in short, a proper Roper girl. Still, she was younger. Jan would not be separated from both her children. She told herself Kim would do just as well in either the British or US education system, depending on her mother's decision.

Jan had always been one to keep her emotions to herself, most of the screaming and shouting inside her own head. If Ray didn't yet realise the depth of her disaffection, she had given him more than fair warning in that year of Martin, the hurricane that clinched Sovereign's decision to get out of the Caribbean.

Grace was buried in May. Jan took Kim back to San Juan to finish her school year, talked to Ray and set to spend the whole of the summer holidays based in Northampton. He and Denis would come back for a spell according to their own schedules and Ray's continued employment status.

The length of her own stay would depend on what happened to Karen. Recovery would be a slow process – weeks if not months of almost total dependence on the support of others. Jan planned for that, although Karen would never allow them to forget the more brutal alternative.

Lucy would have come through with help if not for her unexpected pregnancy. Jan had to admire her sister's talent at the long game, without doubting it was initially as much a surprise to Lucy as to the hapless Greg. Kar had written a characteristically barbed congratulation card, stating that UNDER NO CIRCUMSTANCES was 'Karen or derivatives of it' to feature amongst the child's given names.

She hadn't expected too much from Ange. Still, it was frustrating to be cast as nursemaid also to her. Karen had the gumption to get herself to hospital – at that stage it was still a question more of moral than physical support – and was there when Jan was summoned to their oldest sister's house.

While the police's business there was almost done, they would rather not leave Ange in a state of hysteria. 'Mrs Reed has been in a bit of a scrape today, I'm afraid,' the female one said. 'I'm sure she'll tell you about it herself – you might like to give her another cup of coffee.'

The male officer was less sympathetic. He seemed disdainful of talking to Angela and made a point of taking Jan aside before they left to tell her why. Her sister was apparently known to the forecourt attendant for other purchases as much as petrol.

'At least Ange had the sense to get properly shitfaced before the cops came calling,' would be Alex's later take on the incident. 'Amazing how they've got the resources to pursue women on their own rather than going after the real criminals.' His precious car was not unduly damaged – the odd dent and scratches from the flying pump and overturned bin. His wife was unhurt and not in jail. If he didn't know about her drinking by now, it was probably too late for Jan to enlighten him on that or anything else.

'Ange, you can't go on like this. What if a kid had been walking out of the garage shop – you'd never have forgiven yourself?'

'I know, I know. I wasn't *this* drunk – I only started properly when I got in. I remembered from way back the bottle of brandy we always kept in case Alex was being chased. He says they can't do you for drink driving when you can prove you've had some since you got out of the car, in your own house. I had plenty of bottles to choose from – didn't have to be brandy.'

Jan didn't respond to the tentative smile. 'Whatever, they can still do you for criminal damage, attempted robbery, fleeing the scene of a crime.' To an extent she was making the charges up as she went along to throw a scare into her sister, but went on with more personal conviction. 'And if they bring race hate into it, you're in really deep doo-doo.'

'I explained all that to the police,' Ange wailed. 'I wasn't trying to get away without paying for the petrol – I would have filled the fucking car up first, wouldn't I? They didn't know what to say to that. And I'm normally polite when he serves me my fags, Mr Ahmad – see I know his name. I still bet it was him grassed me up. Wait till I tell Alex about him.'

'I'd leave Alex out of it. If you called the poor man what the police said you did, you're lucky they didn't take you in already. We may have heard that sort of language when we were kids, but that doesn't make it right. For fuck's sake, not even Nana can get away with using that word nowadays. They've probably got cameras covering the forecourt, got your registration number. Don't go blaming someone else.'

'Don't go preaching to me. If you hadn't asked me to take Karen...oh God, I know how feeble I sound. I'm not strong like you lot. I always think because I was the first I got more of Mum somehow than you all did. You think the drink's going to help, and it does for a while. Look at Mum – it wasn't that what killed her.'

'Ange, you're not Mum. You don't have to be. Doctors are a lot more careful about what they prescribe than they were back then. They'd keep a lot closer eye on you, give you something that might really help. We all need to pull together now to help Karen through her op. Do you talk to Alex about how you feel?'

'Don't make me laugh, Jan. And don't tell me you talk to Ray about how you feel either. Maybe Jason would have lapped that sort of stuff up, and look how long he lasted. Men don't want to hear it. They want a good dinner, ironed shirts and open legs – that's all men want.'

'We'll talk tomorrow, Ange, when you've sobered up. Don't start drinking before I come round, else I won't go with you to the garage to say sorry, try to sort out what you owe them. With any luck they won't press charges.'

Jan felt guilty herself for omitting the element of racism when she tried to make an amusing story out of Ange's misadventure – she did get away without any charge but the financial one – hoping to provoke if not a laugh then a cutting comment from Karen. It was hard to see their younger sister so lacking in energy, though she didn't complain of her pains and tiredness. The doctors had to get her to base camp as they called it to prepare for the operation, free of the bladder infections that tormented her. If she was so tired during the day, it was because she was often up half the night. Kimberley bonded with her over books, becoming her library assistant and talking to her about literature when her aunt could rouse herself a little.

Billy never apologised for his initial brutal enquiry of how long she had left to live, probably didn't realise there was anything indelicate in it. He made no further reference at all to the illness. He did start coming round every night though, developing a mini-circuit from work to the Criterion, to his house for a quick shower, Ange's for his tea, Jan's for drinks and cards if either sister or niece was prepared to indulge him, the Criterion again then at last sozzled to his pit.

Kim was always glad to attend him, learning to count up her crib hands with his occasional gruff help. Billy knew the score of the most complicated combinations at a glance, without being able to explain verbally how he'd reached it, only by spreading the cards in sets between them. He was similarly prompt at adding up three dart scores and chalking the total down from 501, yet an early attempt at an electrician's apprenticeship had foundered when he stuck a fuse box upside down on a wall, the text on it not giving him any clue which was right way up. He had always preferred to say he was thick rather than accept any possibility he might be dyslexic, which he perhaps equated with disabled. Most people had taken him at his word.

Billy would bring cider round for his sisters, even after it became clear that Karen was no longer in drinking mode. Jan noticed he was beginning to colonise her fridge with bottles, as well as how much he drank himself, while convincing herself she would rather he did it in her house than in the company of Angela, egging each other on. Any drink problem he had would have to wait its turn if she was expected to do her Good Samaritan bit there as well. She had enough to do watching herself, having taken a conscious step back from a couple of gorilla-fingered Cuba libres in San Juan every night while she was making dinner.

Jan supposed her brother was lonely, without giving the matter a great deal of thought. Their relationship had always been cordial enough but distant even before the physical separations of childhood. She could understand he might be grieving more as a son at the death of their mother than Grace's daughters were. Didn't children always tend to favour the parent of the opposite sex? No, not always. There was no big outward show of grief from any of them to make such judgements easy – they were all Ropers. He still had girlfriends from time to time, never long-lasting and none as live-ins since Sally-Anne, the one who might have been 'the one' if you listened to Ange, whether or not she was to the sisters' taste or ideal specifications. Billy never sought to please them in his choice of women – Why should he? Jan allowed – or otherwise, beyond helping out with odd jobs around the houses of their missing husbands and bailing them out of any motoring emergencies, the latter less common now they could afford to run respectable cars. Nevertheless, the three of them in Northampton were now part of his daily routine for the first time as adults.

If it was hard for Jan not to view Billy's routine as bleak, she told herself Karen's was bleaker. She was also worried about Kimberley not seeing anyone much outside the family since she'd brought her back to England, especially if she was going to stay and study in Northampton.

Graham Dockerty made a good impression from the first night Billy brought him round with his girlfriend. Polite but not too shy to make himself at home when asked, he showed the confidence that had him on the accelerated management trainee programme at GBD, where Billy worked. 'A year or two and Grady'll be my boss. For the minute I'm showing him how the real work gets done. So he can say he's seen the shop floor before he fucks off upstairs.'

'Your Will's one of our key men,' Graham responded to what ranked as high praise from Billy. 'Don't let him tell you different. Only doesn't want to move from the technical specialist to the general management side cos he'd bring home less money.'

Jan had to introduce herself to Graham's young lady, a schoolgirl she would learn only later, a year younger than Kimberley. Marina could already make her presence felt amongst adults, switching the card game from her first appearance from cribbage – 'that's a game for grandads' – to trumps, as apparently knock-out whist was now called. She quickly drew Kimberley into complicity with her against the older generation.

Gary made a couple of visits to his birth mother – stilted affairs. Jan never knew whether it was the right thing to leave them alone or keep them company. There was definitely a constraint between them, and Karen was clearly not in her best moment to be working at relationships.

'Maybe we'll be closer when I've got his DNA inside me as well as the other way round,' she remarked after the last time they met before the op. He also had to be in good shape for the extraction. Their goodbye was without tears, with a hug so timid it showed they were both on virgin soil.

Before they could try to make her better, the doctors had to make Karen much worse. If Gary's stem cells were to have any chance of survival in her body (however good a match they were), its defences had to be comprehensively blitzed to allow them to gain a foothold. She would be in hospital a full week before the big day as they made a systematic assault on her immune system, spearheaded by intense chemotherapy.

She would be put in an almost totally sterile environment at the hospital, in what they learned was called a neutropenic state. Visitors would be kept to the minimum, fully scrubbed, gloved and gowned up. They also naturally had to be free of the slightest cold or any other condition themselves. The family had agreed that Jan would be the only one of them to visit – or rather she had assumed the responsibility as the most practical way. Ange would be a bag of nerves and probably drunk, Billy an elephant in a greenhouse and Lucy was too far away to make daily visits.

They all came to see her beforehand – in case it was a farewell, they all knew but none said.

Tedge had not been told his cousin was ill. Initially puzzled that she wasn't up to roughhouse with him as they had since childhood, he accepted it with his usual placidity. Pete and Shirley brought him along with Nana and Grandad, Jack obviously shocked to see the reduced state of Karen, able only to mutter 'Now then, now then,' as he hugged her while hugging was still allowed. Jan was amazed to see tears in the flinty old bastard's eyes, obviously looking on the dark side as much as his wife was trying to jolly everyone along, insisting that all would be well and Karen would be 'right as rain in no time'.

Joy had persuaded her two men to take a day off work to come up with her by train, as close as ever Henry and Martin, so that Jan sometimes wondered how the boy had found time to raise a family of three – all girls, by a wife like him of Polish origin but unlike him actually brought up in that country. Hanna was very quiet, her English still limited despite twenty years in London and the kids, whose native language it was. Karen had not expected her to come, but appeared ruffled by the absence of Grandad Sess.

'He sends his best, love. He doesn't get out much nowadays,' said Aunt Joy.

'Fine, tell him he needn't bother coming to the funeral either then.'

'Nonsense, no talk about funerals. The truth is we think he's getting Alzheimer's. Not that you all need to worry about that – I wouldn't have mentioned it except I don't want you to think too badly of him.'

'I'm sorry Joy, forget it. Of course he'll be welcome at the funeral. What will I care? Give him my best as well for what it's worth.'

Lucy brought her bump, Greg and Louise up a couple of days before Karen entered hospital, staying at Ange's overnight and leaving before Alex arrived back from the Gulf. He'd arranged a fortnight's leave, to be available up to the transplant and for the week immediately following it, which would be the peak periods of danger. He came round after tea on Karen's last day at home, with Ange, Adam, Little Jan and Suzie all in tow. Billy, Graham and Marina were already there.

'Here you go, Tiger. Plenty to choose from in videos of United glory. Here's half a dozen, job lot.'

'Cheers, Alex. Not sure I'll have time to watch all these before I die!'

'Don't be morbid – you're nowhere near an RIP message in the programme yet. Here's the deal. First match of next season, hospitality suite, the full works for you and me, may swing a box, take a few of these fair-weather fans along an' all.'

'Not everything revolves around United, Alex,' Ange chided him, though his visit and gifts seemed to have cheered Karen slightly.

For the first time, that night they had a full complement of players for the trumps in Jan's kitchen: Alex, Billy, Graham, Marina, Kim, Adam and Little Jan. Only Suzie preferred to stay with her mum and two aunts.

It wasn't long before Alex appeared in the doorway.

'Listen, we've already robbed the kids of all their pocket money, and Grady won't have enough to get his round in if we go on much longer. Any problem if we pop up the Oak, Kar? I mean you're very welcome to come too, you know that, but…'

'Yeah, probably better not, all in all. I'm surprised you've held out this long to be honest.'

'Want us to bring a Chinky back?'

'Would it kill you to call it a Chinese?' Jan snapped.

'Why not?' Karen answered brightly. 'The girls will need some stomach lining if we carry on drinking all alone here. We can say goodbye then, no fuss now…please.'

Everyone was happy enough to take her at her word. She had Alex send her brother, already smoking on the pavement, back inside.

'Billy, I don't suppose you'll be coming back, and don't worry, I'm not going to ask you to miss last orders at your shithole pub. Don't worry about me getting "sloppy" with you either – there's something I want you to hang on to in case…well in case I'm not fit for that season opener.' She gave her eyes a quick swipe with the back of her hand.

Billy didn't seem to know what to do with the slim envelope she fished from her green bag and handed him.

'Keep this for me. It's for all of you really – for later, and no I don't mean it's cash for my round at the pub tonight. I haven't made a will or anything – jack shit to bequeath if you must know – but it's…well, hang on to it, just in case.'

Billy put it in his pocket, accustomed to taking orders from his sister without debate. He ducked to give her a quick kiss on the cheek – an extreme sign of affection from him – before turning to follow Alex.

Jan went out to make coffee, herself the only taker, as soon as the three sisters were alone. Karen broke the silence when she returned.

'I told Ange I'd rather wait to explain to you both together, not that there's much to explain. No need for you even to mention to Lucy, for instance. Whatever you think, I'm not being morbid – I know the odds are in my favour of coming through this next couple of weeks. I'm just being practical, and because I'm me, I found it easier to say all the stuff that needed saying in writing rather than trying to tell you it face to face. Jan, I hope you'll understand that, even if I never did get the lit crit I was looking for from you on "Family Reunion".'

'It made me cry, Kar.'

'That bad, really? Anyway, it's not that I favour Billy over any of the rest of you, and it's *obviously* not because I see him as the family patriarch, lord and master of us all, that I gave him the letter, which is all that was in that envelope. I ended up putting a separate one in the post to Gary, a letter within a letter there, and I'll just have to trust he obeys instructions. It felt quite dramatic – never thought I'd be writing "to be opened only in the event of my death" on anything. Makes you feel kind of important somehow.'

'I was only saying I would have taken better care of it than Billy probably will, and I am the oldest.'

'Mum Ange, here we go again. I think Billy will take care of it. He's a bit of a hoarder on the quiet. More important, I've got no worries about him jumping the gun and reading it. When did you ever see him settle down to read anything?

'I don't regret any of the things I've written, but it's sort of a special letter. It's to all of you equally, including Billy himself, to share just as you like. Still, it's something I don't really want to be out in the world unless and until I'm not. Don't expect any bombshells or recriminations – that's not it. Just sentimental stuff really, the sort of thing us Ropers don't normally do, and I'd rather not do tonight either if it's OK with you both. Deal?'

Jan and Ange reached out each to take one of her extended hands. Karen made sure she was in bed when the others returned, though Jan doubted she was asleep.

20

Weddings: Round Two

The Olly still had one graduate in the next round of Roper weddings. Lucy had been prepared to wait for Greg to settle his divorce, once he'd confessed it wasn't yet a done deal after she was safely moved in with him. As long as she was allowed to keep her own Washtown property in trust for Louise, and treated as an equal partner in a new will, that was enough for Lucy.

It was enough at first, anyway. When Aaron was getting ready for primary school, it started to rankle that she didn't have the same surname as her son. She might have had Aaron christened Roper rather than Brewington, since it seemed unlikely Billy would pick up the burden of continuing the family name. Then again, that would have left their boy without the surname of either of his parents, since she was still a Williams. She would not, of course, be wedding with anything like the flame of her relationship with Tommy. Still, she felt it was time; she would make Greg feel the same way.

The trigger for Little Jan was turning thirty. She and Jamie, already living together for ten years, worked side by side in ReedIT Enterprises, worked properly as technical and finance directors respectively – Ange's directorship was without portfolio or responsibility, purely so that Alex could funnel money to her in the most tax-efficient manner. The Golden Vision had been given golden handcuffs by the bank, spooked by the implications of Y2K, which in the event proved a bonanza rather than Armageddon for him and his fledgling company.

Janette came off the pill, for health reasons as much as the ticking of the biological clock calibrated only in time for her generation it seemed. While she would not have a baby to indulge her mother, she was ready for herself. Call her old-fashioned if you like, she thought marriage should come first. Although she knew nothing of her aunt's design at that point, she was as confident as Lucy with Greg that Jamie would come round to her way of thinking.

Kimberley would later claim she was infected by the rumblings from her cousin. The fierce debate about whether Graham Dockerty had chosen her over Marina or that girl had dumped him for Billy only sparked to life occasionally nowadays. There had been periods of physical separation between Kim and Grady but never an agreed break in their relationship from the time she began at sixth form college in Northampton, through the years of a language degree at Cambridge, and now a promising start to a career in publishing. Meanwhile Grady had moved up the ladder in GBD, as predicted by Billy, a few rungs higher than him though not in the same section.

'Mum, Ange, Janette, I know I said it was to talk about weddings, and that is part of it, but I've brought Graham along – I could tell you were surprised to see him! – because we're worried about Billy.' Kim made her fiancé take a seat beside her at their lunch table in the Oak.

'Yeah, I did think it was odd if Grady was actually showing an interest – more than I can get out of Jamie,' her cousin replied. 'Adam's more excited about it, practically begging to be best man. Don't tell me Billy and Marina are planning on getting hitched as well.'

'God no, it's not that bad – he's probably daft enough for her like all the men are, but it's more about his job.'

Graham focused on his pint. However much he insisted the long-buried thing between him and Marina had never been serious, he had learned it did not suit Kim to believe him.

'Tell them, Graham, unless you're too busy dreaming about what might have been.'

'I've told Kim already, if he's not careful he's going to get the bullet. I'm not talking behind his back – I had a word with him weeks ago. Obviously didn't do any good, and now he's had a formal warning.'

'I thought he was a key man – thought they couldn't do without him?'

'So does he, Ange, that's part of the trouble. Nobody wants to let him go, but we're a big company, have to do things by the book. I mean coming in of a morning with beery breath from the night before, that used to be accepted up to a point, but when you're going off shift more pissed than you arrive, they can't turn a blind eye.'

'Is he really that bad? I didn't think he started drinking till he finished work.'

'Maybe he didn't used to. He's getting worse, and you can't tell him anything. I know everyone laughs at health and safety, but it's a proper thing. People really can get hurt at a plant like ours. The company's bent over backwards, honestly, but HR are gunning for him, ready to pull the trigger, and the union won't go into bat for him this time.'

'And what do you propose we do about it?' Feeling her daughter's hand on her arm, Jan reduced her volume slightly. 'Sorry, Graham, I know it's not your fault, not your problem really. I only hope you're not all expecting me to handle this one. Didn't I have enough with Karen?'

'Karen was ill. It wasn't her own fault – like him.'

'Whose fault, Ange? You're the one who spends every afternoon boozing with him.'

Little Jan stepped in. 'Jan, Mum, can we keep it calm? Everyone appreciates what a fabulous job you did with Karen. And Mum, I thought you'd know better than to blame it on Billy. Don't we all agree alcoholism is an illness? If only because it seems to run in our family a bit, I mean….'

'I suppose I've got this illness myself, have I?' Ange defiantly raised her long vodka glass but put it straight down when her hand started shaking. 'What's it called, pissheaditis, shitfacia? I don't blame illness on the fact that I drink – I blame myself. I know I'm hopeless. Do you think I can make him stop? He sups more at the fucking dosshouse Criterion and with that little bitch than with me – let them look after him.'

'Yes, I see your point.' Kim liked to think she'd picked up a few tips for coping with overwrought contributions to debate at the student union. 'Can we let Graham go off to his rugby? He's feeling nervous cornered with all us Roper girls. You're fine with whatever we might agree for the weddings – can I have that here in front of witnesses, honey?'

'As if I had a choice.' He was already on his feet and backing away from the table. 'Don't forget to order lunch if you're going to continue the conference.' He nodded at the assorted glasses on the table around a tiny, complimentary bowl of salted peanuts.

'I'm sorry Ange,' Jan conceded when the prospective groom had left. 'If we start squabbling, we won't have any chance of helping. I just got this horrible feeling it's all starting again, not so long after nearly losing Karen. She did her bit for Billy when we were younger, when they only had each other – I don't suggest we ask her. He might get her back into bad habits, apart from anything else.'

'As if he'd move down to London anyway,' Little Jan said. 'His worst habit is Marina. God knows how I could ever have thought we were mates.'

'He could live at mine if anyone thought that would help, but I don't suppose it would.' Ange's rage had vanished as quickly as it came. She sounded forlorn.

'It's the old cliché – he's got to want to help himself.' Jan had no wish to suggest that living with his oldest sister would probably tip him over the edge. 'We'll have to talk to him, if we can catch him sober. Will one of you girls have a word with Marina? I mean surely she wants the best for Billy deep down?'

'I don't mind, but I'd rather not do it on my own. I'm not scared of her, more scared I'd end up throttling her.'

'Why's that, Kim? Because of Billy or Grady?' Little Jan was the only one who could get away with that comment.

It was on their third bottle of wine, after a nod to Grady Sobersides in a portion of nachos between the four of them, once Ange had brought the news of Lucy's impending marriage to the table, that the women conceived the idea of a triple celebration.

'I don't know what she's thinking of – probably nothing spectacular.' Kim's face was very red. 'It would make sense to have a joint reception whether she comes in or not. I mean a lot of the guests will be the same and everything.'

'Plus it might stop Ray and Alex getting into a pissing contest about which one gives their daughter the best party. I asked Ray about it – he said whatever our little girl wants.'

'Hey, do you think it might be worth one of them speaking to Billy? He might listen more to someone with a dick, especially to Alex?'

'Can't hurt. I'll talk to him, Luce as well, about the weddings and Billy both.' Not only was Ange keen to offer a positive contribution, there was a point during her daily cycle when she was more than happy to talk to people on the phone. 'We might complain about our old men, but they do spoil you girls. When you think about Billy, he never really had any sort of father in his life.'

'Time to get 'em out of here, Kim, before they get onto Nana Grace and the whole sad saga of them Roper girls.'

Although Lucy grumbled initially about having her plans hijacked by her two nieces, she could see the benefits in sharing costs of a reception, as well as securing a more respectable turnout than she could muster in Chelmsford. Since her first wedding, the slippage of time had claimed her parents, and Nana was gone too. Only when making the funeral arrangements did Lucy find out she was ten years older than Jack. Aunt Shirley set him up with meals-on-wheels and a carer.

Pete and Shirley were more recently, more comprehensively broken by the death of Tedge. It began with a nagging cough, a lung infection becoming pneumonia that carried him off, almost without a struggle at the end for someone whose life had largely been trouble-free thanks to the constant efforts and watchfulness of his parents. Tedge had never smoked, taking so much to heart his dad's strictures against the vice that there was a spell in his early teens when they'd had to school him not to knock cigarettes from the hands of anyone he saw sparking up. The fact they had never ceased to care for him into his fifties, many years beyond the initial life expectations of doctors, did not prevent Pete from blaming himself for his son's end. It was undeniable that Tedge had spent a good deal of his life in the smoke-filled atmosphere of the Service, but hadn't they all, Lucy reminded her uncle in a vain attempt to take some weight of guilt off him.

For the first time, there was no supporting good sense to be had from Shirley. The loss of their boy had shivered the parents apart. Pete threw over at once his lifetime job. 'I can't be in the place anymore Luce, simple as that. If I had to lock it up at night, no Tedge to walk home with, telling me his little stories of the day, I know I'd find myself walking down to the cut instead.'

The wedding weekend became significantly wider in its scope and range. As Jan had predicted, neither of the younger women's dads wanted to be the party pooper in putting a brake on them. The husbands-to-be, less consulted, felt the same way.

The ceremonies were scheduled simultaneously for 12.30 on a July Saturday at Bothorpe Hall in the Northamptonshire countryside. Not only were there rooms available for guests to stay the wedding night in the main building, the family had booked a set of cottages attached to it around a central courtyard for the whole of the weekend. Lucy and Greg would marry on the Friday in Chelmsford, Louise and Aaron dragooned into service as bridesmaid and page boy, with Pete and Shirley as witnesses, before joining the others that evening.

It wasn't so much that anyone took their eye off the ball with Billy, more that it had already gathered such momentum heading downhill that nothing could stop it. Alex told him to pull himself together and learn to drink like a man. Karen told him to come down to London and live with her if he was really set on behaving like a child again. Lucy said she would do everything possible to help him find a new job in the Chelmsford area if he felt a clean break would be the best thing for him. All too little, too late.

Never one to miss a stag party, as he grew older Billy became almost generous when in his cups, earning better than most of the younger crowd with which he was increasingly associating. Before he had to start thinking of what his two nieces' boyfriends might be planning (within the constraints of what the girls would allow), he had a long weekend in Prague.

He remained stubbornly conscientious in never liking to miss a shift. Of course it was a mistake in retrospect to get straight off the plane, dump his bag at home and head for work. It proved to be his last day at GBD.

The next blow was to his health. What he had not spent in Prague, he took to the Criterion during the days when he was technically under suspension before his dismissal was confirmed. Within a fortnight of returning from the Czech capital he was in hospital, yellower than drawer-lining newspapers.

The doctors made no bones that he would have to stop drinking if he was to live much longer. He was not a big man and the cumulative damage to his liver was considerable. He jibbed at Lucy's recollection, or interpretation, of one medical opinion that his next drink could be his last.

Partly on the basis that there was less alcohol in her house than at Ange's, Billy left hospital to continue his recovery under Jan's beady eye until the sisters felt he was strong enough to return to his own home. They all knew the problems would only begin when he felt strong enough again to disregard doctors' orders.

There was no family confrontation of Marina, less materialistic or savvy than everyone had feared since she did not stick around in Billy's house, on which she might have concocted some legal claim if he needed to consider downsizing. Though his career was over, he might still hope for a job. He was handy in many ways apart from the practical management of his own life.

The fact that Marina had decamped to live with one of the younger bloods who had returned in rude good health from the blowout in Prague hurt Billy, however much he professed to be well rid of her. His sisters were certainly not going to beg the girl to come back. Despite suggestions from both their husbands that it would be no more productive, Ange and Jan did pay a visit to the landlord of the Criterion. A crusty old Yorkie, he gave them short shrift.

'Well I don't rightly see that I can ban him. How would that look? He's never given me any bother at all. With all due respect, if I stopped serving everyone whose sister or wife or daughter come in to ask me, I'd end up with no customers.'

'Total waste of time,' Jan told Kim when she asked how their mission had gone later that day. 'Me and Ange were saying, your Graham and Jamie will have to be careful about their stag nights. Not to spoil it for them, but we'll have to make sure Billy doesn't get involved – the last one nearly killed him. Literally.'

'You don't have to worry about Graham. I've told him I don't want to get married.'

'You're joking! I thought it was all your idea in the first place.'

'If it was then I can change my mind, right. No, I don't mean to be flippant, and— Oh God, I promised myself I wouldn't cry when I told you…I just don't think it's the right thing to do.'

'You've got some other man?'

'What does everyone take me for! Why is that the first thing everyone assumes? Little Jan was just the same. The answer is no, thanks for asking. Look, I'm not saying we're going to split up. We might still get married, just not yet.'

'So you told your cousin before you told me? Nice. There goes the two-for-one wedding deal, anyway. And the honeymoon? Isn't it all booked and paid for.'

'I know. If Dad can't get the money back we'll go on it, and we'll enjoy it. We're still friends, still together. Lucky we only asked for money as wedding gifts so nobody else should be out of pocket.'

'If you can still be thinking of going away with him, I assume it's your choice. I mean it's not him with—'

'With another woman? Jeez, is that all you lot can think or talk about – somebody must be cheating? There are other reasons. You probably didn't notice, but when I came in you said straight away "Where's Graham?", like we've already been married thirty years, a couple like you never see one without the other. I'm really sorry about it, Mum, but I think it's the right thing to do.'

'Come here and give me a hug. Listen, I'd never advise anyone to get married if they have any doubts, least of all you. I see too much of myself in you. One last question, are you sure it's not last-minute jitters, nothing more than that?

'All right, all right, I give up – I can see you don't want to go there. I won't say a word against Graham. The wedding might be on again next week for all I know, but you're my priority, always. All I can say, and I'll back you up in front of anyone else on this, is it's better to pull out the night before than the night after the wedding.'

'Maybe don't put it in quite those words, Mum…sounds like the punchline to a dirty joke.'

They were twelve at the top table in the Churchill banqueting hall of Bothorpe House as the waitresses circulated with glasses of champagne: the newly-weds Jamie and Janette, Lucy and Greg; Alex and Ange; Pete and Shirley; Aunt Joy, Jan, Karen and Billy, under protest so that his sisters could keep an eye on him throughout the meal. Ray Roden had grumbled a little that his generously written-off financial contribution to the event did not earn him a seat beside his still-wife but was too superstitious to make thirteen, as she cannily pointed out would be the case in offering at last to have another place set. 'You might want to spend a bit of time with the kids instead of getting pissed again with Alex,' she suggested.

In the end, there had been neither a formal stag nor hen night. The women had agreed that it would be a shame to waste the facility of the cottages (converted from a former farmhouse and its outbuildings) on the Friday night, with the hot tub at their centre the clinching factor.

'Let's make the most of it before the men go to plonk their fat arses in and start a farting contest,' Janette had generously urged, not wanting to hold an outside party when Kim evidently wouldn't be.

Jamie had no such scruples on behalf of Grady. 'If I was him, I'd be getting bladdered every night till it's all over anyway,' he told his bride. Graham's parents had declined to participate in the weekend with the Roper family, while Jamie's lived in New Zealand with his older sister and her young family.

ReedIT Enterprises had scheduled a board meeting for eleven o'clock on Friday 13 July, chaired by Alex who closed it at quarter past, telling Jamie 'Make the minutes look sensible, mate – you know the drill.' When the four directors adjourned to the Cordwainer, Janette made sure to supervise Jamie through a Spoons fry-up before rising with her mother to say goodbye until the next day.

Ange didn't care to know where Alex slept that night. He had been charged by his daughter with ensuring that Jamie got home safely, without suffering any disabling or disfiguring assaults – they'd hired a proper photographer for the wedding – and without the need for police intervention, despite Ange's protests that her husband was not necessarily the best man for that job.

Jan was similarly unconcerned about Ray, who had arrived on the Wednesday with Denis and his latest girlfriend Charlotte. It wasn't really a problem to accommodate her precocious five-year-old daughter Ruby Mae, though Jan felt bound to tell her son it would have been nice to be pre-warned that she was coming too.

'It would have been nice to be pre-warned that Kimba isn't actually getting hitched, Mum,' he replied. 'Not that I wouldn't have come over for Little Jan or anything but still.'

'I have to say I'm glad Janette and Jamie chose the *Reservoir Dogs* theme for the men at this wedding,' Alex began his father-of-the-bride speech. 'Not just because I already owned a funeral suit and tie – this shindig has cost enough already, believe me – but because it gives me an excuse to keep my shades on. Lovely day for the kids, but who knew sunlight could hurt so much?'

'Your shirt's ironed, suit in the wardrobe when you want it,' Ange had greeted him when he arrived that morning, without turning from the tiny dressing table.

'Top of the morning to you too. Don't you want to know how the stag night went?'

'I can guess. Eyes like pissholes in the snow. Did you get any sleep at all?'

'Not much. Too busy wondering if you were sealing the deal with Paddy.'

'Give me strength, Alex. Don't you realise women can be friends? Am I only supposed to hang about with my sisters? God knows you spend enough time with your mates – do I accuse you of having something queer going on?'

'I thought it was only the male hairdressers who were all poofs – more butch than most of them she is. Don't deny it – she makes no secret of it herself.'

'And why should she? What's the matter, Alex, frustrated because you can't smack her like you would if she was a man? Why don't you get your head down for an hour, try and sober up a bit before you walk your daughter down the aisle?'

'You'll make a good pair, you and her with Adam and his latest, I can't keep track of their names.' He started undressing; a quick kip was not a bad idea.

'Don't want to more like. It's Steve – they've been together two years now. You might as well face up to it, there could be a day when you have to give him away as well.'

'Not while I live and breathe. Better to have give him away at birth like Kar did. I always wondered where it could have come from – none of that in our family. Now I'm beginning to see.'

'You bastard. You ever say something like that again, you'd better learn to sleep with your eyes open if I'm around you, which I won't be by the way. We've got three great kids – can we make today about them, especially Janette, not you as per fucking usual? Just let Adam live his life, not yours.'

'Not had your first of the morning yet, my love?' He had so many answers, but let her drone on…

'Lovely surroundings too. A big thank you first to all the Bothorpe Hall catering and serving staff for helping to make this whole weekend so special. I've done a bit of research into the place – apparently it was once a monastery. You know how they separate the men from the boys in a monastery? With a crowbar.

'Please yourselves, I know it's an old one. Speaking of which, old Pete here was too shy to talk, just like he was too shy to join the stag party last night, so he asked me to include today's other wedding in the one speech, which of course I'm delighted to do.

'I think most of us know that Lucy's had some very bad luck in her life, so I hope I speak for all of us when I say we're so glad she's back on track now, with another stag-night dodger. Yes, I did say stag-night dodger, not coffin dodger – Greg's not really that old. Talk about keen though, mate – I mean making sure she don't escape is one thing but to marry Luce twice in the same weekend is really going some. Actually we owe you a big vote of thanks, so we did end up having the three weddings we were all expecting, not just two.'

Lucy and Greg had stood earlier with the younger couple for a blessing rather than a full ceremony. Kimberley, sitting at a round table close to the principal one with her father, Denis, Charlotte and Ruby Mae, made a point of grabbing her recently downgraded groom's limp hand at this point in her uncle's speech. Graham looked much worse than Ray, who had faced some difficulties getting him to turn out when he'd called for him that morning. He was the only one uncheered by the shots the men had all taken before the formal business, or the pints between it and Alex's already dragging speech.

'Before I go on to the younger married couple here today – though not so very young. We all know Jamie is an accountant and it took him ten years to do the sums before he could commit himself to a signature – I want to say a special thank you to my dear wife Angela. Without you, none of this would have been possible. From all I hear, you played a major role in bringing up your siblings along this table – good job with all of them, except what went wrong with Billy? From what I *know*, because I lived it, you had the main role in bringing up our own three children, not just the beautiful Janette here at my side but the equally beautiful Adam and Suzette at their own table there – happy days, kids, no rush to fight over the bouquet when your sister chucks it later.

'It's not true that I didn't like Jamie at first. I've liked him from that very day, all those years back, when an empty car pulled up outside our house and he got out. I'd heard he was studying to be an accountant. I knew he was an extravert one though – check it out yourselves later. When he's got a couple of drinks in him, he'll sometimes look at *your* shoes when he's talking to you instead of his own.

'And as for Janette, what can I say?' For a moment he did falter. 'All the beauty of them Roper girls, with all brains of the Reeds, doubled up, as my dad will tell you if you give him half a chance, because they skipped a generation with me. Right, Simon? I can hear you heckling from the cheap seats. I love you, Little Jan – we all do. Now you have the official blessing to go off and begin a new generation of Littler Jans and Jamies. Preferably Jans though.

'I can hear the grumbles of stomachs wondering if their throats have been cut, so I will ask our friends to start bringing out the food as we all raise our glasses, in respect of both the happy couples here today: to the brides and grooms.'

'How is Pete, Shirl?' Aunt Joy asked as they watched him trail behind Lucy to accompany Alex and Janette in the first dance of the evening.

'Life goes on. You think events like this will help, new chapter and all that jazz, but all I can think about is what a great time Tedge would be having. That would be him dancing with Luce now, trampling all over her feet and her laughing with him. Pete wouldn't have minded giving up his place one bit. Not much of a dancer him, never.'

'I hear you there, gal. I bet if you had a dog lead connecting Henry's ankle to that bar, it wouldn't be at full stretch all night.'

'Doesn't Little Jan look lovely? I did worry her dad was going to spoil it for her when he started off his speech. He seems to have sobered up a bit now.'

'If he has, he must have drunk himself sober. She's probably the first girl he's ever danced with without wanting to screw her.'

'Sounds a bit harsh. Don't tell me...'

'What? No, not me, God forbid, but I think Grace may have been tempted. He was a lot different at seventeen than whatever age he is now – quite the sight for sore eyes. And he knew it. But he wouldn't have got past seventeen if Eric ever suspected there was anything going on. And I'm not saying there was. For heaven's sake, don't ever mention it to Pete. I must have had one too many myself to bring it up.'

'That's all weddings are for us now, Joy. A chance to have one too many and keep an eye out for the little ones. Your three there are a handful. I'm amazed they're still going strong, in and out of that hot tub all afternoon.'

'Sofia will soon be asleep on Hanna's lap or mine I expect, and I shall take the chance to bow out gracefully.'

'We can maybe have one too many more back at the cottages. I expect I'll be putting Aaron Trevor down for Luce. Pete will be wanting a proper drink today. You wouldn't believe how nervous he was about having to make the speech for her. I wouldn't say Alex did a great job, but he took it off Pete's shoulders. He's not all bad.'

'This looks like the party table. See if you can persuade Gary here to stay the night, not trek all the way back to London. I've already told him there's plenty of space at the cottages. Gary, not sure who you've already met or haven't, but here's cousins Denis and Adam – they can do the honours with the others.'

'Stay and have one with us, Auntie Karen, unless yoga gurus aren't allowed to drink. I hear you're well into all that Eastern mysticism shit – I mean stuff – now.'

'Anyone can reinvent themselves, Adam. Sometimes you have to. Speaking of which, when'd you start packing them guns? You're not liable to flip off into a roid rage any minute, are you?'

'I thought I might need 'em against Dad, if you really want to know the truth. I'm drawing back from it now, the bodybuilding. Never got into the steroids anyway – there's enough suppressed rage in our family.'

'Suppressed is right,' Steve cut in, showing how he couldn't link his hands around Adam's bicep. 'Look at the Egyptian.'

'He's talking about Alex, Gary,' Karen said. 'Adam's dad. They just told me it. Go on, Steve.'

'You know, he's neck deep in de Nile about me and his son. Not much of a joke, but then I didn't think much to the ones in his speech either.'

'I'm Charlotte, Gary. If you're feeling lost with all these guys, you're not the only one. I was expecting Den to give me the full-nine-yards briefing on the family while I sat and simpered like Diane Keaton, but he's about as much use as fucking Fredo, forget about Michael.'

'Just this once I will let you ask about my business,' Gary smiled and sat down.

'Your new clean-living lifestyle don't extend to stopping smoking then, Kar?' Alex was at the benevolent stage of wanting to ensure all his guests were having a great time, doing the rounds rather than staying glued to the bar, not caring he was no longer walking steadily.

'So it's you who's been taking the piss out of me to the kids? No, I still smoke when under stress. It's a process. Don't ask me for one though, I'm on OPs.'

'No change there then. I've got a pocketful of cigars anyway. Romeo y Julietas. Grady insisted on returning them to Ray, the fifty he'd given him to hand around as they liked when the wedding was still on. I don't think the poor cunt even smokes, but if I was him I would have kept the cigars.'

'I don't doubt it.'

He did not notice or overrode her tone discouraging further conversation. 'I try to look out for people when I can, but you have to look after yourself first. Your Gary, if I can call him that, seems a decent sort of kid. Have you told him who his dad is yet?'

'What's it to you?'

'Come on, Kar, don't be like that. It was a long time ago. I mean you've never said, but if—'

'If what? Christ on a bicycle, you actually think it might have been you, don't you? How very flattering.'

'No, I mean I know you were a bit wild, and so was I back then...'

'How very flattering that you can't remember if you had sex with me. Or let's say raped me, should we? Wild I might give you, but I was never up for a gang bang, as you and your mates called it. I didn't know all the names, but I remember all the faces on top of me. Trust me, you weren't one of them tipping your filthy muck. Don't give yourself too much credit for not joining in though. If anyone could have stopped them, you could. And you didn't.

'I know I was drunk. You were too, I don't doubt. I gave you a pass on it, I suppose – didn't want to rock the family boat. It's only these last few years

I've realised I was turning all the hurt in on myself. I'm over it, or at least I can talk calmly about it, except to that poor kid. How can I forgive myself that he was conceived in hate and humiliation, not love? What answer do you suggest I give him when he asks who his dad is? Any ideas welcome. Cos I'd have to say I haven't got a fucking scooby.'

The hate and hurt was all in her eyes. From the tone of her voice, she might have been having a pleasant chat with her favourite brother-in-law.

She stubbed her cigarette out in the ashtray between them. 'Stay out here and enjoy your cigar, Romeo. And thanks for asking, I appreciate your concern. Seriously. It might have been a lot worse. You could have married me.'

They were all there at a table, just like they were at a fucking hen party not a family wedding: Ange, Jan, Lucy, Karen – and Paddy, beside his wife.

'Paddy Poo, how are you?' And there was a time when he had half fancied her himself. Perhaps there really was nothing between her and Ange. Weren't they both too pretty? Shouldn't one have shorter hair?

'Fine thanks, Alex. How are you?'

'Fair to middling, how you diddling? That's about the best I can say. Good party though I think.' He gestured airily towards the bar where his mates were still drinking. 'Not wishing you away or anything, but are you OK for transport back to town tonight?'

'Are you offering me a ride? No, only joking, don't worry about me – I'm booked in at the hotel.'

'Must be a good business, hairdressing. I'm sure Ange would have found room to tuck you up over at the cottages if you'd rather. What you looking at your twin like that for, Ange? Did you know these two were twins, Paddy? Not identical else I suppose you might go for them both...'

He hadn't been invited to sit down. Jan rose to take his arm. 'Talking of the cottages, will you come back there with me? I want to go see how Billy's getting on. I suspect they were pretty strong shandies he was having while he was here, and I don't know that Grady is the best company for him at the moment.'

'You got that right, both depressed as fuck I should think – Jilted John and Teetotal Toby. Life's no fun without a woman or a drink. Course I'll come with you, my darling. Never let it be said...'

Jan didn't know whether he was exaggerating his drunkenness so that she would link arms with him or not. She was ready for Ray to question her about leaving the party with her brother-in-law, ready to tell him where to get off. Huddled at the bar as he was with half a dozen men, including Henry/ Martin, Pete and Denis, she had no doubt he would still have one eye on her – like most womanisers, including the one she was dragging away now, he was exceptionally jealous. He only raised his chin at her departure, which she felt wasn't sufficient enquiry to need an answer. She'd already asked if Kimberley didn't want to go back with Graham and her uncle Billy, only to be told that she was enjoying herself too much where she was. Kim was clearly drunk, though not as far along the spectrum as Alex.

He had never forgotten their night in London, one of the best of his life, why did she think Little Jan was named after her? Wouldn't hurt Ange for the world, that was a given, nor Ray if it was up to him, but if they were both free, he had enough to retire already practically, go down to Cornwall together, or anywhere. She liked to travel, right? Not too late yet. Them Roper girls get in your blood. Another go – he knew Jason was just a rebound – tell him there was a chance. Ange sorted with that lezzer, who'd have thought it? He knew she wasn't like that, not Jan. Jan?

'There's no point talking to you, Alex – you won't remember a word in the morning.'

So there was a chance then? She wasn't saying no? She wasn't not saying no just to keep him sweet? He would never hurt her – he never once hit a woman when he was sober, not once. They were already family – keep it in the family. Didn't she miss Washtown? The day of his wedding when he first fell for her – he didn't know it at the time – like a ton of bricks. They weren't that old yet, he wasn't prejudiced, she mustn't think that, live and let live, anything but incest. Her dad, that was fucked up...'

'You what? What did you say about my dad? Did he tell you something? What did Eric tell you? Did he brag something to you?'

Nothing at all, sorry he mentioned it – he was getting confused, bit pissed – like the rumours about himself and Grace – great-looking bird in her day mind – nothing in it. Eric loved his kids, she knew that. Hard as nails he was. What was he going to do, top himself? Had to live with himself – that was hard enough. Don't be like that, never meant to upset her, nothing in it. No, he never said nothing, just me gabbing, what was the other one? Try everything? Yeah Scottish folk dancing, a joke like the ones in the speech, didn't mean to offend, only a joke...'

'It's not a joke, any more than they were. That one we might talk about again. Now pull yourself together, for fuck's sake. I'm not looking after you like some big baby – you can stop leaning all over me now.'

There was her brother lolling back, beckoning them to him with a lazy arm. 'Hey sis, come here in the hot tub with us. Look at these stars, will you? I was just explaining them to Grady. They make you think, you know.'

'Oh Christ, he's pissed as well. God give me strength.' It was sad but Jan had to admit it to herself – it was the first time she'd seen Billy looking happy since she didn't remember when.

Alex was shucking off his shoes, shirt and trousers to join him and Graham in the hot tub. He was not wearing underpants.

21

Munsley Revisited

It was years after Tommy's death before Lucy would consider returning to Munsley for so much as a day visit. When she and Greg were in a position to buy a static caravan to pass their summer holidays, they opted for a site within an easy beach walk of Cromer. More to do for the kids that way, though they would always make a day at Munsley.

Lucy managed the rentals at the van, usually in the off-peak season. Ange and Paddy would quite often take a week or two – mates' rates of course. They lived quietly in Northampton, bothering nobody and benefitting the five kids and four grandkids they had between them.

They did not bother Alex, who could still get worked up about certain things. He had left the house in Northampton to Ange, having another of his own back in Washtown and a bolthole down in Cornwall, too big for one as he always said and used by all of his children on occasion.

When Lucy had raised again the question of Billy's ashes, it was Karen who suggested Munsley. At the time of his cremation, nobody had been able to agree what should be done with them. It wasn't as if there was a family mausoleum or even a plot. Then Karen had disappeared abroad – Billy's money soon burned a hole in her pocket, Lucy said – for almost two years, and all agreed any commitment to a committal had to be a joint one. Then, they mostly stopped thinking of him. When Lucy and Greg announced their retirement to

Washtown as the place they both, after all, considered home, the sisters agreed it was time to end what Karen called the Harry Potter arrangement. They would not just move their brother's remains to a different cupboard under Lucy's new stairs.

They waited until after midnight to return to the beach below the Boat, the eight of them. Ange and Paddy were staying in the van along the coast with Lucy and Greg. Karen had booked two rooms at the Boat – one for herself and Jan, and one for Gary. Alex, miffed not to have received his own invitation but not too proud to take up a grudging acceptance of his presence, was too late to get another room there. Ever the optimist, he made sure Jan knew that he had a double room at the Admiral on the way out of the village.

'Are you sure you want to go all the way in, Kar? We could just scatter them on the edge.'

'In all the scum, no. Don't fuss, Luce, I'd like to.' The night was still warm enough for the other women to be barelegged and bare-armed as she stripped to a lime bikini.

'Does anyone want to say anything?' Lucy was holding the urn stiffly out away from her body, as if she wanted nothing more than for someone to take it out of her hands.

'Let us give you girls a bit of space,' Alex suggested. 'Goodbye, buddy.' He put a hand to his lips and gave a firm farewell pat to the container before shepherding Paddy and Greg a little further back from the tideline.

'You sure you don't want me to take him out, Ma?' Gary asked.

She glanced up from the shorts around her ankles, grateful, a brief shake of the head. He moved back with the others.

And then it was just the five of them. The women each put a hand on the pot. Ange was crying. Jan put her free hand on the back of her sister's neck, bowing her own head. 'Rest in peace, Billy – you'll always be in our hearts.'

'God bless, Billy.' Lucy withdrew her hand as if the ashes had suddenly kindled, reaching to the embrace of her sisters.

Karen took a firm grip on the container, raising it away from the other three like a cup-winning captain, above their heads, still facing the silhouette of the Boat above them. 'Just me and you now, Billy, like old times. You were loved, you know.'

She walked into the sea. Impossible not to wince at the initial chill, but she felt it would be undignified and inappropriate to go splashing and plunging ahead. Good job the tide was in. None of them had thought to check.

'Poor kid. Lucy tells me he never had much of a chance.'

Paddy would tell Ange afterwards that Alex was blinking back tears, though at the time she could have sworn it was a wink he gave her before answering Greg. 'Nobody had a chance with them Roper girls, mate.'

Karen swam in an awkward one-armed crawl, the urn crooked between neck and shoulder blade. It wasn't a costly container, not much disfigured by the masking tape Lucy had though to seal it with for which she was now grateful. She wanted to do it right, let him go in her own time.

Well out of her depth, she stopped swimming and turned onto her back, placing the urn on her stomach as she floated for a few moments. 'Lovely starry night, Billy. I'm glad of that for you.'

First she pulled out the tightly folded note from her bikini bottom. It was soaked of course. No matter, she was only going to rip it up. She didn't care about the paragraphs she had so carefully crafted to her siblings before going into hospital for the transplant. The scrawled addition, found in the envelope about his body at the death, was easy enough to remember: 'Love you all to, sorry Billy.' Spelling had never been his strong point.

She unripped the urn and upturned it onto her belly. She breathed evenly in and out as she tried to feel her sisters close, as her brother dispersed around her in specks of ash and paper. She dismissed the thought of swimming right on, further and further out.

Letting the urn fill with salt water, with a half-turn she lobbed it deeper into the North Sea.

Karen struck out for shore to rejoin Angela, Janet and Lucy, completing them Roper girls.

THE END

THE END

Lightning Source UK Ltd.
Milton Keynes UK
UKHW040637060722
405428UK00001B/10